THE CHOICE

BY PAUL IBELL

To Mary Lou,

Thanks for coming to the launch! x

Love,

Paul x

October '17

Published by Ardennes
27 Old Gloucester Street
London WC1N 3AX

First published 2017

Typeset by Born Group

Printed in Great Britain by Clays Ltd, St Ives plc

A catalogue record for this book is available from the British Library

ISBN 978 1 9998 129 1 1

For Pip Pickering
with love

Chapter One

The ornate Victorian lamps that lined the Embankment gave as comforting a glow as they could, given the freezing fog. They were welcome reminders that this wasn't some formless landscape but a riverside walk, punctuated by lifebelts and ship-themed memorials, only yards from the currently invisible Thames, whose dark, treacherous waters carried the city's secrets out to the open sea.

He stood in a hazy pool of light just a minute or so's stroll from the underground station, resting his back against the lamp-post's metallic firmness. His trench coat's lapels were raised against the cold, while his hat was tipped forward, over his eyes, in a curiously rakish way that made him look like someone in a spy movie. It was an image he always affected at moments like this, as if mocking the authorities.

He had been there for at least fifteen minutes, waiting for something to happen. The agent was supposed to have arrived at ten o'clock. The meeting point's proximity to the tube made for an unusually public rendezvous but this, he had told his embassy contact, made it all the less suspect. What was keeping him? Had he been intercepted? Were the security services now about to emerge from the mist to claim him? They were on to him, that much was sure. It gave an added urgency to the handing over of the latest batch of information. Only a few pieces of paper, in a normal-sized envelope, but important nonetheless. He felt its shape inside his jacket pocket and smiled. He had what he liked to think of as a useful party trick - an ability to pass papers from his jacket or coat to another person's without anyone seeing. A sort of pickpocketing in reverse. Taught him, in fact, by a young criminal he had enjoyed a fortnight's fling with during the war. A skill that had been of great use in several encounters that, to an observer, would have seemed convivial but innocent. Tonight would be no exception. If only they knew, the passers-by, their tentative pace increasing as they saw the station's neon sign: a promise of warmth, light and a train home to the suburbs. The sort of cosiness he despised.

A chill gust blew in from the river, briefly lightening the gloom as it dispersed the worst of the fog. As it did so, he thought he saw a shape come towards him. He stiffened. It didn't look anything like the contact, who was a short, squat man. This one was slim and his outline and the way he moved gave a suggestion of youth. Hard to be sure, given the circumstances, but his antennae were usually reliable on these matters. One reason he had lasted this long. He pulled a cigarette from the pack in his coat pocket, put it to his lips and then, striking a match, lit it. If he was going to brazen this out, he should appear as casual as possible. He drew a deep breath, felt the nicotine rush into his lungs, savoured it, then exhaled. He'd need something stronger when the handover was finished. A double whisky, for starters.

The figure was nearer now. Just the one man. Unlikely to be the Service, then. Or the police. They always operated in pairs, at moments like this. Now he was close enough to see properly, Burgess was pleased he'd been right. It was a young man. In a cheap suit and raincoat. A battered trilby, a little too large for him. His father's or grandfather's, perhaps. A hand-me-down, anyway. So, not a lot of money there. But, despite the unpromising material, he carried his clothes with a certain style. And, walking away from the tube entrance, on a night like this, was clearly looking for something. Or someone. Surely his handlers hadn't sent this boy? He'd soon find out.

'Evening!'

The young man stopped, only a few feet away. His eyes scanned Burgess's face, as if seeking confirmation of something. After the briefest of pauses he replied.

'Good evening!'

The voice was neutral. No hint of cockney, or the provinces, but neither did it have his own clipped, unmistakably public school accent. A grammar school, then, at best. What did come across, though, was an appealing confidence which was both a product of, and major contributor to, an immediately engaging sex appeal. This, like his good looks, was essentially down to his youth rather than any inherent beauty. A connoisseur of such things, Burgess placed him at twenty. He assessed him, much as an art dealer in St James's would a painting brought into his gallery. The boy would have begun to turn heads around seventeen, peaked a couple of years later and would start to lose his looks – replaced by a pleasant but uncommercial blandness – within four or five years at the most. Still, that was in the future. He would do very well for tonight.

'Not the best evening for a stroll,' Burgess volunteered.

'Depends.'

'On what?'

'Whether you're looking - or hiding.'

No, he thought. This was not a Soviet diplomat. Still, as he had always found, complete candour was surprisingly effective.

'You're not from the embassy, then?'

'The Embassy? No! And what would I be doing here, if I was?'

'Meeting me.'

'Sorry. You're in the wrong part of town. I can tell you where it is, though, if you're lost. Which wouldn't be surprising given this fog! It's at the Piccadilly end of Bond Street. Right hand side as you're going up. I don't know the number, I'm afraid…'

'Not the Embassy Club, you idiot!'

'Oh! Sorry. I…'

Burgess checked himself. This wasn't a waiter or club servant to be snapped at. And the boy could hardly be blamed for assuming a stranger was asking about a well-known nightclub, rather than the London outpost of the Soviet Union.

'No, it's I who should apologise. Never in the best of tempers in weather like this.'

The young man tried to restart the conversation.

'I've been to the theatre…'

He was about to continue but Burgess cut in, offering him a cigarette with a casual but compelling gesture. The boy took the cigarette.

'Thanks.'

He also accepted a light, during which Burgess touched his hand with his own, supposedly to shield the flame. He was irritated that his hand shook. Not quite the commanding impression he wanted to make. Damn. He needed that whisky.

'And you thought you'd have a little stroll afterwards?' His voice, at least, was firm. 'As it was such a nice evening?'

The boy grinned. 'Something like that.'

'I had much the same idea. Perhaps we could walk together?'

The boy's eyes, whose colour he couldn't quite make out in this light, widened. Then the grin again. He was up for it.

'Anywhere in particular?'

'I'd normally suggest the Park,' said Burgess, 'but given the cold, and the time, I was wondering if you'd like a drink somewhere round here? Then perhaps walk me home?'

'Which is?'

'I'm staying at a friend's flat in Bloomsbury. Handy for his work. He's in administration. At the British Museum.'

'Won't he mind?'

'He's away. That's why I'm staying there. Unless you'd rather I walked you to yours?'

The boy considered this for a moment.

'No. Yours sounds fine. Mine's further out West.'

That was true, but wasn't the reason he declined. He had a tiny room, a bedsit in a house whose landlady seemed to have almost supernatural hearing - and an insistence that there be no visitors after nine pm. 'Though I don't imagine you'll be having any of those, dear, will you?' she had said, with a hint of irony in her voice, when first showing him around. 'Nice young man like you.' Smuggling this stranger up three flights of creaky stairs was out of the question.

'Then let's go!' said Burgess, with a slight shiver – though whether from the damp or desire, he wasn't quite sure.

'Which way?'

'Covent Garden. I know a nice little pub. And it's close.'

'Good. I'm freezing!'

'Don't worry. I'll soon have you warmed up.'

Chapter Two

The warm, beery fug of the pub, thickened by tobacco smoke, had been an ideal antidote to the cold. The boy's removal of his hat and coat, both now precariously balanced on a nearby shelf, had given Burgess a clearer view of his physique.

'Positively lithe, dear!' he thought with a slight smile, imagining the postcard he'd send to Wystan the next day. They shared a game of writing notes to each other about their sexual conquests, lightly disguised as summaries of sports matches. Wystan's tended to have clever little ditties, too, but that was hardly surprising in a poet.

'You look cheerful!' The boy wanted an explanation for the smile.

'I'm out of the fog and I've found a new friend…'

'I can't imagine you're short of them.'

'No, but I've always been interested in the young.'

'I bet you have.'

'And what about you? Anyone special?'

'Would I be here if there was?'

'Were.'

'Are you correcting my grammar?'

'If you're bright enough to know that, you shouldn't need correcting.'

Tommy sipped his wine, buying time before deciding on his reply: 'But my question remains.'

'You could be seeing a soldier. A sailor....'

'No, thanks. I have my sights set higher than that.'

Burgess drew on his cigarette. 'When it comes to sex, social status is irrelevant.'

'Really?' The boy held Burgess's gaze. 'I thought your sort prefer a bit of rough. Where class, or lack of it, is the whole point.'

'You're not rough.'

'Well spotted.'

'Asking for wine rather than beer was a bit of a giveaway.'

'I should have had the beer. This is awful.'

'Developed a palate, despite your youth?'

'I have friends who've educated me in that side of life.'

As he said it, the boy realised how pompous he sounded. He laughed. Burgess joined in. As always, laughter brought lust that little bit closer.

'Older friends, by any chance? These teachers of yours?'

'Yes.'

'You like the middle-aged?'

'Not specifically. My best friend's a girl about my age...'

'A girl? God help us...'

'Nothing wrong with women. They make great friends. Especially Banya.'

'Banya? She's foreign as well as female?'

'English, but with a Burmese grandmother - and a Burmese name, in her honour. It means Princess, more or less... Grandpa was something high up in the Raj...'

'And developed a taste for the local talent?'

'Yes. A beauty from a very rich family. But a native all the same. Caused quite a stir at the time, I believe.'

'It still would. Is it a problem for her, here in London?'

'No. She's very pretty. And white. But something exotic about the eyes. And very dark hair.'

'Fascinating, I'm sure.'

'Like I said, women make good friends.'

'I try to avoid them.'

'Then you're missing something.'

'Not in my opinion…'

Burgess felt the conversation going in entirely the wrong direction. Which, as a master of the art, unsettled him. He must have been more rattled by the Soviet no-show than he'd thought. Time to get back to the boy.

'Let's move on from Lily of Laguna. I'm more interested in these men friends of yours. They've taught you about wine. What about sex?'

He asked the question just a little too loudly, causing one of the men in the group nearest them to turn and look. Belligerently. Burgess gave him a wink. The sort a man of the world might give to another, when discussing women. That, along with Burgess's colouring, which was an alcoholic red, intensified by the warmth of the crowded pub, seemed to reassure the man, who was himself on his fifth pint of the evening. And Burgess's accent, which had attracted attention as much as the question itself, deterred any further investigation. No point picking a fight with a toff. The police always took their side. The man turned back to his friends, muttering a comment that triggered coarse laughter. The boy, having decided it was now safe to do so, answered.

'I like guys my own age. To look at. But I find older men more interesting. And experienced.'

'Oh, I'm that all right!'

'You don't have to sell yourself. I wouldn't be here if I didn't want to go home with you.'

That was more like it. Burgess seized his chance.

'Then get your hat and coat and let's head off. To my friend's flat.'

'I'd love to.'

Burgess knocked back his whisky then turned and edged – pushed, really, the boy noticed, with a tingle in his crotch at the thought of forceful behaviour yet to come – through the crowded pub, full of men wanting a few more minutes of conviviality before heading home.

They skirted the south side of Covent Garden, along to the Aldwych. As they passed the Strand Theatre and the no.11 bus stop, the boy smiled.

'Yes?' asked Burgess.

'My turn to say nothing!'

As they walked up Drury Lane, side by side, Burgess placed his arm on the boy's shoulder. 'As we're heading back for the night, I think we can share at least one thing before we get through the door.'

'Our names?' asked the boy.

'Exactly.'

Both were used to anonymous encounters. They hadn't spent long in the pub and unless in one of the handful of safe ones, which this clearly hadn't been, it was rare for pick-ups to exchange names or addresses within earshot of anyone else. The boy had expected an introduction on the walk from the Embankment, up Villiers Street towards the Strand - but none had been forthcoming. He had tried to offer his own, but Burgess had interrupted and pointedly changed the subject.

Perhaps he was waiting to get a better look, in case he changed his mind? But he knew that was unlikely. Older men never said no.

'Mine's Tommy,' said the boy.

'How nice to meet you. I'm Burgess. Guy Burgess.'

Tommy was surprised he'd offered his surname. Twice. He chose not to add his own. This was noted, but not commented on.

'We're nearly there. A couple of minutes.'

They had been walking for longer than Tommy realised. Soon after sharing their names, they turned into Great Russell Street and the vast classical frontage of the British Museum loomed up at them, as if forcing its way through the fog like a liner through high waves.

Burgess led him to an entrance to one of the many sets of mansion flats that lined the street. He fetched the key from his overcoat pocket and opened the front door.

'We're on the second floor,' he said, switching on a nearby light to reveal a neat little hallway with a lino-floored staircase offering an alternative to a lift. Rejecting the latter - 'It's a death trap!' – Burgess led the way up, taking the stairs two at a time, giving an impression of eagerness as well as authority. They soon came to the door, painted a rather stylish deep red. Burgess inserted another key, then pushed the door open. He flicked a small brass switch just inside and the flat's little vestibule, hung with Victorian prints of classical sites in Italy and Greece, leapt welcomingly into view.

'Come on in!' he encouraged, nodding towards one of the doors off the entrance hall. Tommy moved past and heard the front door close behind him. Opening the door that Burgess had indicated, he found himself in the apartment's sitting room.

There were two armchairs, both of which had seen better days, on either side of a fireplace. The coals looked tired, the remaining feeble glimmers of red suggesting irritation rather than welcome, as if reproaching Burgess for having left them to dwindle and die while he went out for the evening. Tommy stood in the middle of the room, hat in hand, unsure whether or where to sit. Burgess took control.

'You won't need that!' he said, taking it from him and throwing it onto the nearest chair. 'Or much else…'

Without waiting for Tommy to respond, he pressed himself against him, his left hand cupping itself behind Tommy's head, pulling it forward to meet his own.

His lips, preceded by the smell of whisky and tobacco, pressed themselves firmly, almost roughly, on Tommy's, which opened in a gesture of submission – and excitement. His coat and jacket were pulled expertly off him and flung on top of the hat. Tommy started to undo his tie, prior to taking his shirt off but, ignoring the usual choreography of such encounters, Burgess went straight for the boy's belt, then opened his trousers and pulled them and his underpants down below his knees. As he did so, Burgess sank to his own, his face now level with the boy's stomach. 'Don't speak. Don't move', he ordered, before he went down on him. It didn't take long. Though Tommy didn't speak, he was unable, when he came, to keep silent.

'Naughty boy!' said Burgess, pulling his mouth away. 'You'll wake the neighbours!'

He stood up, as elegantly as he could under the circumstances, then walked across the room to a drinks tray and poured himself a large Scotch, to which he added, with a look of disdain, a splash of water.

'Any chance of a towel?' asked Tommy, who needed to clean himself up.

'There are several in the bathroom. Second door on the left.'

Tommy shuffled his way out of the room and along the corridor.

'Mind if I run a bath?' he shouted behind him.

'Not at all, but I'm going to fuck you as soon as we get into bed, so you might want to wait half an hour…'

Burgess was as good as his word. Fortified by the Scotch, he led Tommy from bathroom to bedroom, where each man undressed himself. Tommy tried to take off Burgess's shirt but was rebuffed. 'I don't believe in valets.'

'And I'm not a servant. I was doing it as a lover.'

'I don't believe in them, either. Too much trouble. Bad for the heart. Especially in my line of work.'

Tommy wondered what it was that Guy did for a living. The accent suggested he might have private means, though his clothes, while well-cut, had seen better days. Especially the shirt, with its frayed collar and cuffs. Not what a high-flyer would wear at the office, surely? However, this wasn't the moment for a discussion about the man's professional life.

Leaving Guy to undress himself, Tommy stripped, threw his trousers and pants onto a nearby chair, then playfully leapt onto the slightly lumpy, faintly damp, double bed. Ignoring its deficiencies, he sprawled seductively, looking forward to what was to come. Burgess, tired and still disconcerted by the non-appearance of his contact, which would mean another, inevitably risky, communication between them tomorrow, decided that the blow job in the living room would have to count as foreplay. He was never very keen on that in any case. Too slushy. For him, sex was swift and straightforward. Which is what Tommy received, gratefully and with noisy appreciation when, for the second time that evening – and just after Guy – he came.

'Ah, the vigour of youth!' muttered Burgess at the sight of Tommy's second burst.

'You're not that old, yourself! You can't be fifty yet…'

Burgess, who would turn forty in a couple of months, winced.

'Let's just say I shan't see thirty again. But I wasn't always flushed in the face. And a little overweight… In fact, when I was your age, I was considered quite a catch.'

'You're not so bad now…'

Saying this, Tommy leant over to the nearby dressing table, picked up the towel he'd brought from the bathroom and dried them both in a few well-practised moves. Then he lay next to Guy, his head on his chest, his arm across his body.

'My dear boy…' Burgess began.

'Dear boy? You're not Noël Coward! Just be yourself.'

'Myself? Ah! In that case I need a little more Scotch.'

'Not yet... Ten minutes.'

Tommy had learned how pointless it was persuading a heavy drinker not to have another glass. But he was determined to have a few minutes of Burgess's undivided attention.

'Ten. And I'm a very good judge of time.'

That was true, but only when he was conscious. To his surprise, he woke suddenly from a brief but deep sleep, to find Tommy, now fully-clothed, his hair glistening after the quick bath he'd had, standing beside the bed, shaking him gently by his left shoulder. According to the bedside clock, it was forty minutes later.

'What? What's?...'

'I'm heading off. Got to get home. Which'll take forever at this time of night. Work in the morning. In a different tie, or people'll notice.'

'Oh! I rather thought you'd stay the night.'

'I'd have liked to. But I can't. Besides which, from what you'd said, I thought...'

Burgess had thought so, too. He preferred it that way. But now, as Tommy leant forward and kissed his forehead, he felt a clenching of the stomach that he hadn't experienced for years.

'Never mind what I said earlier... Would you care to meet for dinner one evening?'

'That would be nice. But I'm afraid I can't really run to meals out at the moment...'

'Don't be ridiculous. I'll be paying. The Savoy Grill.'

Tommy glowed.

So, thought Burgess. Older friends who teach him about wine. Now the chance to dine at the Savoy. Rather an ambitious little thing. Not someone the Comrades would approve of.

'Would you like that?' he asked him redundantly.

'Yes! That would be... very nice!'

'Good! The telephone number of this flat is on a card pinned to the side of the front door. In the hallway. Have you got something to write it down with?'

'Yes.'

'I'm rarely in to take calls, so…' He was now fully awake but, despite wanting to make sure he saw the boy again, longed to go back to sleep. 'Let's fix a time. Tomorrow at eight?'

'Sorry. I'm seeing someone else tomorrow.'

'Let me guess. Even older than me?'

'Very funny. And true, as it happens. But I can't get out of it. How about Thursday?'

Burgess made a quick calculation.

'I was busy too, but I will get out of it. And it'll have to be then, because on Friday morning I return to the States.'

'The States?'

'Yes. My job, though not for much longer, I suspect, is over there.'

'How long will you be away?'

'Infuriatingly, only a couple of weeks, then I have to return. Family commitments. Long-planned holiday. All that. But there's a lot going on in Washington, and I have to show willing now and then.'

'And what's your job?'

'Let's save that for next time. Thursday. Savoy. 8pm in the lobby.'

'Fine.'

A light kiss on the cheek, then Tommy walked to the bedroom door and opened it to leave.

'You'll be there?' Burgess found himself saying.

'Yes.'

There was a slight pause after Tommy disappeared from view, while Burgess assumed he was taking down the telephone number.

'Got it?' he shouted.

'Yes! See you at the Savoy!' Tommy yelled back, to make sure he was heard.

'No need to tell the whole block!' Burgess replied, even louder.

He heard Tommy's light, distinctive laugh, then the door shut behind him.

Burgess turned over in bed and smelt the pillow where Tommy's head had rested. There was a surprisingly pleasant scent, which he hadn't noticed during sex – not least, he supposed, because after the first kiss their heads had barely touched, in either room. When he was young he had preferred to be the passive partner, for which he acquired a reputation, and it was certainly a lot less work, but with age he had come to prefer the active role, which he felt was more fitting when sleeping with a younger man. He had a strong sexual chemistry with tonight's conquest, which started his thoughts down an old, forbidden route - the fantasy he used to have, before he trained himself out of it, that he might have a future with someone. Pointless. His way of life meant it could never happen. 'Bloody God!' he said out loud. 'Just when I can't... No wonder they've banned you in Moscow!'

And with that he turned over again, to face the door and revisit, in his mind, every step of the night's events. He had just reached the moment they'd kissed when, with a little judder, he fell asleep.

Chapter Three

The cathedral blazed with colour, its vast grey walls the perfect foil for the dazzling array of clothes the congregation wore: military uniforms, the gowns of judges, the vestments of bishops and clergy, the sashes and decorations of knighthood. Countesses glittered with diamonds. In a post-war England trying to emerge from austerity, it was a vision of an earlier, grander, world. It was also a fictional one. The kingdom of Murania. The scene was framed by the proscenium arch of the aptly-named Palace Theatre. Tommy was in the audience, watching as a teenager was solemnly crowned, while the entire cast of King's Rhapsody, Ivor Novello's latest musical, belted out his Coronation Anthem.

Soon, the climax over and the new king acclaimed, the congregation processed out of the cathedral. As they did so a figure stepped from the shadows. The slim, dignified figure of ex-King Nikki, who had abdicated in favour of his son. He was swathed in a deeply theatrical cloak that was meant to render him incognito, but which directed all eyes to the man who wore it. The audience, rapt, had suspended disbelief and surrendered to Novello's plot, music and personality some three hours earlier, when the curtain rose. They ignored the incongruity of his costume, for they were focussed on his face. This had always been his greatest asset, launching him as a silent movie star before he moved on to a hugely profitable West End career as actor, writer and composer. As was clear from the centre stalls seat from where Tommy watched the show, Novello's presence still worked its magic.

He stepped gracefully forward, glided the length of the cathedral nave, then picked up the single flower left on the altar for him by his ex-wife (the new king's mother) in a gesture of forgiveness and love. As he did so the curtain fell and the audience exploded in applause. When he came on to take his curtain call, they stood and cheered, just as they had through a thirty-year stage and screen career. Eyes sparkling, he turned again to his leading lady, the beautiful young singer Vanessa Lee, and kissed her hand. At that moment, every woman in the audience could imagine themselves slim, talented and in her place. As they cheered her, they were cheering their dreams. Some ten minutes later, Tommy was standing at the stage door. A determined group of admirers had got there before him but thanks to the continuing bad weather it was a smaller number than usual, so he managed to work his way through to the second row of those waiting for the star's signature. The cluster at the front, who seemed to be rocking to and fro in unison, were clearly regulars, judging by the comments they were making to each other about that night's performance. There were four of them, in their forties or beyond. While they chatted, they kept their eye on the stage door with its comings and goings of cast members heading out for a drink, or visitors calling round and being vetted by the stage door keeper, Jimmy.

A few nights earlier Jimmy had pointed them out to Tommy when he called at the stage door: 'Look at them! Not one of them ever been fucked. We call them the Swayers. It's what they do, while gearing themselves up for a few seconds with their hero. Been doing that several times a week since the Guv'nor was in straight plays back in the '20s.' The Guv'nor was Ivor's nickname backstage, one he'd been given at Drury Lane by the Covent Garden fruit and veg porters who had doubled as stagehands in the evening. Ivor, who had been less than pleased when Noël Coward was given the unofficial but universally-used title of the Master, was delighted to have an equivalent honorific of his own. 'A queen raised to an empress!' as he said at the time. To the Swayers, however, he was, as he had always been, simply 'Ivor'.

'Doesn't he stop for a proper chat?' Tommy had asked. 'Would you, ducky?' replied Jimmy. 'To be fair he does sometimes give them a bit of his time. It's what they live for…'

Ivor liked to receive guests backstage, but Jimmy had let it be known that there was no one in particular in tonight, so Ivor shouldn't be long. The lead Swayer - or the pushiest, at least - had rushed over to Jimmy's little stage door cubbyhole when he waved her towards him. For a moment she let fantasy go to her head: 'Does he want to see me? Us, I mean? In his dressing room?' Jimmy, who wasn't known for his easygoing nature, was about to make a waspish remark when he thought better of it and let her down gently. 'No, ducky, it's just that he's not got anyone grand in this evening so he'll be out soon. But heading off straight away, I reckon. He's looking very tired tonight.' She looked stricken. Jimmy, whose shrivelled heart emerged on random occasions, allowed it a second bout of exercise: 'I thought I'd tell you, so you'd be ready for when he comes out. I know how much he appreciates your being there for him.' The Rolls Royce was already pulled up outside, as after every performance, ready to take Ivor back to his flat, or out to dinner. The woman beamed a thank-you at Jimmy, then scurried outside to warn the others.

Before long, as promised, Novello appeared. There was a moment's slight shock from the less fanatical members of the public when he emerged from the stage door, his exquisitely-cut overcoat buttoned in anticipation of the damp and a fedora clamped down on hair that was unnaturally black, thanks to the dye he had taken to applying many years ago. His face, seen in the rather harsh Soho street lights, was tanned but lined and, though retaining the striking bone structure that had launched a thousand publicity photos, looked some ten years older than it had done, under make-up and skilful lighting, on stage earlier that evening. Despite their involuntary shudder at this evidence of mortality, the fans pushed forward, offering programmes, autograph books and shrill little cries, like young birds squawking for food and love from a returning parent. Ivor's smile transformed the cold night air. Tommy stood, watching, as the Swayers, who always waited for Ivor to speak first - 'Like with royalty,' said Jimmy. 'It's a wonder they don't curtsey.' - had been given their brief ration of Ivor's charm. Then, sensing his moment, Tommy stepped forward.

'Mr Novello! I was wondering if…'

Ivor's eyes met his.

'Of course…! Come along!'

The cluster of fans took notice of the young man for the first time. They looked at him with a mixture of jealousy and the prurient interest with which many of them devoured the gossip in their newspapers over breakfast.

Ivor beamed at them.

'Goodnight, ladies and gentlemen! Thank you again!'

Tommy took his cue, following Ivor to the car door, which was being held open by the chauffeur. Ivor enjoyed the trappings of fame. Once they were inside, the chauffeur shut the door behind them, swiftly took his seat and the car started to move away.

'I wasn't sure if it would still be convenient…' started Tommy.

'For you, my dear, it will always be convenient.'

Tommy blushed.

'How's the show doing, Ivor?' Now the public were left behind, he called him by his first name. It had been Ivor who had provided the stalls ticket.

'Which one?' Novello had two running in London and others still touring the provinces. He was also writing a new musical, set in his native Wales.

'Miss Courtneidge's.'

Cicely Courtneidge was playing the title role of Gay Daventry in Gay's The Word, a musical comedy Ivor had written as a vehicle for her. The venture had worked. Rave reviews, a standing ovation on the press night and the actress's career back on track...

'It's doing very well, thank you. As so it should! It's a lovely show!'

Tommy smiled. Ivor had an infectious enthusiasm for all his musicals.

'But we won't be seeing her later, dear. I'm afraid it's straight home tonight, rather than the Ivy. I hope you don't mind?'

'No, not at all!'

Actually, he *didn't* mind. The experience of being in the most famous flat in the West End was enough for him. In any case, Ivor had another meeting planned.

'Can you join me for lunch on Monday? Rules?'

The restaurant, London's oldest, was a couple of minutes' walk from Ivor's flat. Though the star always arrived by car.

'I'd love to. But my work...'

'Is very important. We all have to earn a living, but it's trumped – as everything always is – by the theatre. I'm sure you can make an excuse. Say you've got a cold. Given this weather, no-one will be surprised. Or take a half-holiday...They do give you holidays?'

'Quite a few! It's the Civil Service.'

Tommy's lowly role in the Whitehall machine had provided the wherewithal to leave home and live independently in London, but he longed to get a job in the theatre. Recently this had become a need as well as an ambition, since it had become clear to the Higher Executive Officer who supervised his team that his heart was not in his work. The man had made his disapproval very clear. The unspoken suggestion was that he move on. Soon.

'So, Monday lunch it is?'

'I'll be there!'

Ivor was pleased. Like all rich men, he was used to getting his way.

'Good! It'll give me something to look forward to, during the day. At the moment I just stay in the flat, curtains drawn and the home fires burning until I have to leave for the theatre. Bobbie's always saying I should get out more. Which I would, if it were summer. But why would I go out more in February? Unless he wants to polish me off…'

'Oh, I'm sure he….'

'I'm joking. We've been together since the Great War and I've been his meal ticket and best friend ever since… Ah! Here we are!'

The Rolls pulled up in front of the Strand Theatre. The chauffeur jumped out and opened the door for Ivor, who didn't so much get out as glide onto the pavement, followed by Tommy, who tried to look nonchalant as he accompanied him. The building next to the theatre was divided into several flats. The penthouse was Ivor's home. The street entrance was just a few yards from a bus stop, but the intimidating grandeur of the Rolls Royce, the protective presence of the uniformed chauffeur and an indefinable regal dignity that Ivor effortlessly projected, meant that no-one waiting in the queue tried to approach him as he crossed the few feet from the car to his front door.

Having got inside, they found the lift, conveniently, was already at the ground floor, at the end of a short, narrow entrance hall. Tiny, with barely enough room for two people, it had carried film stars and glamorous thespians up to smart parties since Ivor had moved in, when his mother was still alive, nearly 40 years earlier. He pressed the button to start the machine on its uneven ascent. As it began the climb, it made little sputtering noises. He smiled at Tommy's frown.

'Sorry,' Tommy apologised. 'But shouldn't someone have a look at it? It made the same funny squeaks last time.'

'It always does. Just think of it as the lift saying hello and welcome back! Mind you, it does play up now and then. Greta Garbo was once trapped in here, with John Gielgud. For twenty minutes!'

'That's put me at my ease…What happened?'

'Johnny emerged, ashen-faced, when the thing finally decided to work and delivered him to my door. He rather breathlessly claimed Greta had interfered with him.'

'Most men would have been thrilled!'

'That's just it… He said for the first time in his life he felt he might respond to a woman's touch. Gave him quite a turn.'

Ivor moved closer - which, given the cramped space, took little effort.

'I imagine she did something like this…'

At which, thought Tommy, any other man would have put their hand on his crotch. Knowing that Ivor was as romantic in real life as on stage, he was unsurprised that, instead of a grope, he had moved in for a kiss.

Shortly afterwards the lift arrived at the flat. Ivor pulled gently away.

'Home at last!'

He opened the front door. At this time of night there were no staff around. Bobbie wouldn't be back for a couple of hours at least, knowing that Tommy was coming round after the show. As Tommy had quickly learnt, Bobbie knew everything about Ivor's life. It was what made him so good at running it. And, on this latest evening with the star, Tommy also knew what was expected of him. Ivor would open a bottle of champagne, placed on a tray next to a cold supper prepared earlier. He would then go into his bedroom to change out of his clothes and put on a silk dressing gown. 'I was wearing these when Noël was still a child actor', he told Tommy on the first visit. 'Yet from the way the press go on, you'd think he'd invented them!'

While Ivor was changing, Tommy looked around the flat, at the books, the *objets d'art*, the two grand pianos. 'A little extravagant, dear,' Ivor had confessed on their first evening together. 'But as my music paid for them, somehow very fitting.' Tommy gradually took off all his clothes, leaving them on the floor as they fell, as if pulled off in the height of passion. By the time Ivor came back into the living room, nearly empty champagne glass in hand, Tommy was half-sitting, half-lying on the largest of the sofas, completely naked and obviously aroused.

After sex there was more champagne, then a relaxed, mellow chat. Ivor loved talking about the theatre and Tommy was genuinely keen to listen and learn. He also had the wit to ask the right sort of questions and Ivor responded to his interest. There was, inevitably, gossip about other stars, their lovers, their dressing room tantrums or fights for new roles. However, Ivor also talked about theatre as a business. Tommy had been honest - another plus point in the older man's eyes - about his ambitions for a career in theatre management. He had spent much of last year doing evening work as a theatre usher, to see what it was like 'front of house', as they called it. He'd enjoyed it, but his ambition was to be a manager, not an actor - much to Ivor's relief. 'Thank God!' he said, when Tommy first told him. 'If you knew how many bellboys think they're born to play Hamlet!'

Tommy reassured him it was the business side he was interested in. He ultimately wanted not just to manage a theatre but to own one. Or to be a producer. He liked the sound of the word, and the aura of success that it carried.

'Really?' Ivor asked. 'I wouldn't recommend it. You're far too nice. Best stick to bricks and mortar.'

The evening ended with an affectionate farewell. The endearments Ivor murmured were as romantic as the lyrics to his songs, but were equally heartfelt. At home, as in the theatre, he made the over-the-top somehow touching and true. Tommy got into the lift and waved a last goodbye. As the door closed and the lift descended, he was on a high.

'I'm Ivor Novello's lover!' he said out loud, looking at himself in the mirror and enjoying the after-sex glow on his face. As he ran a hand through his hair, he admired not just his reflection but the distance he had travelled in the last few months. As he congratulated himself on being bedded by the most powerful man in Theatreland, he also smiled at the knowledge that tomorrow evening he was going to see Guy Burgess again. *Two* men after him at the same time. Two very different men. As a sexual partner, Burgess was undeniably more exciting. Tommy liked that about casual sex. The personal connection so intense, so animal, before the other man went back to a lover, or a wife, never to be seen again...

In a sort of daydream when the lift stopped, he pushed the door open and stepped out to see, with a shock that made him step quickly backwards, that Bobbie Andrews was standing in the hallway.

Tommy had seen him on stage in King's Rhapsody, where he played a wicked Prime Minister. Politicians were generally villains in Ivor's shows, unlike royalty, who were always heroic. Bobbie's face had stared knowingly from many of the silver-framed photos in the flat. Tommy thought he was nothing to write home about, but assumed that was part of the attraction for Ivor - there was no question as to who was the looker in their relationship. What the face did have, seen now for the first time close up and in real life, was a watchful, contained, energy. A suggestion of wit, sharpness and a knowledge of the world. It was the face of man who could get things done. The voice was faintly camp but had a hardness to it, tinged with humour. The mixture made its owner difficult to read, which was the intended effect.

'We haven't met, but you must be Tommy. Unless Ivor's been *very* naughty this evening…'

'Yes, Mr Andrews.' Tommy always found politeness a shield in unpredictable circumstances. Why was he back early? Had he planned a confrontation?

'And you've had a good evening, I hope?'

'Yes, thank you.'

'It's all right, dear. I won't bite.' As he said this, Bobbie offered his hand. Tommy shook it.

'I've come home a little early as I wanted to introduce myself properly.'

'That's very kind.'

'Not really. Just doing my job. Getting a better idea. About you.'

'I hope you don't mind my having been here?'

'Mind? No…. Look, we could talk here, in the cold and looking less than our best in this unforgivingly harsh light but why don't we go next door for a drink? Far more civilised.'

'Isn't the theatre closed now?'

'Not the theatre. The Waldorf. Just a few minutes, then I'll release you and head upstairs to our mutual friend.'

Without waiting for an answer he turned, walked to the door and in a silent gesture that was part enticement and part command, held it open. Tommy walked out onto the street. There were far fewer people about, and of those that were, most looked as if they worked in the fruit and veg market up the road in Covent Garden.

Pulling the door shut behind him, Andrews moved towards the Waldorf's main entrance, Tommy following him. The commissionaire tipped his hat as they approached.

'Bit late, sir, for the bar.'

'Just a little chat, Harry - with my friend here. In the Palm Court.'

'Very good, sir, I'll let Mario know.'

Andrews led the way into the hotel and down a corridor that opened into the Palm Court - a restaurant whose dance floor was famous for afternoon tea dances. Though some table lights were still on, the room was deserted.

He indicated a table. They had barely sat down when a service door opened and a portly, middle-aged Italian appeared.

'Ah, Mr Andrews. How can I..?'

'Two brandies, please, Mario. Unofficially, of course.'

'At once, sir.'

'Are you sure?' began Tommy.

'Don't worry. I've been having the occasional late-night drink here since Mario was slim and pretty. Which gives you an idea of quite how long ago I started… The police won't bother him. Or us.'

'It's an impressive space.'

'Exact replica of the one on the Titanic, I believe. Can't remember which was first, this or the ship's. Either way, it gives the place a slight frisson, especially at night. You can imagine the deep dark waters of the Atlantic somewhere below you.'

Tommy shuddered. 'Must have been terrifying.'

'Yes. The sea's something to be treated with respect. And speaking of respect…'

He paused and as he did so, Mario reappeared with the drinks. Andrews pressed far more money into his hand than two brandies could possibly have cost.

'Thank you, sir!'

'My pleasure. Good night…. Now then, young man.'

He raised his glass. Tommy reciprocated.

'Cheers!'

Andrews sipped his brandy, gave a sigh of pleasure, then replaced the glass on the polished surface of the elegant small table at his side. Tommy waited for him to speak.

'I thought we should have this little meeting so I could put a face to a name. And give you a little friendly guidance.'

'Thank you.'

'You don't talk a great deal. Unlike most young men I've met in similar situations. They tend to chatter away, in their eagerness to please. Nerves, I suppose. Your self-control is far more attractive. And of course you look very nice.'

Tommy smiled, but said nothing, so Andrews continued. 'It's quite simple, really. Ivor has taken a shine to you. You're bright enough to know this little fling is something he's done a hundred times before and, though fun for you both while it lasts, it ultimately means nothing to him. So don't go falling in love. Or persuading yourself, for the sake of your self-esteem, that that's what this is about. Because it's not. It's about you being fresh flesh. And Ivor being charming, famous - and generous. This normally manifests itself in gold watches or ruby cufflinks, but in your case, he tells me, you're more interested in getting on. In the theatre. I approve of that. Indeed, I applaud it. And doing so through Ivor is very clever. Because it will give him great pleasure to help you. So everyone wins. But as you must have noticed he isn't in the first flush of youth. Or, given the state of his heart, of health…'

Tommy moved slightly forward in his chair, as if to prove he was giving his full attention. Nodding his approval of this, Andrews carried on.

'As you'll also have noticed, his lovemaking isn't exactly energetic. No need to blush, dear. Though it's very becoming when you do… He's always been more affectionate than animal in bed and for the sake of his heart I want to keep it that way, so don't try anything too athletic to vary the entertainment. It's youth, beauty and close physical company he wants, not a trapeze routine.'

'He has trouble with his heart? Physically, I mean?'

'Yes. Has for years. His father died of a heart attack. About the same age Ivor is now. So, all in all, though he lives for the theatre and won't stop performing, he mustn't overdo things offstage. Enjoyment, not exhaustion. Now, when are you meeting next?'

'Monday. Lunch at Rules.'

'That soon? Heavens! Sensible to meet at lunchtime, though. Late nights like tonight aren't good for him. And please don't go back with him after the meal. He'll need his energy for the show that night.'

'But if he…'

'Decline. Nicely. I'm sure you'll think of something. He may look rather hurt - he's good at hurt. Did it very well in Downhill, back in '27. For Hitchcock. But he won't mind for long. I'll make sure of that.'

'Mr Andrews…'

'Yes, dear?'

'I want you to know that I genuinely like Ivor. For himself. And I hope that my…friendship with him…'

'Go on.'

'That it doesn't upset you in any way.'

'I've already told you it doesn't… But thank you for asking. Now, it's getting late. I'd like some time on my own, before I go up to the flat. I've enjoyed our little chat. Very helpful.'

Tommy stood up, leaning slightly across the table to shake the hand that Andrews offered - without getting out of his chair - as confirmation that the conversation was over.

'Goodnight, then.'

He went to take his hand away but Andrews gripped it. Not aggressively, but with an unexpected firmness.

'One thing you need to understand. The secret of keeping Ivor happy, is to make sure I am.'

'And I do that by…?'

Andrews let go.

'Don't worry. No sex involved. Just keep me informed if there's anything I need to know. Anything that might affect Ivor. Leave a note at the stage door.'

'You want me to spy on him?'

'That's rather a harsh term. Just keep an eye out.'

'But…'

'I have to make sure everything's fine in our little world. Because if it is, then he can write. And compose. And act. And employ the small army of people who depend on him. He's the swan on the surface and I'm the legs paddling under the water to keep the show on the road. Understood?

'Yes… Goodnight.'

Bobbie Andrews gave a smile that, for the first time that evening, seemed entirely natural.

'Goodnight. And enjoy Rules. The lamb's wonderful…'

Chapter Four

Thursday had been one of those rare January days when, despite the cold, the sky shone with the vivid blue more usually associated with summer. It was past five o'clock, chilly and dark. Tommy emerged from Leicester Square Station and headed up Charing Cross Road. He was meeting Banya at Newbolt's, the second-hand bookshop where she worked. The plan was to go on from there to Maison Bertaux, one of their favourite Soho cafés, to catch up with each other's news. He wanted to see her before he saw Guy Burgess. He hadn't spoken to Banya except on the phone for several days and there was a lot to tell her.

Newbolt's had a distinctive shop window, with a well-arranged display (one of her duties) of antiquarian and second-hand books, most of them either poetry or about the sea. The shop was named after Sir Henry Newbolt, the Victorian poet who had seen life as a game played on the pitch of an English public school. Hugely popular in his day, he had been equally at home on the high seas and wrote many poems celebrating the Royal Navy. He had been out of fashion since the First World War, when comparing battlefields to playing fields, in his poem *Vitaii Lampada,* with its catch-phrase of 'Play up! Play up, and play the game!' had been rendered obsolete and obscene in the wastelands of Passchendaele and the Somme. The shop drew considerable interest from American tourists, for whom its very Victorian window display was an immediate attraction. It also had a local London following because, despite its homage to Sir Henry, it sold volumes of and magazines on modern poetry and had developed a reputation as a place where young poets gathered for regular readings to publicise their work. For them, the contrast between the shop's name and the *avant-garde* volumes and events was something of an in-joke.

Banya's appearance was a complete contrast to the Union Jacks, White Ensigns and Victorian bric-a-brac of Newbolt's window. Petite and slim, her jet-black hair was cut short but with plenty of body, in thick clumps of curls, high off her neck in the latest Italian fashion, though her clothes owed more to the clean lines of Christian Dior's New Look, which had crossed the Channel from France a few years earlier. A small but crucial income from a family trust fund, allied to a knack for a bargain and a flair for combining cheaper outfits with one or two more expensive items, meant she always looked stylish. Another personal touch was her vivid red lipstick. She chose the colour partly for fun but also because it highlighted her white, even teeth. As she liked to joke, they were the least English thing about her.

She and Tommy had met at a play, six months ago, when she happened to sit next to him in the cheapest, most uncomfortable seats at the New Theatre, during a production of King Lear.

When going out with well-heeled friends she would sit in the stalls, but when she was on her own she was happy to sit anywhere, and on this occasion only a handful of the cheapest seats had been available. The main attraction was the old-school star in the title role but despite his undoubted charisma, when the interval came, Banya, at that point still a complete stranger, had put her hand on Tommy's arm: 'What a *ridiculous* old fool Lear is! Please tell me you find all this as absurd as I do!'

He did. She laughed and suggested they give up on the Shakespeare and have a drink. Not in the theatre bar, but further up St Martin's Lane, in a little pub off Cambridge Circus. Enchanted, he agreed and they spent the rest of the evening sharing a bottle of Beaujolais and talking about theatre, ballet, books and politics. The last being something she was more interested in than Tommy, but she made it sound as much of an adventure as anything the arts had to offer. By the time he walked her to her bus stop, they were friends. During the last few minutes at the pub, once the landlord had loudly announced it was high time everyone left - as he valued his licence and the Old Bill were very expensive if they caught him open later than he should be - Tommy had anticipated this moment. She was so unlike the girls he'd known at home, or the typists and earnest young women at the Ministry, that she might want to take things further - either that night or the next time they met. Because it was certain they would meet again. There was still so much to talk about, and a whole city to explore, with someone who would be the ideal companion. Though she was a year younger than him, at a time in life when a year was a major difference in experience, she had the confidence and worldliness of a much older woman. When he went to kiss her goodnight, unsure of where to aim and with what degree of élan, she deftly turned her face slightly away from his to give him a cheerful but chaste kiss on the cheek:

'Thanks for a lovely evening!' she said. 'And I don't mind a bit that you're not… you know.'

'You mean that I'm… you know…?'

'Exactly. Which is womanhood's loss but means we'll get on beautifully for a lot longer than if you weren't. And we'll need *several* bottles to do that particular subject justice… Oh, God! There's my bus!'

She'd slipped one of Newbolt's business cards into his overcoat pocket, pecked the other cheek while he gave a dazed smile, then not so much hopped as soared onto the bus's platform - a legacy of the ballet lessons her mother had put her through as a child.

Now here she was, waiting for him.

'Darling!'

She waved a gloved hand in greeting and his spirits, already high, lifted further, as they always did in her company.

'Hello!' he replied as he finally reached her and they hugged. She was careful to keep her cigarette away from him, holding her right hand out at an angle, using her left to pull him towards her. Though her body was slim, it always felt surprisingly strong. Had she been born ten years earlier, she would be have been a natural recruit for the Special Operations Executive. Tommy could easily imagine her parachuting into Occupied France…

'Do you mind if I keep puffing while we walk?' she asked. 'I've been very good about not smoking recently but I simply had to have one just now and it's got me rather hooked.'

Banya had tried to stop smoking, on the grounds that it eventually had an unfortunate effect on one's lips and she'd rather not have the little lines round them in years to come, but it was such an ingrained habit, and so integral to her repertoire of hand movements, that she found giving up impossible. He colluded in her pretence that she was getting the upper hand of the habit, but he was quite sure this would have been the third or fourth cigarette of her day, rather than the first. She took his arm as they walked to Cambridge Circus then, crossing it, past the Palace Theatre, to where it met Greek Street. She drew deeply on her cigarette, then waved it at the line snaking along the side of the theatre:

'Ivor's still packing them in, I see?'

'Of course!'

'Not that you're biased.'

'I can't deny I like his work.'

'And he you, darling.'

'I won't deny that, either. I aim to please.'

'And the other man you have on the go? The Stranger in the Fog? I can't wait to hear all about him!'

'I'll tell you all once we've sat down… Good. Not too busy…'

They had arrived at Bertaux. The French-run café was popular, but this evening it was quieter than usual. He and Banya had a favourite table, just inside, where they could enjoy the comings and goings, look at the pastries, yet talk with some sort of privacy. The chatter from other customers and from those simply coming in to gossip with the manageress meant they wouldn't be overheard.

Over coffee they swapped their latest news, sharing the excitement of life in London, the adventures they had once formlessly dreamed of now coming true. The war was a childhood memory, peace was the established present and foreseeable future, while the forthcoming election suggested change of a different sort. Not for the better, thought Banya, but Tommy rather hoped that Churchill would get back into power. There was something reassuring in the thought of the old boy returning to Downing Street. Besides, he had much more stage presence than Clement Attlee and seemed to enjoy life more than the austere Prime Minister ever could. Food was still rationed - more than in wartime, frustratingly - but with the Festival of Britain due in the summer and a sense of possibility about every aspect of life, from new architecture to new music, new fashion and the chance of travelling to Europe once again, it seemed a good time to be alive and young, whatever your politics.

'And that's about it', she concluded at the end of a stream of anecdotes about customers at the shop, the love lives of the two girls she shared a flat with, and the literary parties she had been to in the last week. Working at Newbolt's and being beautiful and bright was making it easy for her to begin making her way in bohemian circles. She liked the bookshop but had made no secret of her ambition to move into publishing - and marry a novelist.

'He has to be young, promising - and fertile,' she announced when she first described her plans to Tommy. 'Passionately in love with me, of course, but simply *driven* about his writing. I shall be his muse and his helpmeet. And, in time, the mother of his four children.'

'Four?' Tommy had asked.

'Four', she replied firmly. 'Three boys and a girl, ideally. I much prefer boys but it's only fair to have a girl, too.'

'Very decent of you.'

'I rather thought so…'

Tommy hadn't been sure if she was joking or just completely focused on what she wanted.

Though he was keen to talk about Guy, Tommy was very aware that Banya hadn't said anything about her love life - specifically David, the novelist she had got her hands on a couple of weeks earlier. Writers were two-a-penny in Soho and were easily identified by roll-neck sweaters and leather jackets. He had been surprised she hadn't found one earlier, but when it came to men she was very picky. It was curious that she hadn't mentioned him at all, especially as she was looking happy and well. It can't have been because of a row, he thought.

'What about David?'

'Supplanted.'

'That was quick! Who by?'

'An actor, as it happens. A film actor, so not quite the real McCoy, but he's a darling. And, more to the point, he writes poems. Not published yet, but he's working on it. Getting enough together for a volume. It seems I've already inspired him in that respect.'

'A poet? Aren't they're all nancies?'

'Not this one. Quite an eye for the ladies. One ex-wife and a recently discarded mistress.'

'Sounds like used goods!'

'And Novello isn't? Not to mention the Stranger? Or indeed you?'

Tommy sat up in his chair, backing away from her flashing green eyes.

'Gosh! Got out of bed the wrong side?'

'*Au contraire*, I got out of his bed this morning and couldn't have felt happier. Until you made snide comments about my man.'

'Banya, I'm trying to get your wise advice. Not have a row.'

'Then drop the flippant comments. Can't you see I'm in love?'

'How was I to know? I thought you heart belonged to David...'

'Not any more. Peter's the one for me.'

'And his wife?'

'Ex-wife...'

'And the...'

'Discarded.'

'*Recently* discarded mistress.'

'It's possible she'll fight back, I suppose, but that makes him more of a challenge. Which I'm happy to rise to.'

'Age? Build? Type?'

'Twenty-nine. Athletic. Attractive. Luscious dark hair, but a few grey ones behind the ears, which is maddeningly sexy. He's bright, well-read, and a very good writer. Oh, and he's American.'

'Blimey! What are his films like?'

'I haven't seen any! And to be honest, he seems to play the best friend rather than the leading man, but there's talk of a breakthrough role in a new film. Which he's going to Paris for...'

'I'd love to meet him!'

'I'll arrange it. What could be nicer than to introduce my lover to my best friend?'

'What sort of poetry? Modern or traditional? What does he write about?'

'Darling, so many questions! He says he prefers modern poetry, as a style. Big fan of Auden. Though rather sweetly he also likes Tennyson. At the moment he's writing about me. Three poems already.'

'Does he recite them to you as you sprawl seductively on the sheets?'

'No. He reads them. Not quite the same, I know, but in a way it's more sincere. Like a lot of poets, he can't memorise lines - even his own. Film scripts, yes. Poems, no. Don't ask me why. He told me he once left a sheaf of some really good work on a train. Never saw it again. Heartbroken. A writer's greatest fear…'

'But he must have known what he'd written about?'

'Yes, and the best phrases stayed with him, but he finds when he starts again he can never quite recapture the flow and feel of the original. So they're ruined. He says it's like trying to reheat an old meal.'

'Then let's hope he hangs onto yours.'

'He will, if he knows what's good for him. He's nearly got the volume together and he's planning a few more to go in it. They'll be about me, too. Something to do with the enchanting emeralds of my eyes, apparently.'

'I look forward to the launch party. I'll get him to sign a couple.'

'I'm sure he'd be delighted. And how sweet of you to buy two.'

'Buy?'

'Tommy, books don't grow on trees. Launches are to sell books, not give them away.'

'Guy knows people in publishing. Perhaps he can have a word somewhere…'

'That would be marvellous. Peter's really are very good. Some very funny, but mostly they're what I call proper poems. Sad. Make you wistful.'

'At which point he wraps his manly arms around you?'

'That's the idea…Who's Guy?'

'The man I met the other night.'

'The Dark Stranger? Come on then, let's have the juicy details!'

'He's not dark - more florid, really. And not handsome exactly. He's too old to be that… he looks about fifty. Mind you, everyone over forty looks rather worn out, don't they?'

'How funny! I didn't have you down as a grave robber. But he can't be that bad, if you slept with him.'

'I didn't say he was. Just not traditionally handsome. Or, rather, he is, but in a ruined sort of way. Which was part of the attraction. You can see he would have been good-looking, when he was young...'

'It's the drink, I suppose?'

'Yes - but there's something else. Something I can't quite put my finger on. Something rather sad. Not immediately so. I mean, he's quite forward, which is attractive. Knows what he wants. When he wants to be, he's very funny. But underneath, something isn't quite right. There's something very... unsettled about him.'

'And you're the man to put that right?'

'I wouldn't go that far! I might not see him again after tonight.'

'Why? You said the sex was good.'

'It was. I'll spare you the details...'

'Why on earth would you want to do that? I'm all ears...'

'Because I don't want to sort of jinx tonight. I'll give you a full report next time. After all, there'll be more to tell then.'

'Then why do you think it won't last?'

'He says he works in the States, so it would be very complicated. Besides, he doesn't like boyfriends. Just fucks.'

'Charming.'

'He put it a bit more elegantly, but that was the gist of it.'

'And Ivor?'

He told her about the previous night's visit. The late-night meeting at the Waldorf with Bobbie Andrews.

'I'm not quite sure what to make of him,' said Banya.

'What do you mean?'

'On the one hand he sounds a bit sinister and controlling. On the other, you could say it was all rather sweet. Spending his life looking after a man. Keeping him happy. Nurturing his talent.'

'Like a woman would?'

'Yes! It's not a million miles from my plans. But in another way it's rather pathetic. After all, I'd want my own career, too.'

'You're a New Woman!'

'I don't know where you got that from. New Women were a feature of the 1880s. They wore tweed and went on cycling holidays. Can you imagine me doing either of those?'

'All right, but you've always said girls should get a better deal than they've had. And since the war…'

'It helped… Like the first one did. Shook things up and gave us more to do. And the princesses have played a part, too.'

Banya approved of Princess Elizabeth and her sister, Princess Margaret. She admired Elizabeth's obvious seriousness and the fact that one day she would be Queen - and thus superior to any man in the country. But she also liked the beauty and dress sense of Princess Margaret.

'How *are* Pride and Joy?'

One of Banya's friends moved in Court circles and had passed on the King's quip that Elizabeth was his Pride and Margaret his Joy. So she referred to them as such when she talked to Tommy.

'They're very well, according to Deborah. She saw them at a garden party. Though she only had eyes for Philip. Terribly handsome, she said. Especially in the flesh. As I can vouch for, having seen him once at a polo match Grandpa took me to.'

'Did you flash those eyes of yours at him?'

'Don't be silly, darling.' She lit a new cigarette, forgetting her supposed abstinence. 'That would be treason!'

Tommy watched her draw on the cigarette, then blow a cloud of smoke, elegantly, over his shoulder. He loved the sophisticated way she carried herself…. She pointed the cigarette at him.

'Anyway, we've veered off course, rather, don't you think? Let's get back to Mr. Novello…'

'He wants to see me again.'

'When?'

'Monday. Lunch.'

'Heavens!'

'That's what Bobbie Andrews said.'

'He must be keen.'

'As mustard!'

'So you don't want the Stranger getting in the way?'

'I don't see how he could. Ivor's where my future lies. So Guy' - he deliberately hadn't mentioned his surname, even to her - 'will just be a bit of fun tonight.'

'Where are you meeting?'

'The Savoy.'

'Heavens! Again. He knows how to treat a boy. Either that, or you're getting very adept at gold-digging.'

'That's not fair!'

'Really? The richest man in the West End - or the most famous, at any rate, and he can't be poor - vying for your affections with a mysterious stranger who takes you to one of London's smartest hotels on a second date?'

'I wouldn't have called Tuesday night a date, exactly.'

'First date, then. Even more impressive. It's not exactly egg on toast in a Soho café, is it?'

'Look, it's not as if I asked him to take me there. It was his idea.'

Though Tommy tried to shrug the accusation off, he was on the defensive. He liked to think of himself as a man of the world. Being a gold-digger wasn't part of his self-image. Besides, it was unfair for her to make those sort of comments about money, given her family background. He was about to say this, but thought better of it and changed the subject, asking her about mutual friends who spent as much of their spare time as they could either at the French Pub or the Bar Italia, making a pint or an espresso last most of the evening. Talking about them not only kept him up to date about people he liked, but stressed their circle's modest means - proving that he didn't just associate with the wealthy. However, the Savoy returned to the radar when he realised that he and Banya had spent far longer talking than they'd planned.

'God! Look at the time! I've got to go…'

'I must get home, too. My turn to make dinner and they'll be starving by the time I get back… Their appetites! Anyone would think they were Land Girls, not secretaries.'

They paid for their coffees then walked out, back to Cambridge Circus where their paths diverged - Banya to her bus stop, Tommy south towards the Savoy.

'Have fun! Don't do anything I wouldn't!'

'As if… 'Bye, darling.'

They hugged, then parted. Tommy was looking forward to dinner and the inevitable sex afterwards, but was also intrigued to learn more about Guy Burgess - what he did, where he came from, what he liked, what he thought about life. One of the reasons Tommy enjoyed the company of older men was their different perspective on the world. Given this might be the last time he saw Guy, he hoped to get as much from his conversation over dinner as from his body in bed. After a brisk walk, he arrived at the junction of the Strand and Savoy Place. The Art Deco splendour of the hotel's facade, the canopy with the statue of Count Peter of Savoy, made a welcome contrast to the grime that marked most of the nearby buildings. The architecture, the lights, the liveried doormen, were all of a different world to the one he moved in. Or had done, until he met Ivor. It was an unexpected bonus that Guy seemed to have access to the same sort of places. Tommy adjusted his tie, tightening the knot, checked the angle of his hat in a nearby shop window, then walked up to the hotel entrance as casually as he could manage. 'Here goes!' he said to himself. 'Life!'

Chapter Five

Burgess was in an armchair, in the foyer. He had a newspaper on his lap but wasn't reading it. As Tommy came through the revolving doors he made eye contact with him. The smile was one of welcome but also, Tommy noted, of relief that he had turned up.

This gave him a lift. He had assumed Guy would be looking forward to the meeting too - but confidently so, sure of his charm, armed by experience and fuelled with a middle-aged man's disposable cash. All that, and the understated splendour of the setting, gave Guy a major advantage in the balance of power that always see-saws, unacknowledged but present, between any two people on a date. Guy's smile had inadvertently lost him some of his initial advantage.

As Burgess rose to greet him, he wore the worldly yet genial expression that was his trademark, but was aware he had already given more of himself away than he would have chosen. Too bad, he thought. If anything, it would add to the likelihood (which wasn't really in doubt) that the boy would be willingly bedded for a second time. Sympathy might fuel sex appeal…

'How nice to see you again!' He shook Tommy's hand firmly, with a slight squeeze. He had been known to kiss a man's cheek in public, with a loud 'Mon cher!' to confuse any disapproving voyeurs. On this occasion, and with Tommy, however, he knew it would be a wrong move. The boy wanted to be part of the world of five star hotels, not to mock it.

'And you!' Tommy replied. 'I've been looking forward to this all day!' A slight flush and his eager expression confirmed it.

Burgess was back in charge. 'I'm flattered! Now, we could go into the American bar for a cocktail….'

Tommy's eyes lit up. A cocktail! American!

'But that would be rather a cliché. And besides, I'm sure you're as hungry as I am, so let's go straight into the Grill…'

'You're in charge.' Tommy's tone, though ostensibly upbeat, failed to conceal his disappointment.

'Don't worry! The bar won't go away. We can have a drink there another time, if you'd like. But the Grill is very special and they've kept my favourite table. Which, tonight, is really for you.'

Mollified, Tommy followed Burgess in through the small, discreet door that led off the foyer and into the restaurant. The head waiter showed them to their table. Tommy noticed that, though deferential, there was none of the theatrical bowing and scraping he had seen in other dining rooms, with other men. This was impressive, as was the sense of old-world comfort and discretion, permeated by cigar smoke and the aura of wealth. They sat down and as they did so a napkin was neatly placed onto Tommy's lap - accompanied, across the table, by a wink from Burgess. The menus were set before them by the waiter, whose elegantly arched eyebrow was raised in silent enquiry.

'Two dry sherries, please', Burgess replied to the unspoken question. 'And some of that marvellous fizzy water.'

'Yes, sir.'

'Sherry?' asked Tommy, his spirits dropping again, as the waiter walked away.

'Yes. It sounds a little spinsterish, I know, but it's the ideal aperitif. Gets the tummy ready for what follows. I hope you don't mind if I order for both of us? I'm not being bossy, it's just that I want to share my favourite meal with you.'

'Put like that, how can I resist?'

'Let that be your motto!'

The meal was surprisingly simple, but exquisitely cooked and presented. Pâté and toast was followed by a starter-size fish pie, then, after a lemon sorbet, by a main course of roast beef. Pudding was apple crumble with cream. Tommy enjoyed the food and was impressed with the wine - Sancerre with the pie, Merlot with the beef and Monbazillac with the crumble. Even the coffee that followed tasted special, making it as much a component of the meal as the sherry had been. But his main pleasure was in the conversation, and in Guy's interest in him. Not so much the evident sexual one, as his wanting to hear Tommy's life story. His ambitions. He told Guy about his love of theatre, of how he felt most fully alive when watching a play - or a ballet.

'Ballet? Dear God!' was the reaction. 'What about opera?'

'Oh, I've seen a couple, but it doesn't have the same appeal, I'm afraid. Much less sexy!'

Burgess leant back in his seat and lit up the cigar that had been brought, unasked, with the coffee.

'A brief word of advice. If you want to be a grown-up pansy, then you have to take an interest in opera. No, really… It's the apotheosis of theatre. You get drama, set design, lavish costumes - and sublime music.'

'But the people in opera!' Tommy protested. 'They're so fat! It makes a nonsense of what's happening on stage. Having an enormous woman supposedly dying of consumption…'

'Surely a theatre aficionado like yourself can manage a suspension of disbelief? After all, when you're watching Hamlet duelling with Laertes, you're fully engaged, even though you're perfectly aware that you aren't at the Danish Court. You're in a playhouse on Shaftesbury Avenue and the little minx playing Hamlet will rise from the dead at the curtain call.'

'I suppose so. After all, it's the mix of drama and music that makes Ivor Novello's shows so wonderful…'

'Ivor Novello?' Burgess raised his eyes, theatrically. 'It gets worse! Don't tell me you're a fan.'

'More than that. A friend.'

'Ah! Now we're getting somewhere!' Burgess blew a satisfied ring of smoke towards the ceiling, then sat up in his chair and lent forward, conspiratorially. 'Do tell.'

Tommy was disappointed that the news of his knowing Ivor, which he had assumed Guy would be impressed by, had instead been entirely taken in the older man's stride. Flustered, he spoke quickly, as if to regain momentum.

'I've always loved his music - we had records of it at home, of course. Since I could, I've been to see his shows, too. They really are wonderful. And then one day I plucked up courage and asked for his autograph. At the stage door. He was very friendly and…'

'I'll bet he was. Sorry. Do carry on…'

'He signed my programme, but also wrote a telephone number on it, with a short message. To call later that evening.' Tommy's eyes shone with the memory. Burgess's only looked more cynical.

'Hmm…'

'Anyway, I called. Someone answered. I later worked out that was Bobbie Andrews. His friend.'

'Indeed. Go on.'

'He put Ivor on the phone. We had a nice chat, then he invited me to join him for a drink after the show the next day. I was to meet him outside his flat. The stage door being too public.'

'After which you went inside?'

'Yes.'

This, too, seemed to amuse Guy rather than impress him. 'What's he like in bed?' he asked. His cynicism was replaced by a mischievous energy.

Tommy blushed. 'It's not really fair to talk about that.'

Burgess was pleased at the reply, which confirmed an advantage he had over Novello as a rival for Tommy. 'I see. Not much to write home about, then. As I've heard before.'

'I didn't say that. And where have you heard it?'

'Ivor Novello has been bedding bellboys and aspiring young actors, not to mention singers and dancers, for decades. And not everyone is as circumspect as you when it comes to discussing the experience.'

'I enjoyed it.' said Tommy, loyally. 'And of course he's absolutely fascinating.'

'About theatre?'

'What else?'

'That's rather the point. There seems to be nothing else for him, from what I gather. He lives for the stage. People - real people - mean nothing to him. Except as paying customers at his shows.'

'That's a bit harsh. But even if you're right, he makes no bones about it. The theatre is his world. And as I've been telling you tonight, it's mine too. Or will be.'

'Which is where Mr Novello comes in? As it were.'

'Yes. And why not? He takes a genuine interest in me…' He was interrupted by Burgess's laugh.

'That's very mean of you.'

'I'm sorry, Tommy, but the idea of his jumping on you out of altruism…'

'If he does like my body, that's hardly something to laugh about. After all, I wouldn't be sitting here if you didn't.'

Burgess reddened. For the second time in the evening he was at a disadvantage, but, like an ageing but resilient boxer, he refused to let a painful blow stop him.

'You know,' he said, recovering quickly, 'You're very attractive when you're passionate. Let's talk about passion...'

Emboldened, Tommy threw the spotlight back onto Guy. 'No, let's talk about you. What are you passionate about? Apart from me, of course...'

'Apart from you? Politics.'

'Politics?' This was the last thing Tommy expected. He had anticipated an amusing little speech about the joy of sex - or the pleasures of the bottle, given the part it evidently played in Guy's life, written as it was on his complexion and his belly. His tailor did the best to minimise the second, but with his jacket open and characteristic slouch when seated, Guy's stomach undermined Savile Row's best efforts to disguise its presence.

'Yes, politics. Real life. People. Changing the country.'

'You're looking forward to Churchill getting back in, then? If he does. Mind you, with the mess Labour have made it can't really be in doubt...'

'Is that you speaking or your middle-aged friends? And if the former, you're seeing too much of the latter.'

'You see, Ivor says...'

'Haven't we already established Ivor Novello's the last person to listen to when it comes to current affairs? He's as reactionary as the royals he likes to play on stage. Come the revolution, he'll be lined up against the back wall of whatever theatre he's gracing - and shot.'

'Hang on! Mr Churchill is pretty old-fashioned, too!'

'You seem to think I share your awe for the old bulldog. Let me disabuse you. Churchill is the last person I'd vote for.'

'Oh! You're not a Conservative, then?'

'Conservative? Christ, no! I'm a Communist!'

The volume with which Burgess said this, along with the statement itself, turned several heads at nearby tables. Tommy grinned broadly.

'You?' he asked.

'Yes! And what's so funny about that?'

Where to start, thought Tommy. 'You're not exactly a son of the soil, are you? I can't see you on a factory floor!' He expected a riposte about the masculinity of manual workers, but was met instead with a very different Guy: sitting up straight, his face concentrated, his eyes clear and his voice serious. The intensity with which he spoke transformed him from Byronic roué to a man with a mission. It also, he noted, took several years off him.

'I work for a living, Tommy. I sell my labour.'

'Yes. To the government, you said. Though you're very cagey about exactly what it is you do. But, whatever it is, you can't pretend to be working class.'

'I don't. At least not as the term is generally understood. But in Marxist theory, in the analysis that actually matters, then of course I am. Everyone is, unless their income comes from ownership of land, cash or shares. But though, thanks to our shockingly-ordered society, my experience of life is utterly different from those born into the lower classes, that doesn't stop me dedicating my life to their service.'

'Like Pride did in South Africa?'

'Pride? South Africa? What the hell have lions got to do with it?'

'Sorry! It's a nick-name the King has for Princess Elizabeth…'

'Christ! Don't tell me he's been taking you out to dinner too?'

'Very funny.'

'It would be! Now the late Duke of Kent would have been entirely another matter. And afterwards he'd have had the trousers off you before you'd shut the door…'

'My friend Banya….'

'I thought she was part Burmese, not African.'

'Well remembered!'

'I listen to what you say. My work means I have to remember conversations.'

'I've been hoping we'd get round to your work.'

'I've been hoping you'd finish your anecdote.'

'You've strung it out so much with your interruptions it's sort of died a death. I was going to link what Princess Elizabeth said in that radio broadcast in '47, about dedicating her life to the Empire, a life of service to the people...'

'Ah, I see. Now that's safely out of the way...'

'You can finally tell me something about what exactly it is that you do for a living...'

'I'm charmed by your interest', Burgess interrupted. 'And impressed by your persistence. But no. Not this evening... As I'm heading back to Washington at the crack of dawn - an unfortunate expression, I've always thought - work is the last thing I want to talk about tonight.'

Tommy took another sip of wine. Guy changed the subject.

'You mentioned the election. We'll never get Communism in this country through the ballot box, of course. The Establishment are far too clever for that. But there are other ways.'

'But the result in '45...'

'Was a great improvement on what we had before, but shows the system trying to preserve itself while making merely superficial changes...People bang on about the National Health Service. The Welfare State. Nationalisation of industry. They're all good things, but we still have a King. Capitalism. The class system. We need real change. What we'll get, when Churchill wins an overall majority...'

'When? Then you're sure he will?'

'Yes. People are idiots. They're bored of austerity under Labour and they feel, in a sickeningly British way, that it's time to give the other chap a go. An innings at the wicket. Even though the other chap happily sent troops in against strikers before the First War.'

'And saved us in the Second.'

'He was a necessary evil in 1940, I grant you. But that's over. There are other battles to fight. Bigger ones. Closer to home.'

'At the Savoy Grill?'

'Now you're being flippant. Far less becoming.'

'You're the flippant one. Sitting here, of all places, talking about revolution.'

'We were talking, specifically, about the next election. Which, sadly, is when people, after a brief flirtation with social justice, will try to turn the clock back to the '30s.'

'To peace.'

'To the past. We've already got peace. They've got better housing than before the war. They ought to take themselves seriously. As citizens, not subjects. But, for all their radicalism in '45, a surprising number of them have been indoctrinated into thinking the Tories are the natural ruling class, so they'd better put them back in charge again. It's not that they want to be kept below stairs, behind the green baize door, like their parents and grandparents, it's just that they feel more comfortable when the government minister on the newsreels or in the newspaper photograph is clearly a gent. Given this, who better to vote for than Winston, a cigar-smoking grandson of a duke?'

'Hang on! You sound like you went to public school yourself…'

'I did. Eton.' Guy's pride in this shone from him.

'There you are, then.'

'Where, exactly?'

'You're one of your so-called class enemies. A gentleman.'

'I don't deny it. Which means I know what the bastards are really like.'

'But you had an education.'

'And I want to give a better one to the rest of the country. Which I'd start by closing down the public schools.'

'Why do you hate them? Were you bullied?'

'Not at all! In fact, I loved the place. Happiest days of my life and all that. But that's part of the problem. Because I couldn't agree more with Cyril Connolly.'

'The writer?'

'Him. Looks like a pug, but women find him irresistible, I'm told. His theory is that schools like Eton are so beguiling, they cripple you for later life. You spend too much energy looking back to your teens. Which is madness, of course. We're the only country in the world where it happens. If Italian bankers, Dutch industrialists or Belgian arms manufacturers are feeling nostalgic, they'll think of the older woman they lost their virginity to, or childhood summers in their family's country house. Their English equivalent smiles ruefully as he remembers how he used to thunder down the rugby pitch as a seventeen year-old, or sits there with tears streaming down his face as he remembers singing the School Song in the chapel at the end of term. If he's feeling perkier he gets a semi-hard on thinking about the crush he used to have on the handsomest prefect. Now, don't get me wrong. It's all very compelling. Taps into the same, very English, sense of loss as A E Housman's poetry. A Shropshire Lad made flesh. But it's a national disease. Or among those of a certain class, anyway. I'm as guilty of it as the next man, but where I differ from them - and especially from your Mr Churchill - is that I actually care about people other than the privileged sliver of society I was born into.'

'That's very decent of you...'

Burgess ignored the sarcasm.

'Privilege is wrong. Divisive and wrong. Surely you can see that?'

'It's part of life. It's natural. We're not created equal.'

Burgess reached for his wine.

'We're certainly not treated equally. As for my background, surely it gives me a moral authority to push for change? It can't be dismissed as sour grapes from someone born poor. It's evidently altruism. And evidently just.'

'Bit of a saint, are we?'

'No. Saints are minor deities in a religion that, like all religions, is an opiate. A way of glossing over hell on earth by promising a future heaven far above it. In the sky! I mean, really....'

'Will there be anything else, sir?' The head waiter had appeared, silently but purposefully, at Burgess's elbow.

'No, thank you, Marrott. Oh, unless?' Burgess nodded towards Tommy.

'I'd love another coffee, please.'

'Then make that two coffees. And if you have any more of those delicious little chocolates?'

'Yes, sir.' Marrott slid away.

'He's a good man. Always sidles up to me like that if he thinks I'm getting carried away - and a little too loud. Mustn't upset the other diners, you see. And his name is such a gift.'

'How?'

'Marrott. Rhymes with carrot. Wystan has great fun with that....'

'Wystan?

'W H Auden. The poet.'

'Oh, sorry.' Tommy was mortified at not making the connection, not least because he was a fan of Auden's soundtrack to the film The Night Train, but then he'd only ever seen the poet's name written or spoken as initials. He'd assumed the W stood for something more prosaic, like William. 'What an unusual name! If I had a name like that I'd use it, rather than hide it behind an initial.'

'Hiding has a lot to be said for it.'

'You haven't exactly hidden your politics tonight. And if Mr Marrott has a sort of code word to calm you down, then this can't be the only time you've spoken out like this.'

'Do you know John Buchan's work?'

'Yes. The Thirty Nine Steps and all that. Though I prefer Greenmantle.'

'So do I. You have good taste. Buchan had a favourite phrase, which was that the best place to hide something is under a light. You see, it's the last place anyone looks for it. And that sort of sums me up. Utter clarity is the best disguise. Now, having got that off my chest, it's time to think about fun.'

'You can't stop now! This is fascinating. There's so much to talk about…'

'True, but the night is not young, neither am I and my mind has turned to other things…'

'So, back to the British Museum?'

'Not tonight. I rather thought we'd just go upstairs.'

'Really? You've got a room here?'

'I have. A going-away present. For me. For both of us, I hope. Something to give us some nice memories.'

'That sounds a bit final.'

'It wasn't meant to. I hope we have a lot of memories ahead of us.' Damn, thought Burgess. He had meant to be gallant but sounded sentimental. Time to stop talking and get on with what the whole evening was leading up to.

'But we'll get arrested if we stay here!' said Tommy.

'Not at all. Oscar Wilde did it all the time.'

'Yes. And look what happened to him!'

'He was arrested at the Cadogan. The Savoy would have sent the policeman round to the tradesmen's entrance and given Oscar time to escape. They wouldn't have tolerated one of their best customers in handcuffs.'

'If you're sure it's ok…' Tommy said, doubtfully.

'Trust me. We just have to go through a little routine, that's all. Think of it as a sort of ballet. Swan Lake at the Savoy. With me as the wicked sorcerer and you the young princess in my power. We'll shake hands goodnight, in a very formal way, in the foyer. Then I'll go up to my room, which is number 203, by the way.

Once you've got to the Strand come back and tell the concierge you forgot to take an important document from me and could he please tell you what room I'm in. I'll have slipped him a pound and he plays for our team in any case, so there'll be no problem. I'll be waiting for you.'

Burgess signalled to a waiter that he wanted to pay. A bill was produced almost immediately.

'That was quick!' said Tommy.

'They know I don't like to hang around. Especially when there's a pretty young man in tow.'

'So I'm just one of a long line of one-night stands?'

'How can you say that? This is our second evening…'

'You're very sure of yourself, aren't you?'

'Yes, I am!' He placed several notes on the table and, followed by Tommy, stood up, ready to leave the Grill and begin the brief ballet that would lead to bed.

'The one unshakeable truth about life in this country, Tommy, is that you can get away with anything - anything at all - with a full wallet and an Old Etonian tie.'

Chapter Six

On Monday, a keen Tommy arrived at Rules, at 12.30p.m. precisely. Ivor liked punctuality. 'Unsurprisingly, after a lifetime in theatre…' he had explained over a cocktail, a week or so earlier. 'You see, you can't respond to a cue a couple of minutes after you should have done - or the curtain will have come down, to a chorus of catcalls, by the time you saunter onto the stage. So I got used to being where I am expected, when I am supposed to be there. And I find it very disappointing when others aren't.'

He had made it part of his public persona, since he came to fame and money aged twenty-one, never to lose his temper. When anger needed to be shown or people fired, Bobbie did the shouting or the firing. In such a tightly controlled court, where no unpleasantness was ever allowed to surface, for Ivor to directly express irritation with anyone was the equivalent of total war. So those who knew him kept appointments with a precision normally associated with Swiss station masters.

Rules was one of his favourite places. The oldest restaurant in London, it had been established in the 1790s and specialised in meat - beef, the lamb Bobbie Andrews had recommended to Tommy and, particularly, venison and game. The clientele was mainly middle-aged to elderly, with a smattering of young stockbrokers and the occasional youthfully ambitious businessman. With its heavy, plush Victorian furniture and fittings it could have been a gentlemen's club. Tommy felt he was travelling back in time and up the social scale with every step he took further into the building. This was the sort of place he wanted to become accustomed to.

Ivor, seated on a banquette, beamed at him as he was shown to the table - one of the more private in an otherwise closely-packed room. 'Forgive me for not standing up, dear,' he apologised. 'Doing so means getting one of these charming boys to move the table first, which I'd rather avoid, and besides, when you're very close friends you can dispense with the formalities, don't you think?' The waiters in their immediate vicinity were indeed young and attractive. Lesser tables were allocated to the older staff. Tommy shook the hand that Ivor stretched towards him over the spotless white tablecloth. As always, he was struck by the contrast between Ivor's general manner - beautifully groomed, immaculately dressed and gently camp - and his very firm handshake. A touch of steel beneath the satin.

Champagne was served, lunch ordered. Much as Tommy looked forward to the food, his attention was focussed on Ivor. At first he was distracted by the contrast between his two lovers - the actor at Rules and the diplomat at the Savoy. He thought of his night at the hotel with Guy. The hurried sex at dawn before Burgess left for Southampton to catch the liner back to the United States. But as the champagne took effect he surrendered entirely to the conversation at hand. Monologue might have been a better word, as Ivor reminisced, comparing modern London with the Edwardian city of his youth. Tommy was happy to listen, fascinated by the glimpse of a London that had flourished only forty years ago but seemed as distant as Georgian England, so great had been the changes in the intervening years. They had just finished their first course when Ivor, who had been in full flow, paused, as if suddenly reminded of something he would rather have forgotten: 'Of course, the Great War ruined everything.'

'It must have been awful.'

'It was. Though I, after some abortive attempts to fly airplanes, landed a cushy desk job in Whitehall and spent my time writing musical revues for the West End. All thanks to Eddie Marsh.'

Sir Edward Marsh, who had once been Winston Churchill's private secretary, was a wealthy bachelor who had a penchant for attractive and talented young men. His first major protégé, Rupert Brooke, had barely been buried on the Greek island where he died, on his way to Gallipoli, when Marsh had spotted Ivor at the opera. Now an old man, Sir Edward's silver hair, careful walk with an ebony-tipped cane to keep him steady and immaculate tailoring were still to be seen at first nights at theatres, the opera house and concert halls.

'You were lucky, Ivor.'

'I was beautiful. Luck often attends beauty.'

Tommy felt this called for some sort of response.

'But you still are!'

He meant to be playfully reassuring but seemed to have hit an unexpected nerve.

'Sadly, no. Though thank you for saying so. Distinguished? I hope so. Handsome? I think I can still claim that - given the right make-up and lighting! But that's entirely different from beauty.'

Tommy waited for a compliment about his own youthful looks. It failed to arrive. Unlike the wine waiter, who served each man a glass of Chablis. Ivor thought it vulgar to have more than one glass of champagne at lunch and had already chosen the first bottle of wine to accompany the meal. Encouraged by its arrival, he warmed to his theme.

'Oscar Wilde talked about youth, in The Picture of Dorian Gray. What he said made sense, but youth can only be fully enjoyed if accompanied by beauty. And of the two, it's beauty that's more valuable.'

'And me?' If the compliment wasn't coming of its own accord, perhaps he could tease - or bludgeon - it into making an appearance. Tommy felt confident enough in his own attractiveness to demand rather than wait for one. After all, he was only here because Ivor fancied him. The belated praise was politely produced, but almost immediately moved on from, as Ivor returned to what was bothering him.

'You, darling boy, have of course got youth, so you know what I'm talking about. My point about *beauty* is that it's in a different league. It's a sort of power. Magic, almost. It's intoxicating to know you possess it. At first it can be frightening. It attracts people and situations before you know quite how to handle them. But once you've learnt…'

'But what about people who aren't interested in sex?' asked Tommy, disappointed at being relegated to second or third division to his face. 'Are they immune to beauty?'

'They don't exist! Oh, perhaps there are a *few* who are not smitten - but even they are beguiled. They can't help it. They *want* to be nice to you. There's an unspoken agreement that to be rude to the beautiful is social suicide. It's like being aggressive to royalty.'

'Really?'

'Of course! Just think. You're in a crowded street. In a hurry, like everyone else. Someone bumps into you. Exasperated, you're about to swear at them, or at least pull a face. And if they're ugly, or plain, that's exactly what you do. Even if they mutter a pre-emptive apology, in that very English way, you stay graceless and cross. Not least because, added to the initial irritation, is a glow of satisfaction that the other person has deferred to you by apologising. But if they are beautiful, whether boy or girl, you take one look and the anger disappears. Any apology is accepted with a wide smile. Any lack of apology - for the good-looking can be shits too - far from cheapening them, simply demeans you - your anger at their action is compounded by an unspoken sense of shame that someone so handsome considers you deserving of such shabby treatment. There is no way, a little part of you is whispering, that they would have behaved like that to someone really attractive… A friend of mine, who I was visiting in hospital, once said to me, rather bitterly: 'There is only one true division in life. The proletariat of the sick and the aristocracy of the healthy.' I know what he means, but you can at least rise from your sick bed and join the healthy again. Whereas a more profound and permanent gulf separates the beautiful from the rest of mankind… I may have talent, but it was my looks that started my career.'

Tommy laughed. 'Then, like I said, you were very lucky!'

'I was. But as with everything in life, you pay for it eventually.'

'You've done very well out of life!' said Tommy, gesturing at the white linen tablecloth, the silver and glassware, the opulence of the dining room.

'I have. But my looks have left the auditorium. And that's the price. The sense of loss. I can always write another hit - look at Gay's the Word. Box office tills merrily ringing. But I will never be beautiful again.' As he said this, Ivor's melancholy made him look subtly but noticeably older. As he was speaking, part of him wondered why on earth he was talking like this, on what was, despite the lunchtime setting, a date. The immediate answer was the boy clearly liked him, needed his patronage and wasn't going to get up and leave in search of someone more cheerful. Besides, Tommy's refreshing *joie de vivre* was matched, unusually, by his being a noticeably sympathetic listener, so who better to share his thoughts with, given they seemed in need of an outlet?

'I have compensations, of course, but that's not the point. When I look in the mirror in the morning - first thing in the morning - I see the puffiness round the eyes. The wrinkles. The lines. The face of a man in late middle age. Yet I keep in my head the memory… the exact memory … of what I used to see reflected back at me. What the stills photographers and the newspaper reporters and film directors saw. What the cameramen captured. And the difference is… disappointing.' He trailed off, looking pained. Tommy kept silent, as there was clearly more confession to come. After a brief, thoughtful pause, it did.

'The other day I went to a Turkish bath.'

As Ivor began, the main course was announced. The head waiter, seeing him so engaged, had held back from serving the lamb for as long as he dared, but could wait no longer. Ivor gave Tommy a conspiratorial look but said nothing as the food was presented. Once the staff had withdrawn, both men, with a tacit understanding, had a few mouthfuls from their plates, mutually agreeing on how good the food was. After eating enough to show an appropriate interest, Ivor dabbed his mouth with his napkin and prepared to explain what had happened.

'I hadn't been to one of those places for years. If I want a man, I have only to drop a hint with the company manager and one of the chorus boys will be told to report for duty. One of the side benefits of employing so many actors is I have a range of young men to choose from. Variety as well as vitality. It gives them something to gossip about with their friends and, in any case, they'll get lashings of champagne in the course of the evening.'

'Lashings?' Tommy grinned.

'Of champagne, you wicked boy! I can't stand seeing anyone in pain at the best of times, let alone in bed. Sex should be fun. And romantic. You know what I like…. So, my point is there's no shortage of actors, dancers… you get the picture. No need to go looking. And sex at home is convenient and safe. No chance of a pretty policeman looking for a scalp or a reporter after a scandal.

Besides, I never really liked pubs and I'd rather die than claw my way through bushes and brambles on Hampstead Heath looking for love in the open air. Several friends of mine swear by it, but a twig up your backside and mosquito bites all over your legs isn't my idea of a brief encounter. So… my sex life is normally very straightforward. But the other day, for some reason, I felt the sap rising and thought I'd try something wholly out of the usual. The Turkish Baths in Jermyn Street. Have you been?'

'You bet!' said Tommy. 'Plenty of action once you're there. But there's quite a lot of older guys looking for a quick…' Too late, he realised he was putting his foot in it.

'I'm afraid,' said Ivor, 'that was the problem a fortnight ago. I thought no-one would recognise me with my clothes off. Not least because no-one would expect me to be there. I'd already rehearsed a quip about looking like Ivor Novello and was there a piano somewhere in the building, in case someone did cotton on, but no-one did.'

'The lighting's pretty low.' suggested Tommy.

'Very. Another point in its favour. It would help disguise my age as well as my identity, I thought. Sadly, that was part of the problem.'

'What happened?'

'I went there, dressed down in an old suit and wearing my glasses. Which the public never sees me in. The receptionist barely looked at me as he was too busy chatting to another customer. So far, so good. Then I found a locker, changed into two towels and headed into the baths.'

'Two?'

'Yes, one round my waist and one draped, rather fetchingly, I thought, over my shoulders. Which had the added advantage of covering me up a bit. Since I got ill, I've lost a lot of weight. And I was slim to start with. Anyway… I had a shower then wandered into the first steam room, or whatever the technical term is. Very low lighting, but enough to see there were quite a few people there. Through the steam I spotted a very nice little number. About your age. Muscular. Could have been a labourer. I stared at him - it's not the time or place for subtlety. He sauntered over. He of course, was wearing just the one towel. Very low. And it was clear, from its shape, that he was feeling as perky as I was. I was thrilled, of course. Especially as another man, who I hadn't at first noticed, also seemed to be making a play for him.'

'Did you talk?'

'Briefly. It's not really the done thing, but I wanted to get him out of that room and into one of those more private areas that I'd heard about… So we could move things on. Without an audience. I know I like them, normally, but there's a time and a place… So I said: 'Hi. I'm Nick.' A reference, of course to my role as King Nikki. Well, dear, the colour drained from his face. Or as much as it could, given the increasingly uncomfortable heat in there.'

'He recognised you?'

'No! He thought I'd said, 'You're nicked!' No-one would ever cast me as a copper, so it took me a second to realise the mistake. As he stood back in horror, I made it clear Nick was my name rather than my occupation and reached out to pat his arm encouragingly. Only by that stage he'd moved, so my hand actually connected with his crotch. He smiled and led the way through the steam out of the room into a little corridor that leads off it. We arrived at a very cosy little nook - a small space with a narrow entrance, a sort of arch, without a door and inside a couple of wooden seats, with scarlet cushions…'

'Did he say anything?'

'Just his name. Bert. Which fitted. He went into the alcove first. I sensed the other man, the one who had been after him, was following, so, to stake my territory, I put my hands on Bert's broad shoulders, turned him gently round and kissed him.'

'And?'

'He had soft, slightly sweet-tasting lips, which was a surprise, as he looked so butch. I wondered if he was wearing just a hint of lipstick, but that seemed unlikely, so I just put it down to his natural taste. His tongue was somehow rougher, more masculine. We pulled away from each other for a moment and I could see he'd very much risen to the occasion. He followed my eye, laughed and dropped his towel. Breathtaking! I was just as excited, and practically hurled my top towel from my shoulders onto one of the benches. Even in the throes of passion I couldn't quite bring myself to drop it on the floor. I was about to undo the towel round my waist when I sensed something wasn't quite right. The other guy, who we'll call Bastard, the one I'd thought was going to try to follow us into the room, had stopped just outside, found a light switch - and turned it on. The space was suddenly garishly bright with a horrid, cold, deeply unflattering light. I imagine every line, every imperfection was spotlit. I don't know who was more shocked - him or me…' Ivor stopped, staring over Tommy's shoulder into an unfocused point somewhere towards the restaurant door.

'Yes?' Tommy nudged.

'I'm afraid that seeing me suddenly in such a…*harsh* light seemed to shock him. I swear he actually shuddered. Then Bastard, who'd clicked the switch, stood in the doorway, gleaming with sweat. He signalled Bert to join him. Which, without a moment's hesitation, he did. Pathetically, I gave him my most dazzling movie star smile in the hope - Christ knows why, but it was sort of automatic - that he'd change his mind. He just looked uncomfortable and said, barely looking at me, 'Sorry, guv.' Bastard, crowing, pointed back in the direction of the steam room: 'There's plenty of others back there, mate. Your own age.' Bert looked rather ashamed at this but followed him anyway…'

'I'm very sorry,' said Tommy.

'As was I. More than sorry. Mortified. No one likes rejection but when you've been known as the handsomest man in England…'

His voice trailed off. Tommy instinctively went to put his hand on Ivor's, but Ivor, in public and with an image to protect, moved his sharply back. Almost immediately, however, in an inspired piece of ad-libbing, he passed Tommy the salt cellar, as if that was why the boy had reached across the table. As he did so, he asked: 'Have you heard of a poet called Sir Thomas Wyatt?'

'Vaguely,' said Tommy. 'Was he one of your conquests?'

Ivor laughed so loudly the head waiter looked across the room in alarm. 'Darling, I passed the salt as an alibi. Not so you could pour it into my wounds! Sir Thomas Wyatt was an Elizabethan. Far before even my time! He wrote a poem about falling out of favour at court, and how, once that happened, people who had sought his company when he was in a position to be of use to them, now shunned him. His line about this perfectly sums up where I find myself: the sort of boy who, years ago, would have come bounding over if I'd so much as fluttered my eyelids at him, now runs away when he sees me in anything more revealing than the semi-dark….'

'What's the line?'

'They flee from me that did me sometime seek.'

'Is everything all right, Mr Novello?' The head waiter hovered anxiously at the side of the table.

'With the food, yes. Though I've allowed myself to be slightly distracted in the course of boring my friend to tears. I promise we'll both concentrate on the lamb - and indeed the claret, which is excellent.'

'Shall I hold the pudding for a while?'

'I shouldn't if I were you, Frank. It'll burn your hands.'

'Ha! Ha! Very good, sir.'

'Not exactly music hall standard but we must find humour where we can in this vale of tears… Please tell chef that we'll be ready for pudding in ten minutes.'

'Very good, sir.' A quick gesture summoned the wine waiter, who topped both men's glasses up.

'How nice!' Ivor smiled up at him. 'I do prefer to drink from a full glass!'

Ivor turned his attention back to Tommy. 'Now, that's quite enough of my morbid thoughts on the ageing process. This lunch is supposed to be fun, after all...You should take it as a compliment I can unburden myself like this to you. I can't think of anyone else I would...'

They both knew that of course there was someone else, but he was taken for granted, as if he was somehow an extension of Ivor himself.

'I hope you can always tell me anything that's on your mind,' Tommy replied. 'Provided I can do the same with you?'

'Of course! Which reminds me, we need to do something about your career. I've made a few enquiries and I think there may be a job going before long at the New. Assistant Manager. Which would be rather a good start, don't you think?'

'Good? It would be brilliant!'

The New had been one of London's leading theatres since the Old Vic had been bombed out during the war and its actors had moved across the river to St Martin's Lane, where the New stood, tucked behind its sister theatre, Wyndham's.

'I'm pleased you're pleased. There are others in the running, but that needn't bother us too much. Leave it with me and we'll get an interview arranged. More of a formality than anything else. All the most interesting work comes through contacts, don't you find?'

'I'm sure you're right.'

'Then that's settled! And I'll also set up a meeting between you and Binkie Beaumont.'

Tommy realised what a favour this was. Beaumont was the most powerful producer in London. Find favour with him, and your career was made. The other side of the coin was that people he disliked never worked in the West End again.

'I guarantee he'll like you… The main thing is not to show you're nervous. He likes confident people. Give him that cheeky smile as you go into his office and you'll be fine. Now, let's finish this up and head back to the flat.'

Damn. Tommy knew this was going to be awkward, after Bobbie's injunction not to have sex with Ivor after lunch, but given the job offer he was in an impossible position.

'Can't wait!' he said, with as much enthusiasm as he could muster. Ivor, however, knew a badly delivered line when he heard one.

'Something the matter?' He sounded concerned but there was a dangerous flash of something else in his eyes. Tommy wondered if the hint of anger masked a deep-seated fear. Having had such a shocking experience at the Turkish bath, was he about to be rejected again, by someone who, despite all his help, would rather not go to bed with him? That would be intolerable. Besides, Tommy did want to go to bed with Ivor. He liked him, he found him attractive despite his age and, as a highly sexed young man, the chance to get his clothes off and have his body worshipped was reason enough to go to bed with anyone halfway presentable, let alone a millionaire matinée idol. A brief mental image of himself naked at the flat gave him a hard-on. He would ignore Mr Andrews and hope for the best.

'The only thing that's the matter is not being able to tear my clothes off and jump on you right now!'

Ivor's delighted laugh confirmed Tommy had said the right thing. He followed it with: 'I know it's not the done thing here, but could you ask them to put the treacle pudding in a doggy bag?'

'It isn't, but I could. What on earth for?'

'So when we're back at yours and the treacle's cooled down a little, you can eat it off something more interesting than a plate!'

'Ah!' said Ivor, summoning the waiter to do just that. 'What a pity Mam isn't alive. She'd have loved you and your naughty ways!'

Chapter Seven

Just over a month later, buoyed by Ivor's offer of a job in the theatre and unable to bear the drudgery of office work any longer, Tommy handed in his resignation.

'I can't say this comes as a great surprise,' said the Higher Executive Officer to whom Tommy reported.

'Far from it, I'd have thought.'

Carthston, a classic minor civil servant, from his cheap pin-stripe suit to his air of obstructive officiousness, looked sharply at the young man. He was unaccustomed to being answered back by a junior. He had never liked Tommy, immediately picking up an inherent difference about the boy. 'Touch of the greasepaint - and then some!' he had reported to his long-suffering wife. She, who had had youthful dreams of a life as a chorus girl stamped on by a Methodist father who thought all theatres a gateway to Hell, had an immediate fellow-feeling for the young man her husband so evidently despised. She made a habit of asking about him over dinner, her interest necessarily disguised as a sympathetic concern that the junior clerk had been playing up again. The reality was that the more her husband warmed to his theme, the more she felt drawn to the young man she knew she'd never meet and whose dreams she somehow hoped might come closer to reality than hers ever did.

'In any case,' Carthston told Tommy, 'I accept your resignation. With alacrity and satisfaction. I see…' he looked again at the neatly handwritten note Tommy had presented to him in his airless little office. 'I see you ask whether the notice might take effect from the end of this week?'

'Yes. It'll mean the money's tight for a while, but there's no point hanging around where you're not wanted.'

'Very true. Friday it is. You'll be paid off as at that date. Doing so's highly irregular, but I'm happy to use the authority vested in me to make an exception on this occasion. Though you do realise that such a precipitate departure will lead to gossip and speculation?'

'I can live with that.'

'I thought you might. Very well, it's decided. Now, run along.'

That evening, at home, Carthston described the encounter, taking great pride in what he thought of as the Olympian heights from which he'd put the uppity young man in his place. He was gratified at his wife's smile, little realising that it was one of quiet satisfaction that someone had had the courage to throw in a steady job and follow their hopes for a fuller, more rewarding life elsewhere. She was so cheered by the news that that night, when she returned from the bathroom to the bedroom, where her husband was already tucked up (they slept in adjoining singles) she came over, without face cream or hair rollers, and sat on his bed, deftly taking the book out of his hands as she did so. This was her unmistakable (but rarely given, other than on their wedding anniversary) indication that sex would be accepted. As he responded, gratefully, he imagined that the masterful way he ran the office, as recounted over dinner, had triggered a carnal response in his wife. She, as she closed her eyes, began to enjoy the fantasy that young Tommy, of whom she had heard so much, had taken his revenge on her husband by breaking into the house while Carthston was at a Rotary Club meeting and was pressing his firm young body against her mature, fuller figure before forcing his manhood into her helplessly yielding flesh.

Tommy, having left Carthston's office - he had handed the letter to him shortly before five o'clock - tidied his desk, said goodnight to the three other clerks in his room and headed to the Salisbury, a Theatreland pub on St Martin's Lane. It had a cosy old-world decor of Victorian brass, wood, mirrors and engraved glass, along with a roaring fire in the saloon. It was popular with actors, actresses and the theatre-going public, while for Tommy it had the additional attraction of being next door to the New Theatre, where Ivor had promised him a job. The Salisbury had also long been a meeting place for young men who were not, as a friend of his had put it, of the marrying kind. Tommy knew, and had slept with, a couple of the regulars and hoped he might find one in that afternoon. As he walked into the pub, he saw his most recent conquest, Kevin - a dancer - chatting to some other boys by the bar.

Though it was early, Kevin had the slight flush of someone who had already had a couple of drinks and his greeting, when he saw Tommy, was an affectionate hug. Sensing that he was on to a winner, not least because the fact Kevin was drinking suggested he wasn't working that night, and was therefore available, Tommy decided to make sure:

'Where's the redhead?'

This was a reference to Kevin's long-term boyfriend. His presence or imminent arrival was the only potential complication to what should otherwise be a straightforward pick-up.

'Oh, she's probably flogging herself down the 'Dilly…'

Kevin's smile matched Tommy's. The deal was sealed.

'Then it's safe to get you a drink!' said Tommy.

'No, I'm buying.'

Kevin moved closer to Tommy, his hand on his arm.

'What can I get you?'

'A glass of Sauvignon.'

'That all?'

'And a crisp.'

'Sure there's nothing else?'

'I'm not planning on staying long.'

'Oh?'

'But a quick drink would be nice. Before we go back to yours…'

'You're on!'

Kevin ordered the wine and crisps, then when they were served, clinked his glass with Tommy's.

'Bottoms up!'

'Who's?'

'Yours.'

'You remember!'

'Course I do! Best trip to the swimming pool ever!'

They had eyed each other up in the showers at the Marshall Street Baths - a Soho swimming pool known as a pick-up venue. Their courtship, as Tommy jokingly called it when telling Banya about it afterwards, had taken place in a changing cubicle.

'At least we'll have more room to manoeuvre this time.'

Their drink lasted all of five minutes before they left in a haze of lust. A taxi was passing as they emerged into St Martin's Lane, and Tommy hailed it.

'Are you sure?' asked Kevin, whose finances were ropey that month.

'Just this once. Strike while the iron's hot. Last time I saw you, you were about to move. Have you?'

'Yes. Kensington. Little place off the High Street. Needs doing up though. Not been properly put back together since the war. That's why it's so cheap…'

'Great!. Tell the cabbie the address.'

With that they jumped into the taxi and headed through the traffic to Kensington. Some time later, while Carthston was finally achieving climax with his wife, Tommy was enjoying his second orgasm of the evening with Kevin, shortly after which they fell into a happy, exhausted sleep.

Chapter Eight

The next morning Tommy called the office from a phone box in Kensington High Street. He had planned to tell them he was sick and unable to come in that day, but as he dialled the number he changed his mind and told the colleague he was put through to that he had forgotten to mention a dental appointment for late that morning, that he was sorry, and that he would of course be in after lunch. The colleague, Andy, an attractive boy from Liverpool, briefly teased him but otherwise showed no surprise or particular interest, so Carthston couldn't have made the news known round the office. Of course he hadn't, thought Tommy as he dialled another number. He wouldn't make the announcement until Tommy was there, hoping for maximum embarrassment. Who cared? He was going to go home, have a bath, a change of clothes and then, and only then, make a leisurely way into Whitehall. It was a bright, sunny day, though a winter chill was still resisting the signs of Spring that were sprouting in the London parks and squares. First, though, he wanted to tell Banya the news. The next number he called was Newbolt's.

'Good morning! Newbolt's Bookshop.'

'Yes, I'd like to make a complaint about one of your staff.'

There was a stunned silence on the phone. Tommy burst out laughing, at which she realised who it was.

'Tommy! You beast! I wasn't expecting you at this hour!'

'So it seems!'

'You're lucky to catch me.'

'I wasn't sure I would, but things seem to be going my way at the moment, so I thought I'd try. Right now, I'm on my way home..'

'Naughty boy! Who was it? Ivor or the other one?'

'Neither. A very good-looking dancer with legs to die for. Or under.'

'Little did I realise, when I was being so expensively educated, that my future best friend would be a slut.'

'I think I prefer Romeo. Or Casanova, if you must. Though that wasn't what I was phoning you about. I wanted to let you know I've resigned.'

'When?'

'Yesterday evening.'

'But you haven't had the interview yet.'

'I know, but if Ivor says it'll happen, it will. And fairly soon, I gather. So I'll treat the next week or two as a holiday.'

'Can you afford that?'

'Just about. I've been careful with my cash over the last few weeks, and if there's a problem I'm sure I can get something temporary.'

'Ok. Tell me all about it when we meet.'

'Will do. See you.'

'Bye. And behave!'

Tommy got back to his lodgings in Notting Hill just before ten. The other three lodgers would all be at their desks by now, so he'd have the place to himself. He looked forward to the luxury of using the bathroom without the unspoken but mutually-observed rule that no lodger would spend more than twenty minutes having their morning bath, shave and whatever.

As he stepped into the hallway and shut the front door behind him, he saw the door to the dining room, which was next to the hall, open. He was about to dash upstairs to avoid his landlady but realised that as well as being undignified - and rude - the timing wouldn't work. He'd barely registered the thought when Mrs Yardley appeared, coffee cup in hand.

'Good morning!' She managed to inject an entire paragraph of questioning, commentary and conjecture into that simple phrase.

Though he had lived in the house for several months, Tommy had barely met the woman more than a few times. He'd been told of a vacancy by one of the clerks at work, whose brother was one of her lodgers. Tommy's interview with her had been brief, not least because it was conducted in the hallway when he, late for the appointment because of appalling traffic made worse by the heavy rain, was dripping wet and she, in a bad-tempered way, was wanting to get away and meet a friend, for whom, as she tartly told him, she would now be late. 'And lateness, young man, is something I abhor!' Given the circumstances and that, though indoors, she was already wearing a hat against the weather, which meant her face was thrown into shadow, he had taken little interest in her then or subsequently. She had given him a lightning-quick tour of the house, after which she announced she would accept him as a tenant. It was clear this was because she wanted the matter settled so she could leave to meet her friend, rather than for any liking she may have taken to him. Keeping his distance from landladies was, in any case, a deliberate policy: the less they saw of him, the less they would be inclined to pry. So he knew very little about Mrs Yardley. Now, as she stood before him, right eyebrow arched, the morning sunlight seemed to spotlight her, while the warmth of tones thrown on her by the stained-glass window that was one of the hall's major features, made her look more sympathetic than he remembered.

'Erm... Good morning, Mrs Yardley.'

'You look as though you've had a busy night. No doubt working through it at the office?'

Her voice suggested a worldly amusement rather than sarcasm.

'I'm sure you'd like a bath and some rest, but I've just made coffee. Why don't you come in and have some?'

Under the circumstances, he felt no option but to accept, though wondering how quickly he'd be able to make his excuses and go upstairs to his room. To his surprise, rather than going back into the dining room, where the lodgers took their meals, she crossed the hall to her private sitting room. When he paused, she turned and, looking over her shoulder with an expression that somehow took twenty years off her, said:

'Come into my parlour…'

When he did so, the room was nothing like he had imagined. He had expected a fusty late-Victorian space crammed with objects and dotted with potted plants. Instead, the room was light and airy, a combination of Art Nouveau and Art Deco that, despite their very different styles, somehow worked. What most caught his eye were the theatrical mementos: framed posters, books of theatre history and biography, along with busts of leading actors and playwrights. Nothing like these were in evidence anywhere in the communal areas of her house, or in the lodgers's bedrooms, which were comfortably but very conventionally furnished.

'Here we are…' Mrs Yardley handed him a coffee and gestured for him to sit in an armchair opposite hers, on the other side of the fireplace.

'I had no idea you were interested in the theatre, Mrs Yardley!'

'Why should you? We've barely spoken since you took on the room. I don't see all that much of my lodgers, but you've been rather an extreme example. From your comment, I assume you enjoy the theatre as well?'

'Oh, yes. In fact, I've given up my job so I can work there.' He saw a twinkle in her eye, noticed her shift forward slightly in her seat, as if keen to hear more, and felt emboldened to carry on.

'In fact, that's why I'm back at this hour. I wasn't working last night, I was celebrating.'

'How lovely! With a friend?'

'Yes, he's....'

'Obviously a good friend, if you've been carousing all night. I hope he wasn't late for work?'

She smiled at him, conspiratorially.

Partly because she seemed wiser and nicer, partly because he wanted to keep her onside in case she was thinking of replacing him as a lodger now that he'd confessed, unnecessarily, that he didn't have a regular income to guarantee the rent, Tommy decided not to pretend he didn't know what she was saying. Also, the lack of sleep made him feel a little lightheaded, so his normal guard was down.

'Yes, he's a good friend. But not my best. As it were.'

'You have several...?' She left the word they both understood unspoken.

'Yes.'

'Quite right too. Youth and good looks are bound to attract attention! They certainly did when I was young. A lot of us had gentlemen callers.'

She gestured, with her coffee cup, in the general direction of a table which supported a group of silver-framed photographs of showgirls and actresses, taken, judging by the hair and clothes, sometime before the First Wold War.

'Especially her!'

Politely, he got up, leaving his coffee on a little side table by the armchair, and walked over to the collection. He picked up the most prominently-placed photo which, he correctly guessed, was the one she was referring to.

'I can see why. Who is she?'

'Someone you know. Slightly.'

'Really?' he turned to her, puzzled, the penny still not dropping.

'It's been a very long time since that photograph was taken, but surely if you look very closely...?'

'Good God!'

'Not the most flattering response, but chivalry is a thing of the past....'

'Mrs Yardley! You were beautiful.'

'Thank you. Now, put it down before you drop it, and have some of that coffee.'

Tommy returned to the chair.

'So, were you in the theatre, too?'

'I was. Gertie Gilbert. 'The Girl With A Winning Way' was how they liked to promote me. I was in some musicals, as I could sing a little then, but I was mainly in light comedies.'

'Until when?'

'Until I got married in '17. To a young officer. He was a banker in real life, but in uniform when we married. I was getting a little long in the tooth by then - I was twenty-seven. I'd had admirers, but never quite the right man. Not least because so many of them were already married, with families. I'd never been very keen on young bachelors-about-town. They were often very attractive, of course, but seemed somehow immature. Then before I knew it, I was the wrong side of twenty-five - which was long after most married - so when Bertie proposed, I jumped at the chance of settling down. Not least because he seemed an unusual combination of successful, steady and young. Of course, the war was another factor. The prospect of death was a great aphrodisiac. A case of having fun while you could. He'd been conscripted the year earlier. No call-up to start with, you see, unlike the last war, and Bertie was far too smart to want to cross the Channel to a slaughterhouse. So he waited until he had to, then we got married a week before he went away.'

'I'm sorry. I assume he was...'

'Killed? No. It would have been so much better if he had been. He was badly wounded. No lost limbs - though he had to walk with two sticks the rest of his life. It was his mind that suffered most.'

'Shell shock?'

'Yes. He didn't go mad, as such, so I could still talk to him, which was another of the reasons I liked him so much - he was so well-read and loved to chat about things - but unless he was in here, and with me, he panicked. Eventually he wouldn't leave the house. He had left for the Western Front as my husband and came back as an invalid child. I was a cross between a nurse and mother, rather than a wife. After a while I realised that in order to keep my sanity I needed to go back on stage, however difficult he found it. It helped that he went to bed early so, apart from matinées, when I set off for work he was already turning in for the night. But my career, which was on a roll before the war, never quite recovered. Partly I was getting older, of course, but the critics - and the producers - thought something had gone. Unfortunately, they were right. My famously winning ways weren't really there any more...'

'And when did Mr Yardley die?'

'Quite recently. Or it seems so, to me. Actually, it was nearly ten years ago.'

'Is that when you started letting out rooms?'

'Yes. I don't need the money, fortunately, but I thought I'd like to do something useful with the house rather than have it empty. And besides, I was lonely.'

'But you don't get much company from us lodgers, do you?'

'No. There's a big difference between being a hostess and a landlady. As I quickly realised. Which works both ways. Because there's a gulf between the people you'd invite for the weekend and those you accept as lodgers. No offence intended...'

'None taken... I'm fascinated to hear you were in the theatre.'

'And how wonderful that you're going to be! Perhaps you'd like to have lunch with me one day? You can tell me more. Of course, I'm in touch with what's happening professionally...'

'You are?'

'I may be old, but unlike poor Bertie I like to get about. I should say I go to the theatre.... oh, at least once a week.'

'I had no idea.'

'Why should you? Besides, you're out several nights a week yourself. With your friends, I imagine. Best or otherwise... Any of them on stage, by any chance?'

Tommy felt emboldened to tell her. Not least because, having been confided in, he thought it only fair he should return the compliment.

'Actually, I have. One of them is Ivor Novello.'

Mrs Yardley didn't miss a beat.

'You don't surprise me. You're right up his street. Dear Ivor! How we all loved him!'

'You've seen his shows?'

'Seen them? I was in two of his early plays. By that point, I'd been looking after Bertie for some time and he was in no position to refuse me permission to go back on stage. So, back I went. But that was nearly thirty years ago...'

'I must tell him I know you.'

'He'll be surprised but, I think, amused. Now, before I forget, a gentleman left this for you.'

Mrs Yardley crossed the room and picked up a letter she had placed there, earlier that morning.

'Here we are.'

'Thanks..... Erm...'

'Yes?'

'You didn't see who left it?'

'Twitching my net curtains?'

'Oh, no, I didn't mean that, I…'

'As it happens, I did, because I was about to fetch the milk in. It was a middle-aged man who looked like a depraved cherub.'

'That'll be him!'

'And that… he… is a serious rival to Ivor Novello?'

'He's very different to Ivor, of course, and he's not rich and famous…'

'But has his attractions?'

Tommy blushed.

'Yes. A man of the world. And he's fun to be with. But I do like Ivor very much. And it's thanks to him that I'm getting the new job.'

'But not as an actor, I think?'

'No, as a theatre manager. With an eye to perhaps becoming a producer at some point down the line. Ivor's arranging an interview for me at the New.'

'Then you've given up your, what was it?'

'Civil Service.'

'Before the theatre position is confirmed? Is that wise?'

'Oh, Ivor's sure I'll get it and I have enough to cover the rent in the meantime.'

'I'm glad to hear it! It's an impetuous decision…'

'Actually it's not. I've thought about it a lot. But I grant you some people would think it's a risky one.'

'They would. But if you can't take risks when you're young, then when can you? At least you're sure about what you want. And you've got the best possible person to help you.'

'I have.'

'But your other friend? If he's not of our world, then what does he do?'

Tommy was thrilled at the word 'our' and its implied sense of theatrical camaraderie. In the course of this entirely unexpected conversation Mrs Yardley had gone from being a distant and vaguely threatening landlady into a colleague of greasepaint and limelight. Warmed by her unexpected goodwill and the excellent coffee, he felt sympathy for her widow's need to feel some sort of connection with life, even if vicariously.

'He's a diplomat. I think. He's a bit vague about it.'

'Really? Perhaps he's a spy!'

They both laughed at the idea.

'The important thing is you like him. And Ivor can't claim sole rights to your time. Not least because he's got…'

'Bobbie Andrews.'

'Exactly. Have you met him?'

'Actually, I have. The other day. Do you know him?'

'I haven't seen him for twenty years or so, but I doubt if he's changed much. Maybe a little more bitter with age, but otherwise much the same.'

'Which is?'

'No, you first.'

'That's the problem. On the one hand he's quite cold and calculating. But on the other, he's devoted to Ivor and my friend Banya says…'

'A foreign admirer, now?'

'No, my best friend. A woman. Part Burmese, hence the name. The point is, she has some sympathy for Mr Andrews.'

'Then she's an intelligent girl.'

'She is.'

'Has she met Ivor?'

'No.'

'And this other man…?'

'Guy.'

'How apt.'

'It is, rather. She hasn't met him either but I'd love her too.'

'Will you ask her for her opinion of them?'

'You mean help me choose?'

'Yes. As much as one can in these matters, given it's so much down to physical chemistry between the two people in question.'

'You're a wise woman, Mrs Yardley.'

'Please call me Gertie. In private, you understand. Can't have the other lodgers call me that, or discipline will collapse!'

'I will. Thank you.'

'Now, you'd better not let me keep you any longer.'

'No. I'll just pop upstairs and have that bath.'

'Don't forget your letter…'

'I won't! And thanks for the coffee.'

'The pleasure was mine. And let's have that lunch one day.'

'That would be lovely.'

Tommy shook the hand she offered him. Looking at her, he could see the young woman still present in the bone structure of the sixty-year-old widow. He also noticed the straight and elegant shape of her back and the way she held herself. He wondered if he hadn't noticed this before because she had always, consciously or otherwise, been playing the role of an elderly landlady and carried herself accordingly.

He shook her hand again, for friendly emphasis, then, keen to see what Guy's unexpected presence meant, ran up the stairs two at a time, rushed into his room, threw himself on the ancient single bed and tore open the letter.

Chapter Nine

My dearest boy,

I find myself back in London for a little while. Not the best time of year to be here, but I can think of several ways to warm myself up. All of them involving you. I hope this finds you well. I imagine you won't see it until you get back from work this evening but I thought I'd let you know I'll be at the Stag's Head tonight from about nine o'clock, after an early supper with a friend - one I hope you'll meet soon. If you can, join me there.
Guy x

Tommy read the letter several times, delighted with the news of Guy's being in town and available that evening. He looked forward to telling him about leaving his job. And even more to spending the night with him.

As he lay back, the warm water up to his neck in the vast old roll-topped bath, he thought about his earlier conversation with Gertie. He was pleased that he had found out about her past and was happy to get to know her better, but at the same time, though she was clearly a more worldly woman - indeed, a wholly different woman - than he had thought, he didn't want his landlady turning into a friend. Though he hoped she wouldn't be his landlady for much longer. Once he started at the New he would be able to afford his own flat, however tiny. Living somewhere else would make it possible to get to know Gertie better, and on an entirely different footing. Meanwhile, he would tell Ivor about her. He wondered if he would remember her and, if so, whether she was a good actress. Was there a reason she hadn't appeared in his musicals? After all, they had plenty of non-singing parts. Ivor himself never sang in his musicals. 'I know my limitations,' he had said to Tommy one evening. 'And given I devise, write, compose and star in my shows, singing in them too seems a little over-the-top, don't you think?'

Once he'd bathed and dressed, Tommy headed out to work, Gertie presumably still in her sitting room. His colleagues made sardonic references to his dental visit, not one of them believing his story. Andy, as usual, was the most forward:

'You've got a very nice dentist, Tommy. You know, friendly, like.'

'Yes, he is,' Tommy deadpanned.

'I mean, giving you a love-bite like that. Taking your mind off the injection, was he?'

'What do you mean?' There was no mirror in the room and Tommy was sure he hadn't noticed a love-bite when he was shaving - but you never knew how long they'd take to emerge.

'Or was that just foreplay? You know, before he got his drill out?'

The other clerks found this hilarious. Tommy, with a furious stare at Andy, ran out of the room and into the men's lavatory down the corridor, where he looked at both sides of his neck. He was worried, not by what any bruise would say to his co-workers, but what Guy would think this evening. To his relief, there was nothing really there. Maybe a very slight flush on the right side, but no love bite. Andy had just been teasing. Tommy resumed his seat in the office - to more laughter - with as much dignity as he could muster. The atmosphere remained cheerful through the afternoon, until Carthston came into the office, even more dignified than usual (as he saw it) and smugly triumphant (as the clerks saw it) to announce Tommy was leaving. With immediate effect. His revenge for the boy taking the morning off on some spurious pretext. That would show him. And, he hoped, excite his wife for an unprecedented two nights running. The surprise had the intended result. The clerks were shocked. What behaviour could warrant such an immediate dismissal? Carthston hadn't actually used that word but the way he phrased the news gave the entirely misleading impression that he had caught Tommy at something and got rid of him on the spot. To his surprise, Tommy felt no anger at this unnecessary, spiteful twist. It simply confirmed he was lucky to be shot of the job there and then. Especially as the pay packet handed him would have to include payment to the end of the week. Carthston's timing had the unintended benefit for Tommy of enabling him to shake his now ex-colleagues' hands, then, like them, leave the office as soon as possible for the real world. There would be no time or incentive for a long post-mortem. They asked if he had any plans, to which he announced: 'I've been offered a job in a theatre. Junior management…' As this fitted with what they knew of his social life, any curiosity beyond mere politeness was satisfied. When they made their various ways home by train, bus or tube, any thoughts about Tommy's dismissal related solely to its possible impact on their position in the department. He himself was no longer of any interest. While they scattered to the suburbs, Tommy, as arranged, phoned Banya at the bookshop. They agreed to meet at the Black Jaguar, a new coffee bar with, incongruously for central London, a South American decor. He preferred more traditional venues but generally went along with Banya's suggestions. She, by contrast, liked to experiment when new bars opened. When they met, she hugged him.

'Darling! You look like you've had a busy couple of days!'

'Thanks. I was hoping I was looking seductive.'

She lit a cigarette.

'You always do! Besides, why worry? You know he fancies you. He'd take you if you looked as if you'd just swum to shore from a shipwreck!'

'Rather a violent image...'

'But an imaginative one, don't you think? Actually I'm feeling a little violent myself.'

'What's happened?'

'I was supposed to meet Peter tonight but something's come up. He's having to meet that bitch of an ex-wife of his.'

'Why?'

'Because she's lost a relative of some sort and is in a bit of a state.'

'That's not his problem, is it?'

'My thoughts entirely, but the woman is fragile at the best of times. She got worse during the divorce - emotional blackmail, if you ask me - and now Peter's career is taking off she feels hopelessly left behind. He calls her damaged. I call her vengeful.'

As she said this, Banya pulled on her cigarette with a violence that suggested someone sucking venom from a wound. Tommy was about to fill the temporary pause but was enjoying the character assassination, so kept silent. Banya, noting this, duly stuck the knife in.

'Which is a bit rich as she was the one who wanted a divorce, to marry a more established actor she'd met on the Riviera. Who quite understandably changed his mind about her on closer acquaintance and fled to Hollywood, leaving her high and dry. Now she's had this bereavement, Peter feels he ought to do the decent thing and give her a shoulder to cry on. Which is maddening, but then it's one of the reasons I love him so much. So I bit my tongue - when I'd rather have bitten hers. Seeing you is today's vaguely silver lining.'

'How kind.'

'What about your resignation? How did they take it?'

'Carthston was delighted though unpleasant, which is par for the course. He booted me out today, making it look as if I've left under a cloud.'

'What about proper notice?'

'He was as keen to get rid of me as I was to leave, so he's just paid me off.'

He took the pay packet from his jacket pocket and tossed it onto the table.

'But you haven't been given the job at the New yet.'

'I know... but I'll manage'.

He then told Banya about his night with Kevin and his chat with Gertie.

'A widow with a past! That touch of tragedy that makes women so intriguing...'

'You're not tragic.'

'That's because I'm young. Give it time.'

'There's something about Guy, too. I don't think tragic is quite the word. Mysterious might be better.'

'It really is time we met.'

'I'm not sure he'd...'

'Of course he would. Especially if he's that serious about you. I'm seeing Peter for dinner tomorrow. Why don't you both join us?'

'Wouldn't you rather see Peter on your own?'

'I've plenty of chances to do that. Not least when we go back to his place after dinner.' Peter's 'place' was a vast flat near Regent's Park that his film company had rented for him. It was a far cry from Banya's flatshare in an Islington street still pock-marked by bomb damage.

'Thanks! Of course, I'll ask him, but I've no idea what his schedule is. Let me get back to you...'

'Do. Now, let's have some more Merlot...'

Later, after seeing a mildly tipsy Banya onto the bus home, Tommy walked through Soho to the Stag's Head. Its customers were almost entirely homosexual men, though there were a sprinkling of street girls who came in for a drink in the warm when the weather outside made their pavement patrols chilly as well depressing. Some of them had pimps, but these, by an unspoken convention, left them alone when they were 'resting on the antlers', as regulars called their own visits.

Tommy saw Guy at the bar. He was chatting, in a relaxed but clearly lascivious way, to an off-duty sailor, who was in uniform. The sailor was short, stocky, with very wide shoulders and a backside that was shown (to the furtive delight of the customers) to perfection by the cut of his bell-bottomed trousers.

He felt a stab of jealousy, which disappeared as soon as Guy caught his eye and beamed at him, abruptly ignoring the startled-looking sailor, whose hopes had been torpedoed by Tommy's arrival.

'Tommy! You got my note! This is Simon. He's a sailor.'

'I'd never have guessed.'

'Well, say hello.'

'Hello, Simon.'

'Hello.'

'I've just bought him a drink. Now, what would you like? Sauvignon? Or something stronger?'

'No, that'll be fine. I've been on red earlier.'

'Red with…?

'Banya.'

'Of course.'

Having introduced the sailor, Guy felt he'd observed the niceties and his eye contact was now entirely with Tommy. Taking the hint, and spotting a presentable-looking man in an expensive suit who had just walked into the pub, Simon muttered a goodbye to them and intercepted the businessman before he'd got halfway across the floor.

'Notice,' said Guy, as he waited to be served, 'how that rather predatory young man knocked back most of the drink I'd just bought him and left his glass on the bar. Thus giving the new arrival the opportunity to offer him a drink and start the whole *danse macabre* again.'

'I didn't notice that man arrive. You must have eyes in the back of your head.'

'Ah! Here's service at last...Oh! and Barry and Tom!'

Barry and Tom turned out to be a pair of antique dealers. Barry was English and Tom - originally Tomas - was Hungarian. He had come over to England when the Communists took power. Tommy had heard Guy mention this and was curious to meet him. Tomas was the more talkative of the two. He clearly looked up to Guy, who prompted him to give Tommy an account of his dangerous journey from Hungary to the West.

'And, since I've been here,' he concluded, 'I have done, in my turn, what I can for the Resistance. Sent home what help I could. Guy has been marvellous.'

Burgess gave a self-deprecating shrug.

'I wouldn't say that...'

'Not at all! You see, Tommy, Guy has always taken a great interest in the anti-communist forces in my country. I'm afraid the authorities over there seem very good at penetrating our organisation and arresting people, so we need all the assistance we can get.'

'Your cause is a noble one... but at the moment I've only got eyes, ears and anything else for my friend here!'

He then held forth about Tommy's attractions. Far from being flattered by this, it put Tommy on edge. He wanted to be taken seriously as someone starting a career in the theatre, yet here he was, being presented as some sort of trophy, based entirely on his looks. Half an hour of badinage later they finally left the antique dealers to their evening and walked back to Bloomsbury. Tommy thought it curious the flat was still so readily available and wondered again where Guy actually lived. When he'd asked that before Guy, though explaining that he was, of course, based in Washington, had been doggedly evasive about his sleeping arrangements in London. Ultimately, Tommy didn't really care, so he let the matter drop. At the flat the sex was immediate, rough and exciting. Tommy found himself hugely turned on by being seen as such a sex object that his partner wanted no niceties of speech or behaviour to stand in the way of his getting him naked and fucking him.

Afterwards they lay in bed, with Tommy's head on Guy's chest. His favourite post-coital position. He felt a compliment was in order, so told Guy what he wanted to hear.

'I missed you, Guy.'

'Have you been a good boy while I was away?'

'Can't say I was.'

'Bravo! Much more fun being in bed with someone naughty!'

'I'm glad you're back.'

'So am I. And will be again before long, I expect.'

'Really? They give you a lot of holiday.'

'That's one of the perks of the diplomatic corps. My last proper holiday I spent on a mini continental tour, including Brussels, where, as always, I spent a happy hour or so looking at Wystan's painting.'

'There's a portrait of Auden over there?'

'There may well be in some grand queen's apartment. No, what I mean is the Breughel painting in the Musée des Beaux Arts. Of the fall of Icarus. He wrote rather a well-known poem about it. So I always think of it as his.'

'The Greek myth?' Tommy might not know all Auden's poems, but he wanted to show he had a decent, if largely self-taught, education.

'Technically a Greek myth, yes, but actually the human condition. Though the former is of course simply a commentary on the latter.'

'You don't say?' Tommy appreciated things being explained, but drew the line at being patronised.

'I sense a certain prickliness. Let's talk about something else. I'll save my explanation of the painting - and the story - until we're standing in front of it ourselves.'

'You mean you'll take me there?'

'I will.'

'That would be great. My first trip abroad!'

'You've never left England?'

'How could I? There was the war as a child and I'm only twenty now.'

'Silly me. I was forgetting your youth.' He stroked Tommy's chest, as if admiring the smooth feel of a marble statue. 'I was lucky enough to travel quite a bit before the war - as did Wystan, of course.'

'Was he there when you last went to Brussels?'

'No. I was on my own. Friendless in Flanders. Which wasn't a problem. I went to the museum and pottered about the city. It's charming. Quiet, but charming. I think the latter quality's a little under threat as they seem keen on tearing down old houses and replacing them with motorways. I'm all for progress, but it shouldn't rule out a sense of style.'

'Where else did you go?'

'Here and there.'

'Why so mysterious?'

'Oh… it's just that one day I'd like to have a European jaunt with you. To show you Luxembourg, for example. Beautiful country. For a beautiful boy.'

Guy turned over, his back to Tommy, and swung his legs out of the bed, so he could sit on its edge as he poured himself a whisky. 'I'll save the tour guide bit for then.'

Feeling slightly miffed at the lack of physical affection, Tommy's reply ignored the offer completely.

'And this trip back here?'

'Largely work-related, as I had to make some reports in person. Actually, that's a rather cowardly way of saying I've been hauled over the coals.'

'Why?'

'I can't stand America. The powers that be know it, but won't send me home. Just bloody-mindedness on their part. The other reason I'm back so soon is compassionate leave. Poor Mummy's ill again. Officially, anyway. Truth can be surprisingly elastic.'

'One day it'll snap.'

'Oh, I do hope so. Though unlike you I'd rather not resign. I'd prefer to make them go to the trouble of dismissing me. The embassy isn't any keener on me than I am on America, so when I go in a week or two's time I won't be there for long. When I finally get back to Blighty we may be jobless together.'

'Speak for yourself! I've been promised a job by Ivor. Remember?'

'Ah, yes. Mr Novello. Your other lover.'

'That's not fair.'

'Life isn't. When you mention him, I feel like I'm being painted as the other woman.'

'You as a painting? I like it! Who'd do you best? Any artist. Any period.'

'Botticelli, probably. When I was younger. His models were all so attractive - and he had a knack for making them look almost edible. Now, given a certain amount of excess flesh, I suppose I'd be more of a fit for Rubens. Not sure who'd paint Novello.'

'Do we have to talk about Ivor? At a time like this?'

'When better, given we're talking about sex?'

Tommy propped himself up on one elbow, looking intently at Guy who looked, unflinching, back.

'What's this about? Why do you want to ruin the evening?'

'Because I'm hugely jealous.'

'You're supposed to be a man of the world.'

'I am. But, rather to my surprise, a jealous one.'

'You said you didn't want to be tied to one person.'

'I said I didn't like having my heart broken.'

'There's no reason for it to be even chipped.'

'There is now. You came along and everything changed.'

This was unexpected and unwelcome. Tommy wasn't looking for a relationship with Guy, or anyone else for that matter, and given his stated manifesto at their first meeting, he had never considered the possibility in this case. He knew Guy was keen, but then so was everyone Tommy slept with. A fling couldn't work unless both parties threw themselves into it, but at a very shallow level. No room there for love. Unsure how to respond, he played for time.

'That's flattering, but it's no reason to take against Ivor. He's no threat to you. Besides, you spend most of the time abroad.'

'I know....'

'Well, then. Why spoil it?'

'It?'

He knew some sort of gesture was called for. He equally knew that Burgess would place too much weight on what he was about to say, but that didn't matter. It would do for now.

'What we have, Guy.'

'Then we do have something?'

'Isn't this something?' he answered, disingenuously.

'I'd like to think so.'

'Then show it. By not banging on about Ivor.'

'I'll show it all right…'

And with that he pulled Tommy towards him.

Chapter Ten

Over breakfast, Guy and Tommy agreed that, as Tommy had already arranged to see Ivor that night, he would meet Guy the following evening. Guy hadn't been pleased, but had scraped together the necessary dignity not to object. Tommy had duly gone to the Palace that night. King's Rhapsody had finished a few minutes before Tommy walked round to the stage door, where he was waved in out of the cold by Jimmy. 'Been out front, again, dear?'

'Yes.'

'At this rate, it'll be cheaper for you to buy the theatre!'

Tommy managed a laugh, but as the joke was on him, he didn't find it all that funny. What did Jimmy really think of him?

Jimmy had been a fixture at the Palace for years, seemingly as much a part of the fabric of the building as the safety curtain or the little decorative figures who adorned the theatre boxes. Of indeterminate age - people placed him as anything from forty-five to seventy, depending on their experience of what Soho life could do to a man - Jimmy had worked in the theatre since he left school. Starting as a stagehand, he had eventually crossed the proscenium arch to work front of house as an usher. He had enjoyed this at first, but as the years went by and promotion - to head usher, let alone a management role - passed him by, he became bitter. He blamed his lack of advancement on his looks, and it was true that his slightly ferret-like features didn't help in terms of immediate presentational skills. However, he worked diligently and clearly loved the building. Another point in his favour was a camp humour that amused the other ushers. His decline from repartee to bile seemed to have begun after one too many failures in his private life. Fond of sailors on leave - of whom there was no shortage in Soho, often on the arms of Francis Bacon or John Minton - he had fallen for a stoker from Newcastle who eventually announced that he'd met the girl of his dreams and wasn't prepared to service Jimmy any more, even if he did get a free bed for the night and a cooked English breakfast in the morning…

After a hysterical scene - 'The last time I ever cried over a man, ducky' - Jimmy went on a two-day drinking binge. When he finally turned up for work, he was somehow different. This was assumed to be the temporary result of heartbreak and hangover, but it proved to be a permanent change - one that got more noticeable as the weeks went on. The management, who knew he couldn't be kept on in a role that involved close contact with theatre patrons, found to their surprise they had a begrudging affection for him, so rather than lose him they offered him the post of stage door keeper, when the previous holder of the title astonished everyone by marrying, aged sixty and claiming that her new-found status as the wife of a librarian was incompatible with the job.

Jimmy had jumped at the chance and made the role his own. He was the gatekeeper of the Palace, its communications hub and the chief purveyor of information - the more salacious the better. He combined this role with an undoubted efficiency and enough sense of self-preservation to know when to keep his mouth shut. He was formidable to younger actors - and especially actresses - but projected a certain fellow-feeling for and occasional *bonhomie* towards older cast members. Though he was quick to make fun of them to others, he also had a grudging admiration for the sheer resilience of the Swayers and, like most of the profession, held something of a torch for Ivor Novello. He was subliminally jealous of Ivor's young men, whether chorus boys or outsiders, but his affection for Ivor trumped any inclination to brusqueness and he made himself superficially agreeable to them. With Tommy, for reasons he couldn't explain to himself, he felt a sort of sympathy. The boy's youthful eagerness, the obvious pleasure he got through his fling with Novello, seemed to bring out the best in Jimmy. It was almost as if, instead of resenting someone else's success, he was vicariously experiencing the sort of excitement that he himself might have enjoyed, had he looked very different when young.

'The Guv'nor's expecting you, dear.'

'Thanks Jimmy. How's tricks?'

'I don't know where you get these Americanisms from! Too much Rodgers and Hammerstein, I suppose. In my day - which is far from over, before you say anything - in my day, a trick was someone you picked up and took home.'

'That's what I meant!' Tommy bluffed, with a grin.

'No oasis in the desert, though thanks very much for asking. And in any case, it's been so long I've forgotten what to do… In you go, don't keep him waiting.'

Tommy raised a hand in acknowledgement and walked through the pass door into the corridor that led to a lift and staircase, both progressing to the various levels of dressing rooms, the wardrobe department and all the other essential offices in a theatre.

When he reached Dressing Room One, Ivor was just finishing removing the evening's make-up with cold cream and tissues. The room was full of fresh flowers, while to the side of the traditional dressing table with its surround of light bulbs was a long antique sideboard on which lay various presents, including bowls of fruit and a remarkable range of chocolate. It was as if rationing no longer existed.

Ivor, wearing a surprisingly plain, not to mention battered, dressing gown, greeted Tommy. They kissed on each cheek, then Ivor gestured to an armchair. It was where Tommy sat when they chatted after a show, but equally he always waited to be asked to sit down. As he had quickly learned, there was as much protocol involved with theatre royalty as with the real thing.

As he sat, following Ivor's brief wave, Billy, Ivor's dresser, emerged from the adjoining bathroom, where he had been putting more bottles in the fridge.

'Champagne for our friend!' ordered Ivor, whose own glass was already half empty. Billy poured Tommy a glass and topped Ivor up.

'Thank you, dear. Can you give us five minutes?'

Billy looked surprised - he never left the room until Ivor did, whoever the visitors and whatever the conversation. He was there as dresser, waiter, bodyguard and, given the enthusiasm of some of the less worldly female VIPs, chaperone. Though his face registered surprise, he immediately headed for the door. 'I'll just get a top-up from Jimmy, then.'

'Champagne?' asked Ivor, with a glance at the two unopened bottles in ice buckets.

'Gossip!'

'Ah! Let me know what you hear!'

When the door was shut, Ivor turned away from Tommy to carry on cleaning his face. While doing so he spoke, making eye contact with him via the mirror.

'Speaking of gossip, I've heard some rather distressing rumours myself. And not from Jimmy.'

'Oh! What's that, then? Anyone you know?'

'Yes. Rather well. Hence my concern.'

'Who?'

'You, dear.'

'What?'

'What, indeed! You were seen at the Stag's Head, appropriately enough, with a notorious old tart called Guy Burgess.'

Tommy blushed.

'Your colouring confirms it. Apparently he was showing you off to his friends. As a conquest.'

'Ivor… I….'

'I have a boyfriend, as you know. Perhaps boyfriend is too sprightly a word, given our age, but you know who I mean, so I can hardly come over all jealous and betrayed if you choose to wave your cock around with other people. Had it been just another boy, or some Midlands businessman who'd taken a shine to you, I wouldn't have mentioned it. But Burgess…'

'How do you know him? He hasn't anything to do with the theatre…'

'You've heard me talk about Eddie Marsh…'

'Yes, of course…' A little too often, thought Tommy.

'He may be retired but he's very well-informed and I know from him that this man Burgess is dangerous.'

'Dangerous? He's a diplomat!'

'The sort of diplomat who's considered a cross between an embarrassment and a suspect.'

'What do you mean?'

'I can't think very many people who work for the government are communists.'

'You know that?'

'The whole world knows it! He makes a point of broadcasting it to all and sundry, most of whom seem to think it's a big joke. Eddie finds it very unfunny.'

Ivor removed a cigarette from his monogrammed cigarette case, then, watching himself in the mirror as if rehearsing a scene from a play, lit it.

'In any case, it's very foolish of Burgess. But then drunks are fools. And he's one of the best-known drunks in London. Not a man to be seen with.'

Ivor was going to carry on when suddenly he had a spasm of coughing: a loud, hacking cough that Tommy had heard on a couple of occasions, but which seemed much worse tonight. He stood up and reached for a glass of water to offer him, but Ivor, eyes streaming from the effort to control the coughing, waved the glass away and, instead, reached again for the champagne. He took a large gulp, then immediately looked as if he was about to retch, but the moment passed and so did the cough. He wiped his eyes on a large monogrammed handkerchief that he pulled from a pocket in his dressing gown.

'Thank God for Pol Roger!'

Tommy tried humour.

'You see, drinking isn't all bad!'

'Nor, presumably, is Burgess, or you wouldn't be seeing him. I gather he does have a certain ruined charm. But his politics…'

'I don't share his views, Ivor. I'm not sure he does either…'

'Of course you don't. But it's not your views I'm worried about, it's your reputation. And by extension, mine. That man trails trouble and I don't want you to be damaged by it. Nor do I want him associated with me, even indirectly.'

'Are you asking me to drop him?'

'Yes.'

Tommy had no idea what to say. Ivor simply kept eye contact with him in the mirror. Finally, Tommy found some words: 'Can we talk about this over dinner? It might cheer us both up. And then I can make it up to you back at the flat…'

'Not tonight. As you heard just now, I'm not on the best form at the moment.'

'Your chest?'

'Yes.' Then, with a twinkle in his eye that suggested the lecture was over, 'And my heart! It's so big it makes an easy target!'

'You should see a doctor.'

'I have. Several times in the last month.'

'Really? You never said…'

'Unlike Mr Burgess I can be discreet when I need to be.'

'I wouldn't want to hurt you. You know that…'

'Yes, I do. Which is why I hope you'll come round to the flat before long. Cold cuts, champagne - and cuddles. If that's not too dull after Mr Burgess?'

'No. I'd love to.'

'Thank you. Now kiss me good-night, then head straight home.'

'Won't Billy be back in a minute?'

'He's talking to Jimmy, because that way he can see when you leave the theatre. He won't come back in here until you've gone. That's one reason he's been with me thirty years.'

Tommy gave Ivor a brief but affectionate kiss, then, pulling away, said 'Goodnight' and touched his cheek, gently, with his hand.

Novello brushed his own fingers along Tommy's, then turned back to removing the last traces of make-up.

'Bless you. Good night.'

Chapter Eleven

The next day was a quiet one. Tommy went to the Marshall Street Baths for a swim - and to see what else might be on offer. A youth in white swimming trunks that would have been too small even if he'd had a normal-sized package, let alone the impressive bulge that was his passport to popularity, made his interest very clear, as Tommy swam to the side of the pool after diving in at the deep end.

The boy sat with his feet in the water. This meant that as Tommy half-hung, half-trod water with his arm on the poolside, his face was level with the boy's crotch.

'That was a good dive. You practise much?'

'When I can. What about you?'

'Oh, I like it here. Lots of athletic-looking guys.'

'Too many for my liking! Competition!'

'You've not got anything to worry about.'

'You think?'

'Course! That's a very nice bod you've got. But tell me…'

'Yes?' Tommy smiled up at him.

'After all that exercise… the swimming and diving and that?'

'Yes?'

'You must feel a bit stiff.'

'I'm getting that way, given the view.'

'Me too...'

The boy moved his towel so it was now covering his crotch. He did this in as casual a way as he could, given a couple of swimmers seemed to have cottoned on to the little courtship ritual and were watching from the other side of the pool.

'Then we'd better go into the changing rooms', said Tommy. 'And get those swimming trunks off you. They look very constricting.'

'They are, when you're a big boy like me.'

'Come on then!'

Tommy heaved himself out of the pool and, pretending to look at something to his side, moved as fast as he could without attracting attention to the hard-on that his strategically-placed hand couldn't conceal from anyone who cared to look.

One person who did was the lifeguard. Resolutely straight, with a plump girlfriend who was trying hard to get pregnant by him so she could force him into marriage, he'd seen it all before and it had no interest for him. So long as the queers did what they had to do out of sight, he didn't care. His only concern was the pool itself. He was there to stop people drowning, not police their morals. A couple of detective constables had approached him, some months ago, and asked whether there was much 'messing about', as they put it, in the baths. Because if there was, they warned him, they had a new sergeant who was keen to make an example. The lifeguard had been as nonchalant as he could, while knowing he had to acknowledge some activity to be credible with the coppers.

'Hardly anything, mate.' he had said to the more intelligent-looking of the two. 'We have the occasional guy who hasn't had his end away for a while, so he gets a bit of uplift where he shouldn't when he's in the showers. That sort of thing. Nothing for your sergeant to worry about. I'd stick to the public lavs if I was you.'

After an enjoyably intense and very sticky ten minutes in a cubicle with the well-hung swimmer, Tommy showered, changed, then went home for a rest and a few hours' reading. He had recently borrowed a book about Edwardian theatre from the local library and enjoyed being absorbed in the world it described. With no commitments until the evening, when Guy had agreed to meet Banya and Peter, it seemed a good time to sit quietly and get on with the book. Doing so also saved money, which was an issue, and would be until he started work at the New. What if Ivor changed his mind? It would be a disaster. But as soon as the thought, which always lurked in the back of his mind, found its way forward, he forced his attention back to the book...

Peter and Banya arrived at the restaurant first. Italian, in the heart of Soho, it was a favourite with the theatre crowds. It being eight o'clock, most of these were happily enjoying their evening out, so there was a choice of tables. They decided on one that was against a wall, with a good view of the main room and of the door.

'Always nice to see who else is here', said Peter. 'And as the boys will have to be looking at us - or the wall - we can be sure of their attention. Not that anyone'll have eyes for anyone but you.'

'Tommy, perhaps. Not so sure about Mr Burgess.'

'No. But then he'll have me to look at.'

'Lucky him!'

'I like to think so...'

Peter's sense of humour was closer to England than the East Coast of the United States, where his family lived. This was partly because he'd been brought up to think of himself as quasi-English, given his family traced themselves back to Colonial times, and partly out of his admiration for European culture. Despite this, he was proud to be American, a nationality his gentle but unmistakable accent confirmed whenever he opened his mouth. He ordered four gin martinis which had barely arrived when Tommy and Guy walked into the restaurant.

'Darling!' Banya emerged from behind the table to greet them.

Tommy started the introductions. 'Banya, this is Guy. Guy, this is Banya… and this is Peter Buchan.' He was glad he'd remembered Peter's surname - but as it was the same as his favourite novelist, it wasn't that difficult. 'Enchanted,' said Burgess, kissing Banya's hand.

'How gallant!'

'I'm sure you bring out the inner chevalier in every man.'

'Not every man, I hope!' Peter, who had also stood up when Tommy and Guy arrived, put his arm round his girlfriend's shoulder. 'She's temptation enough as it is.'

'One could say the same for you.'

Burgess gave Peter a searching look, tinged with a wistful longing. It was a ploy he often used with heterosexual men. It invariably discomfited them, giving him the upper hand, or at least an initial advantage. On this occasion, he met his match. Peter returned his look with one of well-bred amusement.

'Of course I am. It's what makes us a perfect couple. Doesn't it, darling?'

Guy responded by sitting opposite Peter, to carry on what looked like the start of a duel, while Tommy, gratefully, sat opposite Banya. He realised Guy was mildly irritated by Peter and Banya having the best seats at the table, but saw him visibly relax once he had the martini in his hand. Waiters appeared, wine was ordered, menus consulted and dinner decided on. Banya seized the moment to turn on the charm.

'It's lovely to meet you, Mr Burgess.'

'Oh, Guy, please.'

'Tommy's told me so much about you.'

'Not too much, I trust!'

'Pretty much. We have no secrets.'

'That's rather dangerous. One should always have secrets. Don't you think, Peter?'

Peter nodded.

'Tommy tells me you're a film star,' said Guy.

'I wish! Actor would be more accurate. But yes, I make films.'

'Anything out at the moment?'

'No, but I'm making one soon. In Paris! They can't seem to make up their minds about the schedule, but my agent says I have to be ready to head out there any moment. Occupational hazard with film, I'm afraid. Still, I'm really looking forward to it.'

'How exciting! It'll be a love story, I suppose?'

'Sort of. Set in the war and about the resistance. I play an American airman who's hiding in a safe house before he can be smuggled out of Paris and down to Spain and safety.'

'And, inevitably, you fall in love?'

Tommy picked up on the frequent uses of the word. It fed a suspicion that Guy had love on his mind.

'I do. With the resistance heroine whose job it is to hide me.'

'Sounds delightful. I look forward to seeing it. You've been to Paris before, of course?'

'No. So I'm very excited about it - though I'll miss Banya terribly.'

'Tell me, how did you two meet?'

'At her poetry shop. I love poetry.'

'Really? That's not something I associate with Americans.'

'I can't think why not. We produced Walt Whitman. And Robert Frost. Not to mention T S Eliot.'

'Who had to come over here to flourish. Like Henry James.'

Tommy gave Guy a warning nudge, which he ignored. Peter, however, rose to the challenge.

'Rather like Auden and Isherwood, going in the other direction.'

'Poets always travel,' said Guy. 'Their sense of direction, sadly, doesn't always match their talent. Who's your favourite living poet?'

'An easy choice. Auden.'

'You have excellent taste. Have you met him? He seems to give a lot of recitals these days. They pay the bills, I believe. Though

I've always thought half the charm of a poet's life is never thinking about bills.'

'Why?'

'Because it would be a painfully pointless exercise. Poets never have money. It's why so many starve...'

'I'm glad he does those tours. Unfortunately I've never been free when he's giving one.'

'Then when I'm back here for a longer period, we must have you to dinner.'

'We? You know him?'

'Very well. He's one of my oldest and dearest friends.' Tommy shot Banya a conspiratorial look. As he had once said to her, for an avowed Communist, Guy was remarkably prone to name-dropping. 'And just as much fun in the flesh as he is on the page. Which is all too rare.'

'What matters is the writing, not the person.'

'Really?' asked Guy, who had already moved onto the wine after knocking back his martini.

'Sure,' argued Peter. 'People love gossip but the only reason they read a poet is if they like their poetry. What survives of us is our writing, not our manners or our love life.'

'*Au contraire*. The more interesting the person, the more people are likely to remember them. They'll read their poems, in years to come, precisely because of their love life.'

'Oh, come off it...'

'Look at Byron. Some wonderful lines, of course, and my favourite poet. But the reason we've all heard of him is because he was a lord, was crashingly good-looking and had lots of sex. And because he lived in exile and died in a foreign war. He's a character. A star. So if you want your poems to be remembered, the best way is to create a scandal in your lifetime. Or, perhaps, by being associated with one.'

'I'm divorced, so I suppose that's a start?'

'A toe in the water. Which is how Byron started his swim across the Grand Canal in Venice, after all.'

'I'm going there this autumn. Less tourists.'

'Good idea. Where better to get inspiration?'

'Especially if I'm there with Banya.'

'My dear girl,' Burgess reached across the table, took Banya's hand and placed it on Peter's. 'I hope you realise what a treasure you have here!'

'And you in your friendship with Mr Auden…' she replied. 'Next time you see him,' said Peter, 'please tell him I admire him very much.'

'He'll be thrilled.'

'Actually, I write poetry myself, in my spare time.'

Guy turned to Tommy with an exaggerated look of despair.

'Oh, dear!'

Banya spoke up for Peter.'They're very good!'

Peter smiled at her, then turned back to Burgess.

'You obviously know a lot about it, Guy.'

'Poetry, or spare time?'

'And as for Mr Auden….'

'Yes?'

'If there's any way…'

Burgess interrupted him. 'Let me guess. You want me to show him your poems?'

'You'll think me very forward and American…'

'The two go together.'

'It's just that I think my newest poems are my best. They're all about Banya. She's my muse as well as my girl….'

Banya beamed. Guy's smile was less straightforward.

'That's quite a responsibility. And a pleasure. I can't think of anything nicer than having your head on a pillow next to one, muttering sweet nothings in verse…'

Peter ignored the implication. Banya and Tommy had tacitly agreed to stop talking, so they wouldn't miss what the others were saying.

'I'd love you to show them to him. Not just for myself, but as...'

'As a sort of expression of your love? You feel it so strongly you want to share it?'

Guy knew he sounded catty, but couldn't help himself.

'You're very perceptive.'

'Then I'd be delighted. It'll make more interesting reading than my little notes to him. Somehow our friendship has evolved into a correspondence. Disappointing, but perhaps inevitable, given my work. And a boon for his future biographers...'

'How will I get them to you?

'You mean they're not in your jacket pocket?'

'Guy, I'm not that pushy!'

'Then give them to Banya who can give them to Tommy, who'll give them to me. *La Ronde.* Like so much of life. Ah! here's the pasta!'

Conversation carried on over the dinner. Poetry was at the heart of it, followed by films. Guy made no secret of his dislike for them as an art form. Peter spiked his guns by agreeing. He claimed he would only consider himself a proper actor when he appeared on stage - and in the West End. Tommy was relieved Peter was able to deal with Guy so well. Especially when he brought Guy's deliberately-placed anti-Americanisms to a halt through the two-pronged response of making it clear that an East Coast upbringing made him as familiar with European culture as most educated Englishmen, and by undermining Guy's English superiority complex by teasing him about how unsophisticated huge swathes of British society were. A Somerset yokel, Peter suggested, was not so different from an Appalachian hillbilly. When they reached dessert the third bottle of wine had been finished and Guy, who would never concede defeat to an American, had at least accepted an armed truce.

After the coffee and brandy had been finished off, they said their goodbyes in a haze of alcohol-fuelled *bonhomie,* then headed off in different directions. As he and Guy walked back to Bloomsbury, Tommy was glad the evening had ended without upset. It wasn't until the meal was safely over that the tension had hit him. He felt exhausted. Thankfully, Guy would do most of the work in bed. Ivor always liked to cuddle up and chat afterwards but Guy simply turned on his side and was fast asleep in seconds. For once, thought Tommy, that would be the most welcome part of the evening…

Chapter Twelve

At lunchtime the following day, Guy walked down Jermyn Street - his favourite in London - to where he had arranged to meet Anthony Blunt. It was an old, highly formal restaurant that he'd chosen, whose tables were set at a decent distance from each other, permitting confidential conversations. As he'd quipped to Blunt when discussing the venue, the customers - and, even more, the staff - were so ancient they'd be unlikely to hear anything in any case. A doorman wearing an overcoat and top hat greeted Guy as he arrived.

'Very nice to see you again, Mr Burgess.'

'Hello, Chubb! All well, I hope?'

'Yes, thank you, sir.'

'Mr Blunt here?'

'About five minutes ago.'

'Marvellous.'

The slim, ascetic-looking Anthony Blunt rose from his chair to greet his old friend. A leading art historian, despite his relative youth, he had undertaken delicate undercover work for the King immediately after the end of the war, ensuring that sensitive letters from the Duke of Windsor were safely retrieved from Germany and placed in the depths of the Royal Library at Windsor Castle.

Now the Surveyor of the King's Pictures, he was at the heart of the Establishment. The perfect place for a Russian spy. His espionage days were, however, behind him. He was long since out of the army, where he had been in a position to pass documents and other intelligence to his Soviet handlers. The palace gossip that he occasionally forwarded these days was of no strategic importance but, he wryly noted, even the Soviets seemed to enjoy behind-the-scenes 'secrets' of the Royal Family. Moscow's preferred reading, he found, was not Pravda, but Tatler. These days his chief concern was his own preservation. Like Burgess, he was an ex-public schoolboy (Marlborough, in his case) who enjoyed the trappings, comfort and privileges that went with being part of the ruling class of a Great Power. Unlike Burgess, his youthful attachment to communism had entirely evaporated - 'the triumph of snobbery over socialism', as Guy had drunkenly dismissed Blunt's confession after a long and alcohol-fuelled evening. Blunt, unlike Burgess, never got drunk, but alcohol, taken in sufficient quantities, started to melt the outer edges of the icy reserve that was his most distinguishing characteristic.

The two men, who had known each other at Cambridge, had been very close when in their late teens. They had never technically slept together, in the sense of spending a night in bed, but one evening, as undergraduates, Burgess had made a pass which, to the surprise of them both, Blunt had accepted. He wouldn't go to the bedroom, or allow Guy to bugger him, but he did let him partially undress then masturbate him to a spectacular climax on the floor of his sitting room. The memory, though unspoken, always hovered between them whenever they met, all these years later. Of the two, Burgess enjoyed their get-togethers more. He liked to be reminded of his youthful sexual prime and he also enjoyed teasing Blunt, knowing how uncomfortable he could make him by raising his voice just that little too loudly when in a restaurant. Blunt's attitude to seeing his old friend was divided between a fastidious dislike for Guy's frayed tie and stained shirts and a certain nostalgia for when he and the world were younger, life less complicated and the war - which had terrified him - just a shadow on the horizon, rather than an enervating six years from which he had not fully recovered. The strain of the difference between his past treason and current position at the heart of the Court was another constant in his life and Guy almost personified this. So although he couldn't help but enjoy his old friend's company, he increasingly found their get-togethers a trial. He had suggested this latest lunch to keep an eye on him. Unless he knew where the loose cannon was heading, he couldn't take appropriate action to avoid being crushed by it.

They ordered drinks straight away but even before they'd arrived, Blunt could see that Burgess was in a good mood, especially when describing the previous night's dinner with Peter and Banya and the way he and Tommy had rounded it off, in Bloomsbury.

'You seem very keen on this boy.'

'Keen? I'm in love!'

'I thought you didn't do love?'

'I don't. But this one's different.'

'Aren't they all? You've always said that was their attraction.'

'When you meet him…'

'Meet him? Are you mad?'

'Oh, too grand are we?'

'Don't joke about these things. You know where I work. I can't be seen to be dining with boys off the street. I'm not Oscar Wilde.'

'He supped with panthers. You prefer to lunch with princes.'

'Can you blame me?'

'I certainly don't envy you.'

'Then let's keep our preferences separate, shall we?'

'Anthony, I'm suggesting a cocktail with him, not sex at the Savoy. We've already done that, of course…'

'Spare me the sordid details.'

'You've never complained before. Hearing my bedroom anecdotes is the nearest you allow yourself to the real thing.'

'No need to rub it in.'

'That's your problem. One does. Regularly. You should stop staring at paintings and have a bit of fun. With men. It'll inform your insight into art, if that's what you need to justify it to yourself.'

'Thanks, but no.'

'I won't give up, so be warned.'

'I am. And I need to warn you, about something much more serious.'

'Oh, dear. I was wondering when we were going to get round to our foreign friends.'

'They're worried about you. You've made a complete hash of things in Washington and your behaviour's drawing attention to The Man in quite the wrong way.'

When discussing Kim Philby, who was also attached to the British Embassy in Washington, though in a far more important role, they always used this code word.

'The Man can look after himself.'

'True, but there's no need to make things more difficult than necessary.'

'I can't help it. I hate the place and the people and the ambassador won't give me any important work to do.'

'A drunk and self-confessed - even if no one actually believes it - Communist not allowed any real responsibility in our most important embassy? In the most anti-communist country on earth? You're surprised?'

'Then why I am there? Why should I stay?'

'Our friends agree. In fact they're rather cross. They want you to come back to England, and soon. They assume you can make enough of a fool of yourself to get sent home?'

'They're right. And not before time. Though I've no idea what work I'll be given when I get back. By His Majesty's Government, I mean.'

'The real work will be keeping an eye on DM.' DM were the initials of Donald Maclean, another Soviet spy working in the civil service.

'I gather he's rather poorly?'

'On the edge of a breakdown. Not least because he's under serious suspicion, according to The Man. And the more nervy he gets, the more oddly he acts and so draws more attention to himself.'

'The solution?'

'Is being decided. But they want you to keep an eye on him. Befriend him. Use your inimitable charm. Put some backbone into him and let our friends know if you find anything they ought to hear about.'

'Why didn't they tell me directly?'

'Because the Service is scenting more than one trace of blood and are keeping a closer eye on everyone. They thought it far safer if I were to brief you, here, than one of them on Hampstead Heath or wherever.'

'But if I associate with Maclean won't that put me under the microscope too?'

'No names!' hissed Blunt.

'Sorry! If I associate with DM…'

'That's a risk you must take. According to them.'

'Might it be a risk you share? Given we're old friends…'

'Yes. Perhaps it would be best if we don't see each other for a little while.'

'How long's a little while?'

'Until you get back, permanently, from the States. Meeting me on your return would be perfectly natural, after all. I'll let you know in due course, once I've had the OK from you know where. Meanwhile, you've got your love to keep you warm.'

'I have. And my God, he does. He's got that energy that only the young possess. I can manage once at night and again in the morning if the hangover's not too bad, but he…'

'Your turbot, sir?'

The white-haired waiter had staggered to their table with the main course.

'Thank you,' said Blunt. 'And now, Guy, I think we should talk about something else. Like art.'

'Very well, then. Nanny always told me pleasure had to be paid for…'

Chapter Thirteen

Wystan Auden was intrigued by Guy's most recent postcard. The ulterior motive for his involvement in an American actor's amateur poetry was very clear - it was a favour to his latest fling. Auden had received countless cards about other boys, but sensed that Tommy was not a normal attachment. Now well past his prime, Guy must be getting sentimental. Needy, even. Middle age did strange things to men, as he knew. Intrigued, he decided to meet the exotically-named Banya. It would give an insight into the poems. Peter's nationality was another deciding factor. America had been good to Wystan and he was minded to repay the debt. As for Tommy, he wouldn't meet him until after his summer holiday on Ischia, the little Italian island he loved to visit - its sun, sea and relaxed pace of life so different to Manhattan.

Going to a poetry bookshop was almost asking for trouble - or attention, which he often found to be the same thing. He winced at the imperial memorabilia in the window, then took the plunge and opened the shop's front door. The little chime, triggered by his action, was ignored by the few people browsing and by the small group huddled over a coffee table, looking at some new volume which they seemed to be discussing. A book club, he supposed. He spotted Banya straight away. Attractive, bohemian, her eyes alert and intelligent. She was dealing with an elderly customer who seemed to be making a two-act play out of opening her handbag to pay for a book. He pretended to be looking at one himself, on the nearest shelf, until the old woman finally found the money, received her volume, indulged in some pointless conversation, trying to prolong the brief window of human interaction, and then, at last, left.

'Excuse me, but I think you must be Banya?'

'I am!' she said, turning to face this new customer. As she did so she almost jumped. One of the world's most famous poets in her shop, asking for her by name.

'Goodness! It's Mr Auden, isn't it?'

'It is. A friend of mine suggested I visit this bookshop - and seek you out.'

'Guy Burgess put you up to this?'

'That's an unfortunately pejorative phrase. One puts people up to mischief. My intentions are entirely chivalrous.'

'Cigarettes post-date chivalry, but I'm afraid I now need one, rather urgently. Can I offer you one too? And a quick coffee? Round the corner?'

'That would be dandy'. Damn. He couldn't help coming out with phrases that were mere conventional politeness in New York but sounded forced and alien, especially on English lips, in London. Still, a small price to pay for life in America.

Banya spoke to a weedy-looking young man who was checking a sheaf of book orders. Improbably, he was her manager.

'Rodney, I'm just popping out for a coffee, if that's OK? You don't mind guarding the fort, do you?'

'Righty-ho!'

As they moved away, Auden gestured back towards Rodney.

'He seems very accommodating.'

'He is. Oh, dear, the book club seems to have got wind of you. Let's go, or you'll be signing things for the next half-hour.'

One of the little group broke off from the others and started to approach Auden. Banya intercepted him.

'Philip! I'm just off for a break with my cousin Andrew. Now, one guess only. Who does he remind you of?'

'Er...W H Auden.'

'Yes! It's a scream, isn't it? Anyway, we must dash. Lots of family gossip to catch up with!'

As they emerged onto the street, she took Auden's arm, a casual gesture that enchanted him. He was already getting an idea for the start and structure of the poem he would certainly be writing. Not as an obligation, but for his own pleasure. By the time they finished their coffees, he had the rough outline in his head. He always let a first draft lie fallow for a day or two, then revisited it. When he did so he would remember this conversation, how she looked, her voice, her perfume. They talked mainly about Peter: his career, his attractions, his ambitions, his love of literature, the family house in New England that Banya longed to visit. She asked him many questions but very few, refreshingly, about his work. She was more interested in what he saw at the theatre, or in the cinema. Of what he made of life in America and whether he thought she would fit in over there, if she and Peter moved there one day. Peter had such an affinity for Europe, for an older culture, she told him, but though she loved it too, she wanted to see the New World.

'Paris is where the eighteenth and nineteenth centuries were made. But New York is where this century is happening. I want to be part of my world - not the past. You can study other people's lives but you have to live your own, don't you think?'

Auden did. He walked her back to Newbolt's, telling her to leave Peter's poems for him at his publisher. 'Faber and Faber. They're good at taking care of precious manuscripts.'

'Oh, I couldn't claim they're that!'

'On the contrary, every writer's work is precious. I promise I'll read them very soon, then give them to Guy to give back to you.'

He saw her frown.

'Yes, I'd be worried about leaving something precious in the hands of a drunk, but I can guarantee that he'd do anything rather than upset you - and his Antinous!'

Antinous was the young boyfriend of the Emperor Hadrian. When the youth drowned in the Nile, on one of the Emperor's visits to his Egyptian provinces, he had him deified. Auden was intrigued that there were more statues of Antinous scattered around the Roman Empire than of most other historical figures. He was amused when Burgess compared Tommy to Antinous in one of his letters. 'Keep him away from the Thames, then!' he had replied.

Banya got the reference, but she wasn't prepared to leave Peter's poems in Guy's hands.

'There's something of the Fall of the Roman Empire about Guy, isn't there? I hope you don't mind, but I'd really rather you leave them at Faber's for me to collect.'

'OK. I'll ask the receptionist to let you know when they're ready. But think kindly about Guy. Without him we'd never have met. Now, I must leave you to it… Remember. Faber and Faber. Tomorrow, if you can.'

'I promise. And thank you!'

'You're welcome.'

As he walked away, he decided to visit the British Museum. To have a look at the statues. An idea presented itself. Banya as Cleopatra? No, a little obvious. A shame the woman wasn't an actress. She'd have been ideal for the role. As he thought this, he noticed that even to himself he'd referred to her as a woman, not a girl, which would have been the word he would normally have used for someone of her age. There was something worldly, in the best sense, that made 'girl' hopelessly inadequate. That might be a starting point. Whatever. He would write to Guy that evening, thanking him for a mission that proved far more stimulating than he could have hoped for. If Tommy was half as interesting as Banya, it was no surprise he'd fallen in love with him. A dangerous state to be in, as he'd often found. If you're in for the long term, then companionship rather than passion was the building block. Guy was never one for strong foundations. That was his problem. Wystan patted the notebook and pen in his crumpled tweed jacket. He had a pub to find, a drink to order and a poem to start.

Chapter Fourteen

Gertie had been touched to learn that her lodger was a friend of Ivor Novello. She often looked back on her youth and the roles she had played in her prime. Ivor represented that era for her and one afternoon, as she sat by the fire with her habitual winter afternoon treat - Earl Grey tea, toast and a slice of chocolate cake - she told herself it was absurd not to at least try to get in touch with him. She wasn't looking for work, even though Ivor had a habit of plucking Edwardian stars from retirement. Phyllis and Zena Dare, for example, were both playing major roles opposite him in King's Rhapsody. Though as they were sisters and one was playing his mother, the other his lover, she imagined the casting had needed all of Ivor's charm.

Making her mind up, she'd crossed the room to her desk, to write a note to her old friend. Posted the following day, she hadn't really expected a reply. Yet, to her delight, by return of post she had a letter in Ivor's large, confident handwriting, inviting her to afternoon tea at the Waldorf.

On the appointed day Gertie wore a 'Sunday best' outfit whose simple elegance suited her perfectly. Edith Evans, a plain woman but brilliant actress, had once told her that she got away with playing romantic leads when younger by thinking herself beautiful. Gertie, no mean actress herself, prepared for meeting Ivor by thinking herself impressive (less of a leap than Miss Evans's) and emerged from the back of the cab that took her to the Waldorf, every inch a lady. It was her tribute to one of Ivor's favourite sayings: 'If you want to be a success, then start by looking like one.' A bellboy took her from the reception desk into the Palm Court, where Ivor was waiting for her at a table for two, slightly set apart from the many others that filled the room.

'Gertie! You haven't aged a day!'

They kissed, as if the intervening twenty plus years hadn't happened.

'And your star is undimmed. How lovely to see you!'

The usual range of food and drink was brought on cake stands and silver trays. The two enjoyed a long catch-up, principally about their shared past on stage, Gertie asking him many questions about actors and actresses with whom she had fallen out of touch. They moved on to his current shows and plans for the future, before Gertie broached the subject of Tommy.

'What a co-incidence that you know my favourite lodger!'

'Yes, isn't it fun?'

'He told you?'

'He did.'

'I imagine he tells you most things.'

Ivor looked at her over his tea cup.

'Most, Gertie, but far from all. One needs some mystery in life.'

'I'm thrilled you're helping him. He needs the encouragement of someone who knows what they're doing. Who better than you?'

'Darling, if you don't stop flattering me, I'll eat your other scone.'

'You're used to flattery. However, I come neither to praise Caesar, nor to bury him. Just to thank him for giving someone a helping hand.'

'I accept your thanks. Humbly.'

As she added strawberry jam to the cream on her scone, she developed her theme: 'It's so important to have someone young in one's life, don't you think?'

'I couldn't agree more.'

'Because at our age the temptation is to look back. It's better to look forward. Like the young.'

Ivor paused. Gertie had hit a nerve.

'It is, but isn't there an element of sadness, too? We won't see the future they build.'

'At least they won't have to fight a war.'

'Don't count his chickens. We've lived through two world wars. He may experience the third.'

'Germany's wrecked, Ivor. They wouldn't dare.'

'Not Germany. Russia. Eddie Marsh thinks…'

'He's still going? Do give him my best.'

'I shall. He thinks if we didn't have the atomic bomb the Soviets would have taken Berlin in '48 then carried on West to the Channel.'

'Then thank God for nuclear fission.'

'Yes. I don't have the energy to entertain the troops again.'

'If you had to, I'm sure you would. I can't think of anyone else in the West End with your range of talent - and vigour!'

Actually, she could. Noël Coward. But she knew, from way back, that mentioning Noël to Ivor, other than in an unflattering comparison, would lower the temperature by several degrees. Especially since Coward's cinematic success with In Which We Serve and Brief Encounter. Ivor's silent movies were now irredeemably dated, while most of his sound films were best forgotten. Ivor languidly raised a cucumber sandwich to his mouth, as if in a silent repudiation of Gertie's faith in his energy. Ignoring the gesture, she continued:

'You're the exception that proves the rule, Ivor. The rest of us are drained. We may put on a brave face but the exhaustion is always there. That's the gulf between us and Tommy's generation. He has such energy. Such *joie de vivre..*'

'And charm!'

'What I find endearing is that despite his ambition there's something very *unspoilt* about him. Which in young men about town is very rare, is it not?'

'Very.'

'So I'm glad that he's in the hands, as it were…'

'As it were…'

'Of such a kind, decent man.'

'Darling, you'll make me cry.'

'You always did, at the drop of a hat.'

'I'm an artist. It's allowed.'

'It is. As is another piece of cake.'

'I shouldn't.' He took the biggest piece on the plate.

'It's none of my business, but as we're having a heart-to-heart, may I ask you something? Personal?'

Ivor nodded his agreement, his mouth being fully occupied with the cake.

'You're not at all well, are you?'

Ivor coped with the cake while Gertie kept eye contact, waiting for him to answer. He took a sip of tea before replying.

'No, darling, I'm not.'

'Yet you go out on stage eight times a week…'

'When I can. My understudy gets more chances to shine these days. But you know how important it is to be there in front of the audience. It's what we live for.'

'I know. But you've always had so much music in you. Don't wear it out before you've shared some more with us.'

'That's the trouble. I think it's becoming a race against time.'

'Then should you be seeing a boy who…?'

Ivor cut in. 'It reminds me I'm alive. It's the romance as much as the other thing. Candlelit dinners. Confidences on the pillow. Champagne at midnight…'

'When you go to meet your maker, there won't be a wine dealer who doesn't go into mourning.'

'Joined, I hope, by a grieving public.'

'Undoubtedly. But please, not yet.'

A bellboy appeared at Ivor's elbow.

'Excuse me, sir, but a message from Mr Andrews. He asked to remind you of the time.'

'Thank you.' He gave the waiter half-a-crown tip then spoke to Gertie again. 'That's Bobbie insisting I have a lie-down before tonight's show.'

'Glad to hear it. Now, I've monopolised you long enough. I know an exit cue when I hear one...'

'Perhaps you're right. You head home and I'll get the bill.' Ivor rose to his feet as Gertie got up - an automatic courtesy learned in his Edwardian youth. 'It really has been lovely seeing you again. I promise I'll keep an eye on the boy. But you're his landlady, so I expect you to do your bit, too!'

They kissed a genuinely fond farewell. Ivor gestured to a waiter who immediately came over.

'Miss Gilbert is leaving. Please see her to the door and make sure there's a cab for her. Goodbye again, darling. Safe journey home.'

As she walked through the Palm Court, the waiter at her side, Gertie thought of Ivor's old world courtesy. He, and she, she told herself, really were of a generation whose ways would soon disappear. She couldn't begrudge him his pleasures. But she would indeed keep an eye on Tommy.

Chapter Fifteen

Guy was half asleep in a leather armchair in the reading room of the London Library. He had gone there after a good lunch at the Boulestin, one of his favourite restaurants. He had rounded off the meal with not one but two strong coffees in a pre-emptive strike against the alcohol's inevitable effects, but despite this he had nodded off almost as soon as he sat down. He had called into his club on the way, and been handed an envelope by the hall porter. Waking up with a start, he remembered the envelope, took it out of his suit pocket and opened it. The handwriting on the outside was Wystan's. He assumed it contained a report about his meeting with Banya several days ago and a summary of his views on Peter's poetry. To his astonishment, when he opened it he discovered a single sheet of paper with a post card attached to it by a paperclip. On the card was written:

'Guy, I've read the poems. There are only a few, but they're not bad and I've left a note to the girl to say so - couched in rather more flattering terms - along with the poems themselves. But its Banya who's the real discovery. This is for her, but it's only right you should be the first to read it. Love or what you will, Wystan.'

The poem was in five verses of four lines each. Beautifully written with a combination of feeling and playfulness that Guy had never seen in Wystan's work before, or certainly not in the way it came out in this piece, which had been titled 'Princess in Charing Cross Road'. Extraordinary, thought Guy, that she had had this effect. Peter would be thrilled. And apart from the tribute it represented from one of the world's greatest poets to an unknown girl in a London bookshop, it would be worth money in years to come.

This was not what he had expected. Or wanted. He felt a sudden stab of jealousy. It was only through a defiant act of self-discipline - one which did more to wear off the two bottles of claret than any amount of caffeine - that he stopped himself from tearing the page into pieces. Pleased at his ability to control himself, he then thought again about this literary surprise. Thank God he hadn't torn it up. For what better way to impress Tommy? Yes, it was written for Banya and for the benefit of her boyfriend, too, but it had its origins in Guy's love for Tommy. Surely he would be moved by the end result?

And yet, and yet... Burgess was an intelligent man, even if his mind was noticeably less sharp than it had been before war and a decade of increasingly heavy drinking had taken their toll. He knew the very fact of his thinking about things to dangle before his lover meant the relationship was precarious. The youth, the energy, that made Tommy so exciting were what would take him away to other men, other opportunities. And though this added a dash of hatred to his feelings for the boy, he knew he was being unfair. He would have been the same as Tommy. Indeed, he had been, twenty or so years ago. If he played the poem as a card then the game was lost. He was torn between knowing that it already was and hoping, desperately, that it wasn't. At Eton his debating powers had been famous. He could, as an intellectual exercise, be given almost any theoretical case and, despite overwhelming odds, argue its cause so brilliantly that his fellow pupils would laughingly applaud him and vote him the victor. If he could achieve that with others, then surely he could persuade himself.

And why not? Didn't he deserve a little happiness? More than that. An enduring happiness, with a remarkable boy. Admittedly, one, as he remembered thinking when he first saw him, who would lose his looks in a few years. But sharing those years would be worth it, surely, whatever the cost in terms of self-respect? Indeed, he argued, as if in a one-man debate with himself as both contestant and audience, surely it was a case of gaining self-respect rather than losing it? Wouldn't having Tommy at his side and in his bed be a real achievement? A source of envy among others? Admiration that the old roué could win such a prize? As if Priam rather than Paris had managed to carry off Helen of Troy. He thought of Christopher Marlowe's play, Dr Faustus. Helen of Troy was a prize there, too, and a cause of Faust's ultimate damnation. Marlowe's own life ended in a violent, bloody death. Supposedly in a tavern brawl but actually at a government safe house and at the hands of a member of the Elizabethan Secret Service.

The Secret Service. There was another ingredient in the bubbling cauldron of his life. 'I'm on to Macbeth now!' he thought before bringing his focus back to the colleagues he had betrayed so successfully for so long. The horizons here were closing in on him almost as much as in his love life. Too bad. He was in too deep. But wasn't that another reason to cling to Tommy? A life raft of sorts, something decent and affectionate in a sea of deception and intrigue. Someone whose only real interest, other than sex, was the theatre. When he first started sleeping with Tommy he found this narrow focus rather juvenile. A flaw in the boy's character. Now, it seemed refreshing. Noble, even. Yes, he insisted to himself, he needed him. Though wasn't this being the nearest he'd got to love in many years damning in itself? Perhaps it wasn't love? Just a terrible infatuation? He couldn't even claim it to be an all-consuming one. It filled him with joy, it stabbed him with despair, it made him almost physically sick with jealousy, it ate up an alarming percentage of his energy. But it didn't consume his devotion to the cause he had been dedicated to for so long. That was untouchable.

Imagining the inevitable triumph of communism, picturing himself on a parapet, in a line-up of dignitaries reviewing a parade of the British People's Army - these thoughts were a welcome antidote, just now, to images of Tommy's chest, the shape of his buttocks, the surprising firmness and strength of his legs. Calmer now, though cruelly aware that nothing was resolved and nor would it be, he made himself re-read the poem before putting it back in the envelope and returning it to his jacket pocket. He would show it to Tommy. On Monday night, when they'd arranged to meet - Guy having cancelled something else important to do so - would be the night of the poem. A reassurance and a rekindling. Pushing all doubts aside, he told himself that it would be perfect timing, with a perfect result. All would be well, when he saw Tommy on Monday night.

Chapter Sixteen

Tommy drank some coffee as he dialled Guy's number. He'd had a note from Bobbie Andrews with the first post, at around seven. The two princesses, Elizabeth and Margaret, were being brought by Queen Mary to see King's Rhapsody on Tuesday night. Tomorrow. The next time Ivor was due to see Tommy. They hadn't met over the weekend, which Ivor as usual spent at his country house, Redroofs, in a little village outside Maidenhead. And he hadn't been well enough to see him after the show for several days prior to that. So, Bobbie wrote, Ivor was hugely keen to see Tommy. He had a present for him. Something special. And he wanted to see him anyway. To tap into his energy. Tommy imagined the bitter little smile on Bobbie's lips as he wrote that line. Damn. He'd have to rearrange tonight with Guy. He wouldn't be pleased, but after all it was only a case of swapping the two days over. Not a big deal. The phone rang for nearly a minute before a sleepy voice answered.

'Burgess here.'

'You took your time!'

'Oh! It's you… What do you expect at this unearthly hour?'

'It's eleven. I waited 'til now to give you a lie-in.'

'Eleven is early.'

'I'm glad I've caught you. I'm very sorry, but we can't meet up tonight.'

'What do you mean?' Sleepiness had been replaced by a mix of hostility and alarm. His planned evening, the romantic gesture, collapsed around him. Nothing would be well.

'It's Ivor.'

Fully awake and hurt that he should be so casually thrown over, he tried to keep a lid on his bitterness. As usual, flippancy was his first line of defence.

'He was tomorrow's dance card, surely?'

'That's the point. He can't see me tomorrow because Queen Mary's coming to see the show. With Pride and Joy.'

Burgess felt an added layer of anger. Being a victim of his lover's concern for Novello was one thing. For it to be compounded by the presence of royalty made it even worse. And as for these fucking stupid nicknames… Who did Tommy think he was? Part of the Margaret Set of blue-blooded young men who danced attendance on the little madam?

'Oh, well, if the Germans are coming to call…'

'Guy, you shouldn't call our royal family that. You know they're…'

'Oh, fuck off…'

'God, you got out of bed the wrong side!'

'Actually, as we've already established, I'm still in it. May as well stay here, now.'

'Oh, come on! I'll see you tomorrow instead.'

Yes, thought Burgess. And in the normal run of events that wouldn't matter. In fact it was absurd and undignified to query it, let alone have a hissy fit. But he couldn't stop himself. Like someone drawn by a horrifying compulsion to the very-edge of a cliff, he felt himself marching towards disaster.

Tommy tried to make amends.

'I'm sorry if it's a pain, but you know how ill Ivor is. Which is why I've been able to see so much of you recently.'

'Oh, that's the reason is it? And there was me thinking you did so because you enjoyed my company. And just how ill can he be if he keeps appearing on stage?'

'It's his job. He gets an energy from it. You know… Doctor Theatre and all that.'

'How heartwarming. So, tonight's a sympathy fuck, is it?'

Tommy slammed the phone down. He looked around, checking no one else was standing outside the phone box. Slamming it down had been entirely spontaneous. He didn't normally have a temper, but Burgess's attitude had pressed a button; he hated being talked down to by older men. His irritation wasn't helped by Banya having warned him this would happen. He'd caught her just outside Newbolt's before she started work, and persuaded her to pop round the corner to the nearest café.

'Are you sure you'll go round tonight?' she had asked.

'Yes. The note said not to bother with the stage door, but just go to the flat after the show.'

'That leaves you the earlier part of the evening…'

'No. I'll have to see the show.'

'What are you talking about? You've seen it dozens of times!'

'It's different from the everyday world', Tommy said airily. 'When you're in the business you can watch the same show, or ballet, or opera, endlessly. You notice the differences in each performance. In the reaction of the audience. Each audience is subtly different.'

'You don't say?' Banya didn't like being patronised either. 'Look, Ivor can't expect you to see the bloody thing every time you have sex, surely? Why not cut the theatre part and see Burgess? At least you'll have met him, even if you have to head off.'

'How would you like to meet someone who you had planned to spend the night with, only for them to head off to have sex with someone else?'

'Fair enough… Darling, can I make a very improper suggestion?'

'A threesome with you and Peter?'

'Absolutely not! And I'm alarmed the idea even entered your head… No, what I was thinking was, why not see Burgess first, then pop round to Novello's flat long enough to keep him happy, after which you can go back to Guy and spend the night with him? For dessert, as it were.'

'That's even worse!'

'Really? He might be turned on knowing that whatever happens between you and Novello he'll still get his hands on you at the end of the evening.'

'And I thought women were the nicer sex!'

'I'm just trying to help. Because if you phone Burgess and simply cancel, he'll be furious. I would be too.'

'But if I tell him Ivor's ill…'

'Tommy, the deal was Ivor tomorrow, Guy tonight.'

'But that's the point! I don't *belong* to either of them. The deal was never that he was going to fall in love. And expect us to live like a pastiche of a married couple.'

He re-ran the conversation through his mind as he stared at the phone, unsure of what to do now.

After a few seconds, he took a deep breath then called the flat again. The phone was answered immediately.

'Ran out of pennies, did we?' Burgess's voice had an unpleasant edge to it. Conciliation clearly wasn't on his mind.

'Look, I really am very sorry about tonight…'

'So you said. But not sorry enough to see me.'

Desperately, Tommy tried the alternative.

'What if we meet this evening, for dinner, but…'

'But you go round to see Novello once I've fed and watered you?'

'That's unfair…'

'But not, unlike your suggestion, offensive. You must be mad if you think I'd agree to that.'

'But what', began Tommy, though he was sure what the result would be, 'if I came round to your place after I saw Ivor?'

'For sloppy seconds?'

'I doubt very much if he has the energy for hanky-panky.'

'I don't. It'll be Doctor Theatre earlier in the evening then Doctor Hard On when he opens your shirt.'

'Even if that's true, some people might be very happy with me coming round after. Making them the main event. Having my whore's body helpless in their hands.'

Tommy had never tried phone sex before but he found himself spontaneously getting into it. He'd have to try it again. Not with Ivor - but it would go down a storm with Kevin. Sadly, it was lost on Guy.

'Yes, some people might be very excited. And, if you were a casual trick, I would be too. But I thought we were rather more than that to each other?'

'It's just that tonight, as I've tried to explain…Look, I'll call you tomorrow morning and…'

The line went dead.

OK, Tommy told himself. Guy would have to cool his heels. He was going to see Ivor. And to emphasise the point, he'd make an evening of it and sit through the show again, too.

Chapter Seventeen

The curtain fell on King's Rhapsody after another sold-out performance. Knowing he had half an hour to kill before arriving at Ivor's flat, Tommy decided to get a drink. He walked down Charing Cross Road, then turned left just past one of the entrances to the Leicester Square tube. He followed the little alleyway round the side of Wyndham's Theatre and the back of the New, peeked at the brightly lit windows of Sheekey's fish restaurant, then arrived at the Salisbury.

The bar was busy, but Tommy had a knack for finding a space and insinuating himself into it. That and a well-practised cheeky grin at the barman got him served far sooner than should have been the case, to the undisguised fury of several older men standing near him.

'Think you're special, do you?' asked one.

Tommy beamed at him as if sharing in a remarkable stroke of luck. This could have backfired by annoying the man even more, but tonight it seemed to work and there were no further comments. Tommy took his wine from the barman, gave him the money and a good tip, then walked towards one of the semi-circular red plush benches that lined the walls. There was no room to sit down, but the group of young men who occupied it looked inviting.

Among them was Kevin.

Tommy moved towards him. As he did so, he felt a shot of lust. Kevin wore clothes that showed his contours to good effect and Tommy's memories of what he looked like without them were fresh in his mind. The dancer was talking to a couple of friends. As Tommy arrived, there was a convenient break in the conversation. He tapped Kevin on the shoulder.

'Fancy seeing you here!'

Kevin turned, but though he smiled a conventional welcome there was a warning in his eyes.

'Oh! Hello, Tommy. How are you? What are you up to these days?'

He nodded his head, almost imperceptibly, towards the back of the pub. There, having come up the long flight of steps that led up from the basement and the men's lavatories, was Kevin's boyfriend. Tommy knew him by sight and as 'the redhead', but he had no idea of his name. If Kevin had mentioned it he'd forgotten it the moment after.

'Patrick, this is Tommy. He was an usher and soon he's going to be a theatre manager!'

Tommy tried to hide his irritation. Ivor's job offer - or, more specifically, his suggestion of one - wasn't supposed to be public knowledge. He had told Kevin, but on the condition he kept it to himself. Now, here he was shooting his mouth off about it, in public. Never trust a queen, he thought.

'Hello.' Patrick was tall, slim and moderately attractive. The thin-skinned type always alert for trouble or an insult, he immediately sensed a connection between Kevin and Tommy that went beyond a casual friendship.

'So, Tommy, what brings you here tonight?' The hostility was veiled, but evident enough to suggest Tommy make his excuses and leave. Tommy had a split second to decide how to react. As Kevin had mentioned the job in front of two friends he would certainly have talked to Patrick about it, in which case Ivor's name would have been mentioned.

'I've just been to King's Rhapsody.'

'That old tosh!'

Patrick was obviously looking for a fight. If there were to be one, thought Tommy, Kevin would be a casualty. A shame, but unavoidable.

'What makes you say that? It's doing great business.'

'Because it's so old-fashioned! Give me an American show any day.'

'American musicals are great, but so are ours…'

'How generous of you. To Novello, I mean. Poor old queen. When's she going to pack it in and retire to Eastbourne?'

'Why would he do that? With two hit shows in the West End?'

'Twice as much tat, then.' Patrick looked at Kevin. 'You were saying that only the other day, weren't you, ducky?'

'Bit of an expert on musical theatre, are you, Patrick?' asked Tommy.

'Evidently more than you.'

'Now, remind me. Your job is?'

This was, Tommy knew, a sore point. Kevin had told him how much Patrick hated working behind a shop counter. His ambition had been to be a dancer, like his boyfriend, but not having the level of talent to earn a decent living at it, he had reluctantly given up, though maintaining an increasingly unrealistic hope of returning to the stage one day.

'None of your business.'

'Perhaps not, but I'm sure I… Ah, yes. Now I know where I know you from. I was killing time the other day, before seeing a friend. I popped into Boots. Where I saw you. Behind the counter.'

'We all have to work at other things while we're resting.'

'Seems to me you're the one who should be heading to Eastbourne, not Ivor. All washed-up at thirty.'

Patrick was twenty-five but his already receding hairline and correspondingly older looks was an even sorer point than his job. Kevin hadn't mentioned this, but Tommy guessed. The fear of ageing fitted with the bitter, bitchy personality.

'In fact, I admire you coming in here, Patrick. All of us theatre types. You know, earning a living in the industry rather than just fantasising about it. Must be very painful for you. Now if you'll excuse me I'm going to dinner.'

'With Ivor?' said Kevin, who didn't want to lose all chance of a repeat encounter with Tommy, especially as he had been thinking about leaving Patrick for some time - as the redhead had come to realise, adding another chip to his shoulder.

'No,' Tommy lied. He didn't want Ivor's name mentioned again in front of this group. 'Another friend.'

'You have more than one?' asked Patrick. Tommy wondered whether he had any sense of how catty and bitter he sounded to other people. He decided to fight fire with fire.

'More than you, dear, anyway. 'Bye, Kevin. And having met your boyfriend, I can see why you're thinking of leaving him.'

With that he moved past Kevin, giving his shoulder a theatrically concerned squeeze. There was a commotion behind him, but whether it was Patrick having a go at Kevin, he didn't turn round to find out. The calm of Ivor's flat, the coolness of his champagne and the gentle pleasure of his love-making had never seemed more enticing. But he still had time to kill before he could ring the bell and get in the creaky old lift up to the penthouse.

It didn't take long to walk from the Salisbury through Covent Garden - already stirring with preparations for the next morning's market - to the Aldwych. Knowing he was ahead of schedule, Tommy carried on walking as far as the ruins of St Clement Danes. One of so many Wren churches shattered by enemy bombing during the war, it had been reprieved from demolition but was, like much of the capital, waiting patiently to be restored to its former glory, nearly six years after the end of hostilities. Tommy stood beside it for a while, then turned and walked back to Ivor's front door. He pressed the bell and after a short pause heard Ivor's voice on the state of the art entry phone system. Ivor didn't like gadgets, but as he and Bobbie didn't have live-in staff, Bobbie had insisted on having it installed. Tommy said hello and then heard the buzzer open the lock. He made sure the door was closed securely behind him, then went up in the lift, accompanied by the usual shudders and jolting, to the flat.

Ivor opened the door. He was in a silk dressing gown that resembled a kimono: a complete contrast to the old thing he wore in the dressing room at the Palace.

'You came!'

'I have. And I can't tell you how pleased I am to see you!'

'Music to my ears…'

Tommy went in and automatically listened to see if they were alone.

'Don't worry, there's just the two of us. Bobbie's gone to the Savoy with Zena and Phyllis, for a nightcap. Time for ours…'

Ivor handed Tommy a glass of champagne. They clicked glasses.

'Let's have a sit-down first,' said Ivor, who looked exhausted. Tommy sat next to him on a long, comfortable sofa, and held his hand.

'This is nice', said Tommy. 'And when we go next door we can just have a cuddle, if you like.'

'Thank you, ducky. You know me well.'

Tommy was fine just lying down with Ivor, but they both knew that - whatever Bobbie's reservations and despite what they'd just said - one thing would lead, however gently, to another. The thought, plus the physical proximity of a man who fancied him, and the effect of the hastily knocked-back wine at the Salisbury, were giving Tommy a hard on. He felt relaxed (apart from his groin) and happy.

Their heads moved closer to each other in preparation for a kiss when suddenly, jarringly, the doorbell rang. Then again. Insistently.

'Bobbie?' asked Tommy.

'He must have forgotten something. God knows what. And very unlike him not to have his key. Look, just pop into the loo for a moment, would you? He knows you're coming, but I don't want him to have it rubbed in his face, in his own home…'

'OK.'

'Good. You'll be able to hear him, so you'll know what's going on and when he's left. Like Billy, in my dressing room!'

The buzzer went again. Tommy stepped into the lavatory, holding his glass. There was a brief knock on the door. It was Ivor, with the champagne bottle. He quickly topped up Tommy's glass. 'Can't have you dying of thirst, can we?' Then he went to the front door and lifted the phone that was linked to the door entry system. Tommy listened intently and heard Ivor say: 'Sorry, darling, I was in the loo!'

There was a pause and then Tommy felt something in the atmosphere radically change. The next snippet of conversation was very different. 'No, you can't! Go away! How dare you?'

Tommy couldn't help himself. He came out of the lavatory and into the hallway. Ivor looked ashen, the receiver in his hand. Someone at the front door was clearly raving at him.

'What is it?'

Ivor ignored him and placed it to his ear again.

'Put that way you'd better come up after all. But for God's sake, lower your voice.'

He pressed a buzzer to open the street entrance door, then replaced the phone and turned to look at Tommy. 'I'm afraid we have a visitor - and a very unwelcome one.'

There was the distant noise of the front door being slammed unnecessarily forcefully, then the churning of the lift.

'Who is it?'

'Your friend Burgess. Perhaps now you'll see why I advised you to drop him.'

'Ivor, I... I'm...'

'This is not the time. Can you do lunch tomorrow?'

'Yes.'

'Check first with Jimmy, at the theatre. I'll leave a message at stage door.'

The lift, which had taken a while to make its way up, arrived - and out stepped Burgess.

'What the hell are you doing here?' demanded Novello.

Burgess didn't say anything. He just walked forward, as if to drag Tommy out of the flat and back down to the Aldwych. Furious at the man's presumption, Ivor started to shut the door.

As he did so, Burgess moved forward with surprising speed, throwing himself against the door with his shoulder, in the way Tommy had seen policemen do in numerous cops and robbers movies. The effectiveness of the manoeuvre took all three men by surprise. Ivor managed to keep his balance as he stepped sharply back, even though the edge of the door had caught his face, but Burgess stumbled and only just avoided falling over. The effort deepened the flush on his cheeks and he momentarily looked as if he was going to have a seizure.

Tommy slammed the door shut, wishing Burgess was on the other side of it. As he did so, he shouted 'What the fuck are you doing?' at the intruder.

'I'm having a showdown with your friend here,' Burgess replied. He looked towards Novello, whose left hand was clutching his face, which had a savage mark on his forehead, already starting to form a lump. There was the beginning of a bruise on the cheek and a trickle of blood from a nostril.

'That'll be purple by the morning,' said Burgess with satisfaction, his voice slurred with drink, 'but I'm sure you're used to make-up...'

Tommy was horrified at the thought of Bobbie Andrews coming back from the Savoy to find Burgess in the flat, having assaulted Ivor in his own home. Without replying, Ivor scooped some ice from the ice bucket, wrapped it in a cloth and held it to his face. He was in pain and shaking with a mixture of shock and anger, but the steel that had seen him through nearly forty years in show business kicked in and he found himself remarkably calm. On the other hand, he had always had Bobbie there as his lieutenant - though, given the circumstances, he was glad he wasn't around now. He gestured towards the drawing room where, only minutes earlier, he and Tommy had been sitting together. Burgess smiled in triumph.

In the few moments it took all three to get into the room, Ivor had fully recovered from the initial shock. He was sure the nose wasn't broken, despite the force of the blow, so any injury, however unsightly, was cosmetic and temporary. That crucial issue settled, he was now ready for whatever this ghastly man had in store. Clearly the central part was a sort of duel over Tommy. Very well, then. He would cope, by seeing himself as others might: not on stage so much as on film. And after all, had he not been one of the great stars of the silent movies? He was more than a match for a jealous drunken boor with a second-rate job in the Foreign Office or wherever this idiot government employed him. In his mind's eye he saw himself on screen, dressed in fencing whites, perhaps with the added detail of silver and gold epaulettes on his shoulders, walking purposefully across a castle courtyard towards the intruder, the steel of his sword laughably superior to the drunkard's cudgel.

'Tommy, do you mind offering Mr Burgess a glass?'

Tommy looked at Burgess who hesitated, then gave a curt nod. Tommy filled a glass and gave it to him.

'And I think I need a little top-up. Then help yourself.'

When all three had full glasses in their hands, Ivor raised his in an ironic toast.

'Happy Days!'

Burgess snorted, but took a large gulp of champagne. Tommy sipped nervously at his. He was sitting, though a little apart, next to Ivor on the sofa, as if he had already made a choice.

Ivor began. 'I presume you're here about Tommy?'

'I am. He's in love with me, he's coming home, and he won't be seeing you again.' Burgess's slurred voice revealed the evening's heavier than usual intake of alcohol.

'That's rather up to Tommy.'

Tommy stared intently at his lap. He had no idea what to say and was aware, in any case, that words on this occasion belonged to the others. It was their duel. He was just the prize. Ivor launched the first sword thrust.

'Tommy can make up his own mind. But if any normal person were asked for their opinion, you wouldn't stand a chance.'

'Intelligence and the general public? Since when did they go together?'

'They're often a good judge. Or jury. You can deny them intelligence, but you have to grant them common sense.'

'They know fuck all, most of the time.'

'Ah, there speaks the man of the people.'

'Far more than you.'

'Really?'

'I have their interests at heart.'

'I appeal to their hearts. That's why so many come to see my shows.'

'They come because you're a modern religion. An opiate. Flocking from the factory to the theatre to escape from reality into a make-believe world which in your case is all the more pernicious because you peddle the same ludicrous nostalgia as the monarchy.'

'Theatre doesn't hide the human condition - it reveals it. It speaks truth through artifice. Unlike politicians.'

'Truth? Aeschylus, yes. Sophocles, generally. Shakespeare, perhaps. But your Ruritanian rubbish? And your balding friend with his name-dropping characters?' The reference to Coward's thinning locks had the opposite to the desired effect. Ivor took an uncharacteristically unkind pleasure in the contrast between his excellent head of hair and Noël's increasing lack of it. Unwounded, he nevertheless reacted to the personal nature of Burgess's comment.

'Typical left-winger. Claiming the high moral ground, yet resorting to personal insult.'

'You actually think you're capable of a political debate?'

'Isn't that what we're having?'

Burgess laughed derisively. 'Another drink!'

He waved his now empty glass at Tommy, who stood up to replenish it then sat back down on the sofa, this time a little nearer Ivor. Registering this, Burgess decided that if Novello wanted a proper argument he'd give him one - and wipe the floor with him. Tommy would have no option but to be impressed. But before he could speak, Novello struck again.

'Even the comrades recognise the need for theatre. The Soviets promote ballet every bit as much as the tsars used to. They may stage operas about factory workers and happy peasants toiling for the Motherland, God help us, but the point is they're staged. And over here, where we're free, there's always been a time and a place for every type of theatre. People need showgirls as well as Shakespeare.'

'Smoke and mirrors. You lure them into red and gold playhouses designed like palaces, to keep their minds off storming the real thing. You make royalty sympathetic through stage romances. You pretend to offer escape from the system but the truth is you're a propagandist for it. I gather your latest offering even has a coronation on stage.'

'I'm glad you keep abreast of my work. Yes, it does. And goes down a treat. After all, the King's coronation in '37 was hugely popular. And when, in due, course, Princess Elizabeth…'

'Balls!'

'Look, Burgess, if you can't offer anything more…'

'Oh, but I can! Speaking of the underbelly of society, let's move on to your prison sentence….'

Ivor blanched. The one great trauma in a life that had otherwise been a progression of well-dressed success from his early twenties onwards, it had hit him all the harder because of the contrast between a prison cell and the country house that had been at the centre of the case. It was something that was never mentioned in his circle after his release from Wormwood Scrubs, where he served one month for petrol rationing offences during the war.

'Here you are, claiming yourself as a representative of the people, waving your little mirror at them. Yet when push came to shove, with the V1s raining down, you were prepared to break the law so you could travel down to your country house each weekend in your Rolls. Rather than sharing a train carriage with the little people. You're lucky the magistrate gave you just a month. No, it was two, wasn't it, but you managed to pull some strings, thanks to Eddie Marsh, and get it halved on appeal…. How very English. One rule for the plebs, another for the wealthy.'

'It was a travesty of justice.'

'And that's the system you're defending?'

'I'd rather face a British court than a Soviet one.'

'Much good it did you.'

'I thought what I was doing was legal. I have a very bad chest. And heart. I barely got through pneumonia the previous year. I needed the warmth. Not much to ask, given the amount of war work I've done…'

'You call playing the piano in a French field war work? When I think of the suffering of the Soviet people in the siege of Leningrad…'

'I went to France shortly after D-Day to entertain the troops. I've seen soldiers, in the field, before and after battle. Which is more than you've done. And why is it you and your sort always have more sympathy for foreigners than your own people? Unless, for some reason, the foreigners are American.'

'Communism is an international movement. We don't recognise national barriers.'

'Really? Then why do the Soviets call the fight against Nazism 'The Great Patriotic War'? They seem very keen on the Motherland. Strange you've overlooked that.'

'What's strange is sitting here having a half-cocked argument about politics with a raddled old queen who can't keep his hands off young men.'

'Pots and kettles.'

'I'm twenty years younger than you.'

'And?'

'Your day is over....'

'I should have known better,' thought Ivor. Arguments all too often turned into the verbal equivalent of fights in the street - where men who fancied themselves with their fists ended up flailing at each other, their arms thrashing wildly like little children: without skill, discipline or discernment. He tried to shift gears by bringing the discussion away from the abstract onto the specific. Tommy. The reason Burgess had come to his home and created this appalling scene.

'Let's talk about the future. I'm in a position to help Tommy.'

Tommy looked up. At last, some news about the job.

'As he knows,' Ivor continued, 'I've arranged an interview for the role of Assistant Manager in a West End theatre, and a personal introduction to Binkie Beaumont.'

'Another one of your lilac mafia? Your self-regarding little clique?'

'Self regarding? That's rich, coming from a man who never seems to leave the house without an Old Etonian tie.'

Tommy spoke for the first time. 'Has Mr Beaumont said when he'll see me?'

'Yes. He phoned me this afternoon. His office in Shaftesbury Avenue, next Wednesday, at 11 o'clock. I was going to tell you later. Bobbie's in charge of arrangements.'

Burgess, infuriated at being ignored, as if he were no longer in the room, broke into their discussion.

'I suppose the casting couch is primed and ready?'

'Binkie's not like that.'

'Actually, from what I hear he is. Though perhaps, as Tommy's your bum boy, he'll keep his hands off him.'

'Why do you have to be so offensive? I'm doing him a favour…'

'Won't do you any good. He'll still leave you for me.'

'He can do as he pleases. He's a free agent. You're the one in a jealous rage.'

'You're not helping him, you're pensioning him off. I love him.'

'If you did, then you'd want his best interests at heart. You wouldn't dream of making this scene.'

'What I wouldn't dream is kicking a boyfriend out of his own home for the evening so I could have my end away.'

Ivor went pale with anger.

'Leave Bobbie out of this.'

'Why? He's very much to the point, I'd have thought.' Burgess sensed the weak chink in Novello's armour. 'What a pathetic existence that poor little man has. Half-secretary, half-pimp, with a life sacrificed to satisfying your every whim - including fucking twenty-year-old would-be theatre managers.'

'How dare you!'

'Proud of holding up a mirror to the rest of us, apparently, but not so hot on looking in it yourself. What's reflected back isn't very pretty, is it? And tell me, what's it like pushing sixty and knowing no one finds you attractive any more? Not so much a profile, more a frayed old wallet.'

Ivor was exhausted. The attack hit home, partly because, seeing the drunken horror that was Guy Burgess made him realise how lucky he was to have Bobbie as his partner. Partly, too, because it contained an element of truth. For all the enjoyment his work gave the public, his private life was, essentially, a selfish one in which his pleasures, his convenience, always came first. Bobbie was at the top of a whole hierarchy of people who ensured his life was luxurious, well-run and exactly as he wanted it. Bobbie had been right when he said he shouldn't see Tommy tonight, that he was too tired. But no, he had to have his way and Bobbie, as ever, had gone along with it. What made Burgess's verbal assault so painful was the truth at its heart. He had been going to end the fling with Tommy. The job was a farewell present. He liked the boy, but it was time to move on. He had had hundreds, literally hundreds of eager young men over the years. Bobbie was the only man who mattered.

Then there were Burgess's cheap jibes about his looks. He would normally have shrugged them off, but they touched on a concern so profound, so central to his self-image, and so recently hammered home in the cruellest possible way at the Turkish Bath, that now, exhausted, unwell, furious at this appalling intrusion into his home and unable to see a way of bringing it to an end, it was as if he had received a physical blow more painful than when struck by the edge of the door as Burgess burst into the flat. He felt his heart beginning to beat faster, a rushing noise in his ears and a tightness beginning to form in his chest.

'Just go. Please, just go!'

'Ah!' Burgess scented victory. 'The great debater! The champion of his cause! 'Please just go!' Ha! Not unless Tommy comes with me.'

Seeing Ivor's increasing distress, Tommy tried to reason with Burgess.

'Guy, can't you see he's ill? Please, do as he says.'

'If you come.'

'I can't! He's ill. I've got to look after him 'til Bobbie gets home.'

'Quite the little threesome!' Guy spat out. As he did so he had a moment of clarity, amid the alcohol-fuelled rage. Even more than with the phone conversation earlier that day, it was as if he were watching himself, from a slight distance. He was appalled at his own behaviour, but it was far too late to withdraw with even a shred of dignity. He would have to stay, here in the flat and on the same grotesque track until he got Tommy to come home with him. Until he'd won. It didn't matter how unwilling Tommy was, or how angry. Getting him home and to bed was Guy's best - his only - chance of making things right again between them.

There was a sudden crash as Ivor, pain now blocking everything else out, toppled forward, breaking his fall on a small table whose china ornaments were smashed by the impact. Tommy leapt up from the sofa to help him, screaming at Burgess: 'Just go! Do you want to kill him?'

'I think I've made my position quite clear…'

'Your position?' Tommy's voice rose in incredulity tinged with panic. 'For fuck's sake! Go!'

The sight of Ivor crumpled in a foetal position on the floor, shattered china around him, suddenly had a sobering effect - as did the realisation of complete humiliation and utter failure. Feeling physically sick himself, the plans and hopes he had that morning now as wrecked as Novello's health, Guy staggered across the room, into the hallway and pulled open the flat's front door. The lift was still there, its emptiness mocking him. In a moment Tommy was behind him, pushing him into the lift, ignoring Guy's hand, which tried to take his.

'See you at the flat,' said Guy, ludicrously. 'I'll be waiting up for you.'

Seeing Tommy rush forward, he prayed the boy was about to kiss him. The delusion only lasted a second, as Tommy reached in, pressed the button marked 'ground floor' then slammed the lift door in his face.

Inside, Ivor had pulled himself up onto the sofa, and was trying to sit upright. Tommy took the nearest cushions to hand and put them behind his back, propping him up more comfortably. As he did so, Ivor put his hand on Tommy's.

'Thank you, my dear, but I'm rather beyond cushions now…'

'The bastard! I'm so sorry…'

'So am I. I never wanted you to have to deal with something like this.'

'Me? I'm the one who caused it. By having anything to do with that stupid…'

'Yes, but that's not what I was talking about.'

Ivor's face was now paler than ever. Tommy inadvertently thought of Hitchcock's famous shot, in The Lodger, of Ivor's heavily whitened face as the title character, staring enigmatically out of a window. All that was missing was the shadow of a cross upon it, representing the martyrdom that seemed to be his character's fate - until the final reels produced a happy ending. No such rescue was in sight.

'What I meant was that you may be about to deal with a corpse.'

'This is no time for jokes, Ivor.'

'That's the point. My heart… the pain. It's the same as when my father…'

'Christ!'

'I need you to do two things. Call my doctor and get Bobbie back here. Doctor first.'

Though the pain was crushing, the crisis brought out the administrator in Novello. He was, at this moment, not so much the matinée idol as the businessman who had built a small empire from his talent.

'What's the number?'

'I normally know it, but for the life of me I can't remember. Go to the phone. There's an address book. His name's under H for Headley. Best doctor in town...'

Tommy knew the book - it was small, elegant and had a very expensive-looking leather cover with a jewelled eagle on it. Ivor had proudly pointed it out to him on an earlier visit - 'It belonged to a Romanov princess. It came out of Russia in her luggage, on a British warship. St Petersburg to the Aldwych. You see? Even my phone book's romantic!'

Tommy found the number and dialled.

'He's an insomniac,' Ivor muttered from the sofa. 'He'll be up.'

He was.

'Headley. Who is this?'

'I'm a friend of Mr. Novello. I'm at his flat. He seems to be having a heart attack. Please come at once.'

'On my way'.

'I think he's...' but the phone had already gone dead.

'He's not far,' said Ivor. 'He has a flat in the City. Thank God. Now get Bobbie. The Savoy's in the book, too.'

Tommy phoned the hotel switchboard and asked for the concierge.

'Hello? Is that Mr Hazel?'

Tommy was familiar with the two main concierges at the hotel and thought he recognised the man's voice when he was put through to him.

'Yes, Hazel speaking.'

'It's Tommy. Mr Novello's friend.'

And Mr Burgess's, thought Hazel.

'Good evening, sir. What can I do for you?'

'Mr Andrews. I need to speak to him. Urgently!'

'I think I know where he is, sir. If you give me a moment, I'll...'

'Please! Hurry! It's very important!'

'Very good, sir.'

A few seconds, the sound of someone walking very fast on the marble floor of the foyer, then:

'Yes?'

'It's Ivor. He's…'

'How ill?'

'Very.'

'I told you. You ignored me last time and now…'

'It wasn't me! Guy Burgess…'

'Burgess?'

'He came to the flat. He was angry I was here. It wasn't my fault! Ivor let him in to avoid a scene…'

'Pour him a small brandy. Small. Talk to him. Keep him calm. You've phoned the doctor?'

'On his way.'

'As am I. Now get on with it…'

Tommy put the phone down and turned to face Ivor, who, on realising that Bobbie was coming back, looked slightly less ashen. Feeling stronger himself, Tommy went towards the drinks tray.

'Bobbie thinks a little brandy will…'

Suddenly Ivor cried out. A mixture of pain and frustration that his life would end this way, after such a scene. Leaving the brandy, Tommy rushed to the sofa and, unable to think of anything else, hugged him, then stroked his head, his fingers gently pushing through the still-thick hair that had been one of Ivor's defining features. As he did so, traces of dye stained his fingers but he carried on for what seemed ages but was actually only a few minutes. If only the doctor would get there. He could then hand Ivor over to someone qualified to know what to do. Ivor's breathing became more laboured. Then his whole body slumped, as if all the energy and strength had left. Looking directly at Tommy with eyes in which fear and anger had been replaced by a calm acceptance of the inevitable, he said: 'I think I'm going… Tell Bobbie I would have liked to have said goodbye.'

'I'll tell him you love…'

'No need. He knows…'

There was a long but surprisingly peaceful sigh, then silence.

Tommy kissed him, as if to somehow tempt him back to life. After a few moments he pulled back, unsure what to do next. Should he leave him sitting up, or lie him down?

There was the sound of a key in the front door and it swung open. It was Bobbie. His face bathed in sweat, he must have run from the Savoy. He instantly saw that Ivor was dead.

'The doctor?'

'Any moment, I hope.'

'Good. Help me get him onto the bed.'

Bobbie silently took Ivor's top half, his hands lifting him under the shoulders, while Tommy took the feet. Together they carried the body into the main bedroom and laid it as comfortably as possible - as if he were only ill, rather than dead - on top of the bed. As they did so, the entry phone rang.

'Let him in,' said Bobbie.

Tommy spoke briefly to the doctor, then buzzed him in at the street door. Knowing it would take a couple of minutes for him to get there via the lift, he wedged the front door open then went back to the bedroom. As he stepped inside, Bobbie got up. While alone, he had been lying on the bed next to Ivor. As he stood, with his back deliberately to Tommy, he wiped his face with his hands, but when he turned the tears were evident - his whole face glistened with them.

'The second worst thing is he went without saying goodbye. The worst is, I shall never be able to talk to him again.'

'His last words were of you. He told me to apologise to you for exactly that. That he wasn't able to say goodbye.'

Tommy instinctively went to put his hand on Bobbie's shoulder, a universal gesture of comfort to the bereaved. Far from accepting it, Bobbie stepped back a pace, sharply, to avoid physical contact.

'And you think that's any help? That I hear his last words from a casual fuck who he was spending the evening with, while I dutifully drank a nightcap I didn't want, in a bar I didn't want to be in?'

Tommy flinched, as if slapped. Turning away, Bobbie walked into the bathroom. Tommy stared at Ivor's body, as if for guidance. He heard the sound of taps and splashing water. A moment later, having dried himself quickly and imperfectly with a towel, Bobbie re-entered the bedroom, now firmly back in control of himself, as they both heard the sound of the lift announcing its arrival outside the flat.

'You weren't here, understand? Headley won't ask. He'll professionally forget seeing you on your way out. I will not allow this grotesque event to be the way Ivor Novello left the world. Got that?'

'What will you tell the press?'

'I'll think of something. A final fiction. In which, as ever, I'll play a supporting role.'

'I'll call tomorrow, Mr Andrews.'

'Why?'

Tommy had meant to see how Bobbie was managing, in the aftermath of the disaster. The other reason, essentially subconscious but just enough above the surface for him to feel shame while saying it, had been because he wanted to keep a connection so he could be sure the job interview would still go ahead.

'Hello?' Dr Headley, waiting in the doorway, didn't want to come in, in case he saw something he shouldn't. His last midnight heart attack patient had been pounding away with his mistress when the death occurred.

'In here, doctor!' shouted Bobbie, who then put his face a few inches from Tommy's before saying, very quietly: 'Forget the job at the New. Beaumont won't see you next week either. Your career in theatre is dead. I never want to see or hear from you again. Now fuck off.'

As Tommy ran out of the bedroom and towards the front door, he passed the doctor in the drawing room. He was pretending to be searching among the instruments in his medical bag, so as not to look at him. The boy himself could barely see the doctor through his tears.

Chapter Eighteen

'And then what happened?'

Tommy and Banya were in the window seats of a café in Covent Garden, the following morning.

'I knew I didn't want to go home straight away and the last thing I was going to do was go back to Burgess.'

This was the first time Banya had heard Tommy call him Burgess rather than Guy.

'Go on.'

'When I left, I walked through the Aldwych and carried on down the Strand, past what's left of St Clement Danes, into Fleet Street. I just wanted to put some distance between me and what'd happened. After I got to St Bride's I turned down an alley towards the printing presses. There was noise, and energy and activity… It was like that scene at the start of The Lodger - all those vans emerging from the back end of Fleet Street with news of the latest murder victim. Only this time I almost felt it was me who'd just killed someone.'

'Tommy, you didn't…'

He slammed his hand on the table, causing the cups to shudder and spill coffee on the chequered tablecloth.

'I know! I said almost…'

Banya put her hand on his, gently. She didn't take his outburst personally. She knew he was exhausted. Her touch calmed him.

'Then what happened?'

'I just walked around, feeling terrible. Eventually I found myself back on Fleet Street and sort of headed automatically up the hill towards St Paul's. Halfway up, I realised it would be closed. Then I saw a cab and as I'd got a bit of cash on me I flagged it down and asked to go to Piccadilly.'

'Why there?'

'Lights. Action. Company.'

'And?'

'I've never been there so late! There were still people around - well-off, on the town, thinking themselves very bohemian out at that time of night. I thought I'd walk as far as the Ritz. Ivor said we'd go there together.' He imitated Novello's voice. 'When the weather's better, dear...It's such a lovely dining room but its best seen when there's some spring sunshine coming in...' Now it'll never happen. Not with him, anyway. I walked up the 'Dilly as far as the colonnade on the pavement side of the hotel, then crossed over the road and started to walk back. I'd got to the junction with Bond Street when I saw a friend. He was ahead of me, but I called out his name so he'd stop and say hello. I just wanted to talk to a friendly face, so I started on about something very superficial - just a bit of theatre gossip, really, when he put his hand on my shoulder and said: 'Tommy, it's lovely to see you, but I've got to get down to the Circus. I'm working tonight.'

'What as?' asked Banya.

Tommy gave her a quizzical look, as if to say she should have been able to work it out. Then she did.

'Oh, I see. He's on the game?'

'Only part-time,' Tommy said, defensively. 'He's got an office job during the day. Selling insurance. But he earns some extra, a couple of nights a week. This was one of them.'

'Selling himself? Poor boy!'

'Not really. He's got the looks and he's using them.'

'Yes, but there are other ways.'

'Like mine? Look where that's got me! Ivor's dead and the life I've planned is over.'

'We need to get you home.'

'Sorry. I've been banging on and haven't asked you a thing… How's Peter?'

'Getting ready for Paris. They've stopped messing him around at last. He leaves in a couple of days. I got his poems back from Auden. Peter wants to take them with him but I asked him to leave a few of them with me for a little longer. It's pure sentimentality. It'll be like having a bit of him with me while he's away.'

'Didn't he want them published?'

'Yes, but in France. He thinks it would add an extra cachet to them, being brought out there, given all that's going on there since the war: Sartre, Camus, and that lot… Still, it'll give me an excuse to go over and visit him.'

Tommy touched her arm.

'You don't need an excuse.'

'No, but carrying his poems over the sea…'

'Romantic.'

'Funny what love does to you.'

'In your case, not in mine.'

'You weren't *in love* with either of them, were you?' She spoke as if Burgess was as finished as Novello.

'No. Which makes it all the more horrible. It's not my love that's messed things up but Burgess's. Old queens. They're toxic. What was I doing with him?'

'Come on. Let's get you safely back to Gertie.'

Banya signalled to the waitress, paid the bill, despite Tommy's half-hearted protestations, then led him out of the café and onto the pavement. There was a light rain, more of a mist than a shower, but it wasn't long before a taxi emerged. The driver, seeing Banya wave at him, pulled over with a delighted look on his face. He was less than thrilled when she explained that the cab wasn't for her but for her friend. Could he please take him to Notting Hill? She opened the door for Tommy, kissed his cheek and as he settled on the back seat of the car, asked: 'What will you tell Gertie about last night?'

'God knows! She was very fond of Ivor. Burgess may have taken away the roof over my head, as well as my career.'

'Give her more credit than that. Now, home and straight to bed!'

Banya closed the door and the taxi drove away.

Chapter Nineteen

When Tommy got back to the house, all he wanted was to sleep. He let himself in as quietly as possible. The net curtains remained un-twitched. He sighed with relief but then, as if on cue, Gertie emerged from the dining room, carrying a coffee.

'Tommy!' She was about to ask him what on earth the matter was, but the look on his face stopped her. Playing for time, she offered him the cup.

'I made this for a friend who was coming over but has just called to cancel. A pity for it to go to waste!'

It wasn't much of a lie, but presenting him with a choice made him stand still and think. This was enough to do the trick. Confused as to what to say, he simply burst into tears.

'Goodness!' Gertie put the coffee down on a nearby table and moved with surprising speed across the hall, to place a comforting hand on Tommy's shoulder.

'Come on, in here!' She led him into the sitting room and sat him down, before retrieving the coffee from the hall table. She closed the door.

'There! A little privacy. Now, what's happened?'

Tommy couldn't answer at first. Being treated in this sympathetic way by a woman somehow took him back to childhood. He needed to sob: a combination of expressing his pain and relief that a woman was about to make it better. Gertie sat patiently until he was able to come out with an explanation.

'It's Ivor. He's dead!'

Gertie looked intently at him but said nothing, so Tommy tried to explain.

'I was at the flat last night. A drink after the show. Then that bastard Burgess came round.' He saw her question in her face. 'The man you saw the other day. Who left a note.'

'The ruined cherub?'

'Nothing holy about him. Especially now he's murdered someone.'

'Murdered?' Gertie was appalled.

'Not literally. But near as touch it. He created such a scene… a jealous, drunken, pointless scene… that Ivor collapsed. Had a heart attack. He's dead.'

'And Bobbie?'

'I called him. He was at the Savoy. He rushed round. So did the doctor. But it was too late. He'd gone. Gertie, it was awful! Now Bobbie hates me. He said I can forget my job. I hate Burgess. I never want to see him again. The worst thing is, Ivor warned me about him. Said he was a bad influence. Playing with fire. He was right. And now he's dead. Everyone will blame me. I can't bear it.'

Gertie practically forced some coffee into his mouth and he at once felt stronger, though as much from confessing as from the caffeine.

'Have you told anyone else?' In one way she was thrilled at the idea of being the only person, other than those directly involved, to know about the night's events. On the other, it was a big responsibility. One better shared.

'Banya, of course.'

'Banya?'

'I told you about her. At the bookshop.'

'So you did! Silly of me to forget. I think you mentioned she's a very good friend?'

'Yes.'

'Then a good person to have on your side. When did you tell her?'

'Earlier. I've just left her... I won't even be allowed to go to the funeral. To say goodbye. After all he's done for me. All he was going to do...' he broke into sobs again.

Gertie put her hand on his shoulder. 'However bad they are, things always look a lot better after a good sleep. Which is what you need right now.'

'How's sleeping going to stop Bobbie Andrews hating me?'

'It won't, but it might help you stop hating yourself. Which would be a good start, don't you think?'

For a moment Tommy wondered if she was going to tuck him in too, but she simply offered him her arm, as if she also needed support and together they walked to the foot of the stairs.

'I have some things to do, but up you go.' She nearly suggested a long warm bath first, as a sort of ritual washing-away of the previous night's trauma, but she remembered that the lodgers kept their razors in the bathroom. In his current state of mind the combination of depression, bath and a cut-throat razor was best avoided. Touched by Gertie's kindness, Tommy slowly walked upstairs to bed.

Chapter Twenty

Exhausted, Tommy was still sleeping when, past eleven o'clock, Gertie left the house. By the time she arrived at Newbolt's, he had emerged from his room and was soaking in the bath, while listening to the radio. He had no idea his landlady was on a mission. Gertie's journey had included a brief detour to browse in some other bookshops, timing her arrival for the earliest that any shop assistant would be likely to go for lunch. Newbolt's door jangled to announce her arrival. A handful of people were browsing, while a couple of slim young men with over-long hair were striking poses in a corner - as conscious of how they looked to the customers as they were of the literary argument they had self-consciously entered into.

She saw a young woman near the heavy Victorian table that served as a counter. The girl was pretty and had an unusual, continental-style haircut. That must be her. She was putting on a lightweight raincoat - ready for her lunch break. Gertie smiled to herself - she seemed to have a knack for making an entrance at the right moment. Banya was talking to the person who was taking over from her. Gertie liked her voice - it was educated, but with a lightness of touch and a casual confidence that had nothing of the county set or hockey pitch about it. She didn't want to loiter before approaching her - looking like a slightly batty customer wouldn't get things off to a good start - so she strode purposefully towards the desk.

Misinterpreting this, Banya cut in: 'My colleague will be delighted to help you. I'm afraid I'm on my lunch hour.'

'Actually, it was you I was hoping to speak to. On a matter of a personal nature. About Tommy.'

Banya looked puzzled. 'You're a friend of his?'

'A recent one. If you've heard of me at all, it's as his landlady.'

Banya excused herself from her colleague, then gave Gertie her full attention as, in unspoken agreement, they walked towards the shop's front door. Banya asked her if she'd like a coffee.

'Thank you, yes. It seems to be all the rage these days. When I was young, it was nothing but tea. Still, one must move with the times.'

They found somewhere, coffee was brought and Gertie, after the general pleasantries about books that had filled in the time between Newbolt's and the café, got to the point.

'I've heard about what happened with Ivor. Mum's the word, of course, but I know you know too… The thing is, I think it's very important, for Tommy, that he attends the funeral.'

Banya took a sip of coffee before replying.

'I'm sure he'd love to - if love is quite the right word - but Andrews is furious with him. He's killed off Tommy's chance of a job in the theatre. He's hardly likely to invite him to the funeral.'

'He's just lost the man he's been with for over thirty years. And, if it's not too vulgar to mention it, not just his lover but the breadwinner. So there's bound to be a lot of resentment. Hating Tommy gives him an outward focus for it and stopping the boy getting the job will give him a sense of power at a time when everything else is crashing down around him.'

'Which is why Tommy hasn't the faintest chance…'

"'Say not the struggle nought availeth…' I rather think that, if things are presented the right way, Bobbie might find Tommy a salve rather than the opposite. It'll go against the grain with him, but he may come round to it.'

'Why are you so keen on the idea?'

'I feel sorry for Bobbie and for Tommy and I think it would be good for both of them. Healing. And I have personal reasons… I don't suppose we can get a glass of wine here?'

'Sadly not. We could head off to a pub though, if you like?'

'I would, but I'm sure your lunch hour is precisely that, so let's make do with another coffee…'

'And your reasons?' Banya persisted.

'A long time ago, I was a good friend of a well-known actor. He was married, with two daughters and a son, to an actress. He gave her a title, money, fame, position. And children. But throughout his marriage he had many affairs, which broke her heart. She was a woman of the world, she knew the score. But though she could play the most fearsome roles on stage - I saw her as Volumnia in Coriolanus and was simply terrified of her - her love for him was her Achilles heel. And their children, who were in their late teens when I first met their father, despised him for his behaviour but, because they loved him too, and because hating him would have further broken their mother's heart, they focussed their anger on the women in his life.'

'Of which you were one?'

'Ah! There's the rub! I was not. We indulged a little safe flirting when we first met but for some reason he never pounced. In fact we became very good friends. We enjoyed each other's company, we had similar interests and I became not just a friend but a confidante. His children assumed the worst and on the rare occasions when we bumped into each other - usually in a theatre foyer - they looked at me with pure venom. Yet they were on quite good terms with two women friends of their mother, with both of whom, unbeknown to them, he had been sleeping. For years. I found their misplaced dislike of me and fondness for his mistresses quite amusing until the night I opened the evening paper on the way home, only to see he had died - of a heart attack. I sent his wife a note of condolences straight away. In it I asked to be told of the funeral arrangements as, naturally, I wanted to pay my respects. I got a letter, the next day, from his son, saying that I was on no account to attend the funeral and that he was distressed that a woman who had caused his mother and sisters such pain by her behaviour would have presumed to contact the family at such a difficult time.'

'How awful for you!'

'I threw the letter on the fire and made no mention of it to Bertie. My husband. But I was deeply hurt at the absurd injustice of it all. Though now I come to think of it, injustice is always absurd. I would have loved to have taken a cab to their home and told them the truth about the entirely platonic nature of our friendship. But they wouldn't have believed me. They wouldn't have *wanted* to believe me. I was too convenient an outlet for their grief. Bobbie's anger is similarly misdirected. Not in quite the same way, because Tommy was, after all, Ivor's lover. Bobbie needs to lash out, even though part of him knows he's lashing at the wrong person. It's Burgess he should hurt, but the boy is the easier target. What's needed is a way for Bobbie to feel better about himself. Which he will in time, if he acts with decency now, rather than spite. He'll realise that, if we play our cards properly. He may have been second fiddle all his life but he's an intelligent man.'

'Do you have a plan?'

'Yes. It might sound batty, but I'm going to pay him a visit, at the Palace. Given our old acquaintance, where better to meet than the theatre? I'll lay the groundwork, and get him to agree to see you. I have a hunch that, if he does, he'll soften.'

'Not a man, I imagine, who'll be easily swayed by a woman?'

'*Au contraire*. Men of his sort may not want to sleep with us, but they're often very sympathetic to our femininity. As are all men, really. If they're not play-acting the stud, then what they're looking for is a mother, an aunt or a sister to take their side. To make things better, as when they were little boys. If we can just get you as far as his dressing room, then I'm sure something can be done.'

'That would be wonderful. But we don't have much time.'

'We don't. So I'll get cracking. I'll phone or send you a note if I can get you an appointment with him.'

'OK. Here's my phone number. If I'm not there you can always leave a message.'

'Thank you. As Henry Irving once said, 'Here's to our enterprise!''

Chapter Twenty One

Two days later, Banya arrived at the stage door of the Palace. Gertie had phoned to tell her Bobbie Andrews would see her. Banya had started to thank her, but was told to save the congratulations for after the meeting. 'Telephone me as soon as it's over!'

She pulled open one of the dark double doors and saw, to her right, sitting behind a counter, a tired-looking Jimmy. His was an exhaustion born not of a lack of sleep, but of stress: his own over Ivor's death, and having to deal with everyone else's, once the news broke. Showgirls in tears as they arrived at the theatre each day. Bouquets of flowers from fans. Newspapermen pretending to be members of the public, hoping that while they were talking to him they'd see someone or something that would give them the idea for a new angle on the story - or, better still, doorstep a quote from a passing actor or stagehand.

'Good morning. I'm Banya Sanderson. I think Mr Andrews is expecting me.'

Jimmy's listless manner suddenly improved. He had gathered something of what her visit was about from Gertie's previous appearances at the stage door and Bobbie's veiled announcement that he was expecting a visit from a young woman.

'Yes, miss. He's expecting you. Hold on a second, please.'

He telephoned through to Bobbie and told her his guest was there.

'Yes, Mr Andrews. Thank you... He says to go in, Miss. Through these doors, then straight ahead. Dressing Room One. The Guv'nor's.'

Banya thanked him and was soon at the door of the star dressing room. She could hear nothing through the door. She knocked and just about heard a faint answer. After a second or two it was repeated, more forcibly.

'Come in!'

Inside, the room had been left exactly as it was when Ivor was last there, except that a space had been cleared on the surface of his dressing table, which Bobbie was now using to do paperwork. He rose as Banya came in and his voice sounded far stronger than she had expected. He saw this register with her and explained:

'Mr Novello had the door more or less soundproofed, so he wouldn't hear the chorus boys scampering about, especially as they have a penchant for filthy jokes at the tops of their voices. A good idea, except one can barely be heard when visitors knock.'

'I'm glad that's the reason. You didn't sound well.'

'I'm not, really, but that's another story. Well, a related one, given Ivor's demise. Which is why you're here, of course. Gertie Gilbert told me all about you.'

'It was very kind of her to approach you.'

'She's a nice woman and an old friend. I was glad to be back in touch. A shame about the circumstances.'

'You've kept his room as it was?'

'Yes. The understudy's taken over as Nikki but he didn't feel comfortable about having this room. Not that I gave him much choice.'

'It's good of you to see me.'

'I was intrigued by what Gertie said about you. So, here we are... Tea? Biscuits?'

'Yes to tea, no to biscuits, thanks. I love them, but they're so fattening.'

'Not something you have to worry about, from the look of you.'

'Nor you.'

'Thank you. People say it's because venom and fat don't mix.'

'Why would they say that?'

'Because when you run a business you can't afford to be sweetness and light. Here we are....' He handed her a cup of tea. 'Now, go ahead...'

'It's about Tommy.'

'So I gathered.'

'He hasn't sent me. He doesn't know I'm here. But I am, because I know how upset he is about what happened. He was very fond of Mr Novello...'

'Not enough to keep Burgess away from him.'

'He couldn't have known Burgess would turn up at your flat the way he did.'

'Ivor warned Tommy about him. A warning he chose to ignore.'

'I can imagine how you feel...'

'Really?' The voice was still calm, but sounded distinctly bitter. '*You* can imagine how *I* feel?'

'Yes, though I'm not presuming to say I've ever felt anything like it myself. But surely the disaster that happened was down to the behaviour of someone in a jealous rage precisely because Mr Novello...'

'Oh, for God's sake call him Ivor. Everyone did and it's less of a mouthful.'

'Because Ivor was so important to Tommy.'

'Not least because Ivor was getting him a job.'

'Yes, which was very kind of him.'

The statement, simple and true, touched something in Andrews. His anger was overridden by affection for the man he had lost.

'He was a kind man.'

'So I've heard.'

'I first met him during the war, you know. The Great War, that is. We were both invited into a box at the opera by Eddie Marsh. A waitress was serving champagne when she tripped on the edge of a chair and spilt a glass of it down Eddie's shirt front. He was furious - largely because he was embarrassed in front of the young men he wanted to impress - but Ivor just laughed, that lovely laugh he had, and told her he'd done exactly the same thing at a party earlier that week. Then he took a napkin and patted Eddie's chest, which thrilled the old boy. He blushed scarlet. 'You see?' Ivor said to the girl. 'That little mistake has made an old man very happy!' I fell in love with him at that moment.'

'He could have had anyone in London. You were the man he chose to spend his life with.'

'Yes. And now I'm burying him. At fifty-eight.'

Banya wasn't close enough to put her hand on Bobbie's arm, though that was her natural reaction. Instead she paused, as if in acknowledgement of the awfulness of the situation, before coming to the point of her visit.

'The funeral's next week, I believe.'

'Yes. Golders Green Crematorium. He wanted to go up in flames like some sort of Wagnerian hero. He liked Wagner almost as much as he enjoyed Lehár.'

'What I'd like to ask, because Tommy never would… is that you allow him to go to the funeral. Not lining the roads, as the public will, but to the chapel; at the service. A way of him paying his last respects. It's what he would most like.'

'One doesn't *like* going to funerals. Personally, I can't stand them. Nor could Ivor. He wouldn't be going to this one, if he didn't have to.'

Banya laughed and suddenly the atmosphere lightened. Bobbie joined in. Having done so, he looked slightly shocked at himself, then pleased.

'Thank you! That's the first time I've laughed since he died. Which deserves a little reward.'

He leant back and opened a small drawer under the dressing table. From it he took a letter.

'I opened the original envelope, to see what was inside. You could call it prying, but it was a dead man's letter and I'm his executor, so technically I was within my rights.'

'What does it say?'

'It confirms the date and time of the job interview he'd arranged. It makes it clear the boy will get the job. And he also makes it clear, very tactfully, that this is a farewell present. The fling was flung and Ivor was moving on, as he always did. Nicely phrased, but clearly bringing down the curtain.'

'I'm sure Tommy will understand. And be very grateful.'

'You can also give him this...'

Bobbie sat at the desk and wrote something on a stiff, embossed white card, then put it, with the letter, in an envelope which he passed to her.

'Here's his invite. He'll have to bring it with him if he wants to get in. Security's tight. As is space, so it'll admit just one. I'll tell the ushers to sit him between Jimmy and the Swayers. They're a group of old fans who were, in their way, also close to Ivor.'

'You mean Jimmy actually leaves the theatre?'

'Very rarely, but this is a special occasion, after all.'

'This is very kind. And generous. And the job?'

'Is his. It wouldn't have been, had I not seen Ivor's letter, then been approached by Gertie and now you, but...'

'Thank you. I'm very grateful.'

'Thank Ivor. I've spent over thirty years making sure he got whatever he wanted. I'm not going to fail him this very last time. Now, if you'll excuse me I have a lot of other things to look after. Getting him safely sent on his way is almost as much work as putting on one of his shows.'

Banya stood up, then crossed to where Bobbie had himself stood up to say goodbye. She offered him her hand. He swiftly took it but rather than shaking it, he brought it up to his lips, continental-style, and brushed it against them. The gesture didn't come naturally to him, but it was what Ivor would have done and, here in his dressing room, it seemed the right thing to do. After a brief smile of farewell, he sat back down at the desk and busied himself with some paperwork as Banya, without another word, left the room, holding the envelope, and Tommy's future, firmly in her hand.

Chapter Twenty Two

Crowds lined the streets leading to the entrance to Golders Green Crematorium, as if for some sort of royal procession. Which in a way it was. One of the kings of the theatre world making his final appearance. The trees along the route were still bare of leaves, the skeletal branches making a contrast with the round, padded figures of mourners - most of them women - who were heavily hatted, scarfed and overcoated against the March wind.

Limousines and taxis dropped the invited guests at the entrance to the crematorium, and it was here that the taxi Tommy had taken from Golders Green tube pulled up. There were several cars ahead of him at this point, temporarily blocking the way in, as they disgorged VIPs ranging from Hollywood star Linda Christian to newspaper baron Lord Beaverbrook, a neighbour of Ivor's in Jamaica, where Ivor, like Noël Coward, had kept a holiday home. Needless to say, Coward poured scorn on Novello's house and his own did indeed have a far better location, on a cliff overlooking the Caribbean. Another little niggle between the two men. The throng of celebrities meant that Tommy was some way from the police guard at the front of the building, where they and a long line of ushers were keeping the tearful crowds on the pavement, as they had been all along the approach roads.

Tommy paid the driver, who had been talking all the way from the tube about the Novello shows his wife had enjoyed. He then began to walk to the gates, when a man wearing a well-cut but old and frayed overcoat and a hat pulled down low on his face stepped off the pavement and into the road, ignoring the 'Oi!' from the nearest policeman. Before Tommy realised who it was, Burgess had reached him and given him the sort of close hug that one grieving person might offer another.

'Get away from me!' hissed Tommy, not wanting to have anything to do with him, but not wanting a public scene either. Having got this close to the funeral, he wasn't going to let Burgess ruin his chance of attending it.

'Tommy, I'm so sorry!'

Guy pulled back but did so in such a way that he was now standing in front of Tommy, who had no choice but to listen to him, unless he were to push past - creating the incident he so wanted to avoid.

'I really am desperately sorry. Please, can we meet? Just once? Please?'

'Forget it!' Tommy glanced towards the policeman, who had kept his position in front of the crowd but who was looking towards him in case he needed his help. 'Now get out of my way - or shall I ask that copper to move you?'

'All right. I understand how you feel.'

He stepped back towards the pavement, so Tommy could walk past him towards the gates. As Tommy did so, determinedly looking straight ahead and avoiding any eye contact, Burgess said: 'When you get inside, check your overcoat pocket.'

'Now then, sir, let the young gentleman move along.'

A police sergeant, who had been watching them from the other side of the road, had decided to intervene.

'Of course, officer,' said Guy. 'I got rather carried away. I'm very upset about Mr Novello. Crushingly disappointed I couldn't join my friend inside.'

Burgess's accent did its usual trick and the sergeant immediately adopted a less assertive body language. Tommy, meanwhile, kept walking until, to his huge relief, he arrived at the gates, showed his invitation and was let in.

An usher took him to his seat, which was about half way down the row of pews, between several Swayers on his right and Jimmy on his left. All greeted him with a warm handshake but few words, the women keeping a handkerchief in their hands, their eyes filled with tears. Jimmy wasn't weeping at that stage, but when, during a brief address, the vicar mentioned Ivor's well-justified reputation for kindness, Tommy heard him give a stifled sob. The service itself was fairly short, while the music was mainly classical, reflecting the relatively highbrow taste Ivor had always shown in private. His coffin was in a light-coloured wood and looked small and vulnerable as it arrived, born on the shoulders of only four undertakers, so slight was his body.

Afterwards, the mourners passed a line-up of some of his closest friends, supporting Bobbie Andrews, who stood very slightly apart from the others at the head of the line. When Tommy passed him, he was unsure whether to offer his hand but decided to do so. Andrews took it and gave his usual firm handshake in return, though Tommy could see that the top of his crisp white shirt, on either side of his black tie, was damp with the tears that had fallen during the service. Neither man spoke.

There were vast crowds of people lining the cloisters immediately outside the chapel, waiting for the VIPs to emerge, which they did, processing between rows of onlookers, some of whom, once they'd spotted the person they hoped to see, turned their attention to the banks of flowers that lined the edge of the lawns just beyond the cloister walls. There was a reception mentioned on the invitation, but Tommy had only wanted to be there for the funeral, so he allowed himself to be swept along by those leaving for their cars, walking immediately behind Cicely Courtneidge and Jack Hulbert. Close by was Vanessa Lee, who played the Queen to Ivor's King Nikki in Kings' Rhapsody. An exquisite singer and talented actress, her other recommendation was her beauty, which Ivor had enhanced by paying for her to have a nose job. In later life he had developed a slight eccentricity, offering the same procedure to several of his women friends, not all of whom appreciated the implication behind the offer. Leaving these stars to their chauffeurs and their cars, Tommy grabbed one of the empty taxis that had been allowed to station themselves just outside the gates. He was worried about another ambush from Burgess but mercifully this didn't materialise. This driver was far less talkative than the one who had brought him. The only conversation was about their destination.

'Where to, guv?'

'Hyde Park Corner, please.'

A journey of that length, when he could get the tube, was unusually extravagant, but the thought of being crammed up against other passengers on the hot and crowded Northern line back into town was unbearable. He would spend what was needed to have a solo journey down to the Corner, from where he could walk through Green Park and St James's Park towards the Thames. He had arranged to see Banya by the river, but wanted to kill the time beforehand somewhere quiet and soothing. Having told the driver where he wanted to go, he sat back and, having resisted the temptation until then, reached into the right hand pocket of his overcoat. Nothing. He tried the left hand pocket. Just his house keys. Panicking, despite himself, he reached for the least likely space - the pocket at chest level inside the overcoat. There he found a small envelope, with his name on it. Tearing it open, he saw a sheet of expensive-looking notepaper, on which was a very brief note from Burgess:

Tommy, I cannot apologise enough, but what's done is done. It was terrible, I admit. By contrast, the happiest event in my life was meeting you, in that wintry fog. In the envelope is a ticket for the Royal Ballet at the Opera House tonight. Theatre as a cure for the soul and ballet as the art form where Russia leads the world. You see? I can't keep politics out of anything. But my feelings for you trump everything else. I hope what's left of yours for me will bring you to Covent Garden tonight. And if they need a little extra encouragement after the bruising they'll have had at today's funeral, may I mention that I have something poetic to pass on to Banya? Something she and Peter will be delighted with. In sackcloth and ashes,

Guy x

Chapter Twenty Three

It was seven o'clock, and Guy had been waiting by the portico of the Royal Opera House since six. The performance was at seven thirty but he was worried Tommy would get there early, only to change his mind and leave - hence his own arrival long before. All around, oblivious to his agony, cheerful crowds were arriving for a night at the ballet. The men were generally in dinner jackets (before the war most would have been in white tie and tails), the women wearing their best evening outfits, hair specially done, jewels on display. Guy couldn't help resenting the general atmosphere of well-heeled conviviality, while as a political animal the sight of the upper middle class at play triggered his most violent fantasies of proletarian heroes storming the centres of privilege at bayonet point. So, though he leant against a corner of the portico with what he hoped was a certain louche elegance, his coat collar up as it had been on the night he and Tommy met, his face presented a stern and self-absorbed glower, strikingly at odds with those of the balletomanes and socialites around him.

Despite himself, he couldn't help noticing a slim, dinner-jacketed youth who was looking at him with what seemed a more than casual interest and a slight smile on his artificially red lips. Guy grinned back at him. His heart wasn't in it, but after so many years of cruising for sex, the reaction was automatic. At that moment, he felt a tap on his right shoulder. It was Tommy. That was who the red-lipped boy had been looking at. 'Damn!' he thought. 'The indignities of age.'

'Aren't you trained to avoid being taken by surprise?' Tommy asked. Guy relaxed a little. Humour was a good sign.

'I'm a Communist, dear, not a commando!' he replied. 'I'm pleased you came.'

'You should be. I wasn't going to. I'm actually here for Banya. You said you have something for her?'

'I did. We can talk about that later. For now, let's have a drink. But as we're outside, let me point out a little regal curiosity that I've been staring at since I got here. Anything to avoid the smug faces of the *haute bourgeoisie* having a night on the town.'

Burgess pointed across the road at the imposing stone facade of Bow Street police station. 'See anything unusual?'

'Not really.'

'The light!'

'Oh! Yes, it's white.' Traditionally, lights at the entrance to police headquarters had blue glass. There had been, a few years earlier, a British movie about a young gangster, played by Dirk Bogarde, and the policeman he shot. It was called The Blue Lamp. 'What's special about that?'

'Because, my dear, when Queen Victoria used to come here in her carriage, she noticed the coloured light outside the newly-built police station and thought it indicated something more conventionally advertised by a red one. Her courtiers, hugely embarrassed that she should even know about such things, reassured her that a blue lamp was entirely respectable, indicating the presence of the Metropolitan Police, but she swept aside their protestations and announced: 'Coloured glass is vulgar. I want it replaced!' Hence the only white lamp outside any police station in England. You see, if all else fails I can earn an honest bob as a tour guide. Now, let's get that drink!'

They made their way in and, after leaving their hats and coats at the cloakroom, climbed the imposing flight of stairs to the Crush Bar, which lived up to its name. Guy somehow forced his way to the front of the queue without causing a scene and brought two glasses of champagne over to where Tommy was standing.

'How did you manage that?'

'Confidence on my part and nervousness on theirs. Nobody wants to stand between an alcoholic and his tipple. Cheers.'

Tommy raised his glass, to return the salute. 'Your health!'

'I was scared I'd never see you again.'

'You wouldn't have, if I hadn't received your letter. And, more to the point, seen you in the flesh at the funeral.'

'That was what swung it?'

'Oddly, yes. You looked genuinely sorry. And rather pathetic.'

'A picture was worth a thousand words?'

'Sort of.'

'Good. And soon we'll watch beautiful young people moving delightfully on stage, wallow in the music, weep at the tragedy - then head home.'

'Yes. Separately.'

'But I thought you wanted…'

'To see you. To talk a little. I'm not going to bed with you.'

'I see.'

'You said you had something for Banya. That Peter would like. That's really why I'm here.'

It might be, officially, thought Burgess, but Tommy would not have come if there wasn't a tiny spark still alive, despite what happened in Novello's flat. So, there was hope. However small. The last little voice at the bottom of Pandora's box.

'I'm thrilled you're here, but under the circumstances, I'm afraid I'll have to save Auden 'til later.'

'Isn't he here tonight? Isn't that the surprise?'

'No. Well, not in person. More importantly, on paper. You see, I commissioned a poem from him about Banya. A gift to my lover's best friend.'

'I thought this was an apology, Guy - not emotional blackmail.'

'I'm rather desperate. Love can drive you mad. As the Greeks knew. As this ballet shows.'

'Desperation isn't very attractive.'

'True. But my life has certain problems…'

'Which you never share. Isn't love about sharing?'

'You sound like the motto on a greetings card.'

'Don't sulk. You can't expect me, after all that happened…'

'Yes, yes. I understand you're in mourning. Still, life must go on.'

'It must. Which is why I'm here.'

'Then there's a chance for me?'

'An Auden poem would certainly help.' Two could play at blackmail.

The bell announcing five minutes before curtain up rang loudly, cutting through the background noise of people talking slightly too loudly over their wine glasses.

'If you're not coming back tonight, can we at least go for a walk tomorrow? See things in the clear light of day and all that?'

'Perhaps. For now, I'd just like to see Swan Lake.'

Chapter Twenty Four

The next day, Tommy did meet up with Guy, this time at St James's Park. For a walk. It was mid-afternoon, and nothing else had been planned. Tommy was prepared to see him, but turned down an evening meeting. Mid-afternoon was a safer, less charged time of day.

Many of the trees were still bare, but there were flowers at their bases and yellow swirls of daffodils among the grass. The lake was the area's main attraction, and the two men walked towards it as they set off from their meeting point on the edge of the park.

'How are you?' Guy went to put his arm round Tommy's shoulder but, sensing his disapproval, he adapted the move into an avuncular pat on the back.

'Fine, thanks. And thanks again for last night.'

'You're welcome. It's always so much nicer to see something like that with someone you love.'

Tommy tried not to wince. Couldn't Guy see that banging on about love was counter-productive? After all, whenever it came to sex, Guy's technique had always been the opposite of romantic.

Disappointed at the lack of response, Guy put a brave face on it: 'It'll be something nice for me to think about back in the States.'

'You're going again? You hate it! Why not just leave?'

'I have things to do before I can shake off the dust of America and plant my feet back on the springy turf of St James's.'

'How poetic.'

'These daffodils would make anyone lyrical.'

'When are you going?'

'Tonight.'

'Blimey!'

Tommy stopped on the path. Burgess stood beside him.

'Not a phrase I'll hear over there…'

'When will you be back?'

'Not sure, my dear, but I'll let you know as soon as I do.'

'So, this is your last night here for a while?'

'How perceptive of you!'

Guy always adopted a comical expression when teasing. This came from years of making quips to working-class boys who became sullen or turned nasty, depending on their temperaments, unless he almost theatrically telegraphed that he was joking. This wasn't necessary with Tommy, but it was a habit Guy couldn't shake off. Tommy wondered where Guy would suggest them heading next - Bloomsbury or the Savoy? He was gearing himself to refuse either option when, to his astonishment, rather than suggesting sex later on, Guy ruled it out.

'Speaking of commitments, I've a longstanding one to stay with a friend tonight, so I'll have to keep my hands off you until I come back for good. Assuming you'll be more receptive by then, having finally forgiven me…. On the other hand, the bushes over there are terribly dense, so if you feel like a quick one…'

Tommy started walking again.

'Guy! It's broad daylight.'

'Which makes it all the more exciting.' Guy threw a regretful look back. 'I was on my way to a meeting in Whitehall once, when I saw an eminent professor emerge from that very thicket, looking terribly pleased with himself. Followed, a short while later, though heading in a different direction, by a guardsman in full regalia. At eleven in the morning!'

'How long have you got?' asked Tommy, changing the subject.

'For this walk? Oh, plenty of time. Then I thought we'd get some tea together at Lyons Corner House at Charing Cross, before I have to see a man about a dog. As it were. Let's do a couple of circuits of the park then head up to Jermyn Street, where I've ordered you a smart jacket, a couple of shirts and a rather super tie.'

It was an unsubtle form of apology, and a compromising one at that.

'Really?' Tommy knew he should reject it, but he needed some new clothes. They would help him make a good impression in his new job. He would accept the offer, but with no sense of obligation.

'Really!' Guy had often joked with Blunt and Auden about the exchange of goods for gratitude: 'The capitalism of cock' was how he liked to describe it. In this case it would be sex deferred, but he had wanted to leave Tommy with a good impression, especially as his trump card - two orgasms before sleep - couldn't be brought into play this evening.

Tommy was determined not to ask about Guy's bedroom arrangements for the night, so latched on to the forthcoming gifts and tea as a way of avoiding the subject, unaware that his enthusiastic anticipation confirmed Guy's theory about the transactional nature of so many relationships. Tolerating each other's company while misinterpreting each other's thoughts, they walked on through the cold, bright March sunshine while, a few hundred yards away, a detachment of Grenadier Guards were smartly marching from Wellington Barracks towards Buckingham Palace, from one of whose tall picture windows Anthony Blunt was, in a brief reverie, gazing out towards St James's Park.

Chapter Twenty Five

Banya's plans had been thrown. She had expected to meet up with Peter and a friend of his, an American sculptor who was visiting London on his way to Paris. This was to be Peter's last night in London and he wanted to pick his friend's brains about aspects of Parisian life. All this went out the window when the sculptor caught a stomach bug after trying the delights of a typical English café where, un-typically, the eggs of the traditional English breakfast proved to be off. Banya had been perfectly happy with dinner for two, but when she heard Tommy was free she decided to ask him instead.

'You're sure Peter won't mind?'

'Why should he?'

'The last time he saw me I had Guy in tow…'

'Then he'll be all the more relieved you're on your own. Though he's going to hold Guy to his promise of an introduction to Auden.'

'I'm sure he'll arrange one.' He didn't sound it.

'You don't think he'll deliver?'

'He's dangled something else - something vague - about Auden in front of me but there's no sign of it so far. Makes me wonder about the personal introduction. Especially as Peter'll be in Paris from tomorrow.'

'Perhaps Auden will be there at some point? He seems to travel a lot...'

'The thing is, Guy's very happy to tell people about his friendship with Wystan, but less ready to share him with anyone - especially if they're young, male and attractive.'

'We'll just have to rely on Mr. Burgess's finer feelings,' Banya laughed.

'Don't hold your breath. Anyway, what time and where?'

'Banjo Joe's at eight o'clock.'

This was a new Soho eatery, whose name came from the occasional musical 'entertainment' that the owner liked to provide. There was also a piano and a regular pianist who provided a more conventional musical accompaniment to the chatter of the restaurant's mainly young and arty customers. The food was unadventurous but cheap and plentiful.

Tommy arrived just before eight, to find Banya and Peter together at a corner table. The three had dinner, Tommy giving them a description of the night at Swan Lake and the walk in the park earlier that day.

'Sorry you've ended up with us, rather than your beau,' said Peter.

'He's not my beau. I feel I should be apologising for barging in on your last night before France.'

'Not at all. We invited you, remember?'

'Banya did.'

'Same thing!'

'I'm glad you did, then.'

He meant what he said, as he genuinely enjoyed Peter's company, though as the evening wore on and Peter's attention turned more and more exclusively to his girlfriend, Tommy felt increasingly alone. At first the wine compensated for this, as it did for many of life's problems, but by the time they'd finished the cheese and started the brandy his relaxed resignation had soured into a combination of self-pity and sexual tension. His friends were going to spend the night together. What was he supposed to do? Throw confetti at them as they headed home? Applaud their success while manfully ignoring his own failure? He found himself having a bitter conversation with himself as he looked around the room, irritated by the many couples he saw, locked in their own little world of happiness and desire.

Once a suitable interval had elapsed, he made a polite lie about feeling tired and left. He had suggested asking for the bill but Peter insisted on paying.

As he stepped into the neon glare of a Soho street, the working girls were in evidence, some of them on their second or third customer of the evening, taking them back to tiny, over-perfumed rooms at the top of creaky wooden staircases in decaying Georgian townhouses.

A party of sailors on leave, accompanied by a pair of ill-matched sugar daddies, swung into Tommy's path from a side street, in search of a new pub to explore. One of the sailors caught Tommy's eye, but the last thing he wanted was a courtship in front of the whole group, so he ignored him and carried on towards Cambridge Circus. From there he could go down Shaftesbury Avenue towards Piccadilly, then through St James's Square and on to the park, but he didn't know where Guy was spending the night - he'd been unsurprisingly evasive about the location of his 'friend's' flat. Given that St James's was very much Guy's territory, he didn't want even the smallest risk of bumping into him.

Charing Cross Road was as busy as ever, but once he turned into St Martin's Court the crowds, the traffic and the noise they made, vanished. The little dog's leg of a passageway took him behind Wyndham's and the New Theatre, whose stage doors backed on to each other, and then into St Martin's Lane. He crossed over and disappeared into Goodwin's Court, a tiny alleyway which contained a row of the oldest private houses in central London - dating, it was thought, from the 1690s. He walked through the court, whose chocolate-box bow-windowed houses were dark, save for the two at the far end, whose occupants were in and enjoying themselves, judging by the sound of a piano coming from the bigger of the two homes. Soon he emerged into Bedfordbury, the street that ran behind the London Coliseum, one of London's biggest theatres, and down to the Charing Cross Hospital.

Along the southern side of the Coliseum was Brydges Place, even slimmer than Goodwin's Court. Essentially it was a canyon between the bricks of the Coliseum on one side and assorted nineteenth century buildings on the other - including the back door to a pub, and a low-ceilinged archway which offered an alternative exit, about half-way along the passage. Running along part of the wall was a public urinal. The whiff of stale urine on the floor and the unpleasant tang of the freshly-delivered variety in the trough itself gave the alleyway an acrid smell. This didn't put off the handful of men who lingered there, not actually using the trough, but exposing themselves to each other once confident in their own mind that their neighbour wasn't a policeman hoping to make an easy arrest for indecency.

Tommy had never been keen on 'cottaging', as frequenting public lavatories in search of sex was called, but he knew that young guys from out of town would find their way there, and he would be ideally placed to offer them something rough and ready in a more private setting. Sure enough, as he waited a small but sexually significant distance from the other men, there appeared a tall, well-built boy about the same age as him. Tommy's intuition told him he was inexperienced and that the thin sheen of sweat that the lamps above the urinal picked out was one of nervous tension as well as excitement. He stood at the young man's side before the newcomer had had a chance to get his cock out.

'Evening!'

The boy turned towards him, liked what he saw, and stopped fumbling with his fly. This was the signal Tommy needed.

'Let's go somewhere.'

Giving a simple nod, followed by a shy but pleased smile, he followed Tommy who, confidently, led the way without looking back - a modern-day Orpheus in the underworld. He only turned round when they had left Brydges Place and were standing in Bedfordbury.

'Hi.'

'Hello.'

'You know this area?'

The boy shook his head.

'I do. So you're in good hands.'

The two walked side by side the short distance north to Goodwin's Court, into which Tommy led the way. About half-way down the alley it was almost dark enough not to be spotted by anyone coming in at either end, but with enough light to see as well as feel each other's flesh. Tommy unbuttoned the boy's shirt, revealing his stocky, muscular torso and his now achingly hard nipples. After paying them some attention with his fingers and then his tongue, Tommy moved down to his trousers, opening them and getting to work on the impressively large cock. The boy came incredibly quickly. Men usually wanted to leave straight afterwards, guilt as well as pleasure on their faces, but this one seemed happy - keen, even - for Tommy to turn him round, bend him over and then, using only spit as a lubricant, to enter him. This was the opposite of Tommy's usual sexual role but something about the stranger's passivity, and a sense of power that the encounter gave him, drove him to do what the boy showed every sign of having wanted all along. Soon they were both cleaning themselves up and getting ready to move on.

'That was great. Thanks.'

'Thank you,' said Tommy. 'Where are you from?' He knew better than to ask for a name or profession.

'Leicester.'

'Well, Leicester lad, welcome to London!'

With that Tommy kissed him on the cheek - the only face-to-face contact they had had during their encounter - and walked away.

Sitting on the top deck of the bus going home, forcing his gaze through his own reflection and out onto the street life below, Tommy quietly enjoyed the afterglow of sex. Despite the disaster of Ivor's death, life went on...

Chapter Twenty Six

Tommy's bus-top optimism seemed fully justified when the interview at the New went swimmingly. Not long after, he received a letter offering him the position of Assistant Manager. His first weeks shot by. He loved every minute. The theatre manager he worked for was an old-school type, steeped in West End history but on top of the latest trends in writing, in design, in acting and even in marketing - something Tommy was interested in, but hadn't expected to learn anything about. Most theatre managers seemed to be confirmed bachelors, but Ralph was happily married, with two grown-up children. He had married young, was still in his early forties, yet had the grey hair and courtly manners of a man twenty years older. He had a splendid office in the upper reaches of the theatre, in contrast to Tommy's base of operations, which was little more than a glorified store room. Indeed, half the walls were lined with boxes full of theatre programmes for the current season. Ralph tended to invite Tommy into his own office for a drink at the beginning and end of the week. During the first such session, he explained that, 'When it comes to running the public side of a theatre, in my experience the job boils down to two issues. Lightbulbs and lavatory paper! Everything else is secondary...'

Bearing this motto in mind, Tommy quickly realised that his role was essentially to make sure all the small practical details were provided for. Ralph chose all the staff, from the ushers to the barmaids, and they reflected his taste in people as much as the competence or character of the individuals themselves. What he was looking for was people with the sense of duty you might find in the staff of a traditional country house, but with the important addition of loving theatre, too. He preferred drama school students as ushers and old ladies as barmaids. One of them, whom he had joyfully inherited from his predecessor, had been serving in the dress circle bar when Queen Victoria died.

Tommy enjoyed calling backstage to check everything was properly arranged in the actors' dressing rooms. He was less comfortable dealing with the electricians and carpenters, but that was partly down to their natural inclination to tease anyone young. He knew he couldn't stand on his dignity at this early stage without antagonising the people he'd have to work with for years, but he made a mental note of the various incidents and was determined to establish his authority once, as Ralph put it, he'd 'earned his spurs'.

The public were something of a revelation. There was a vast difference between being a member of the audience and dealing with them as a dinner-jacketed representative of the theatre. True, he'd had inter-action with them before, when working as an usher, but ushers were almost invisible to many theatregoers, whereas managers stood out in their dark finery; visible authority figures to ask for help or to make complaints to. Or, on rare but memorable occasions, to thank for a wonderful evening. Some of the public seemed to regard him, despite his youth, as some sort of oracle, though others could be deliberately bolshy. This created one or two awkward moments, but he stood his ground and made sure he observed Ralph as much as possible, picking up the tricks of the trade from a veteran performer.

A perk of the job was giving free tickets to friends or family when there were spare seats at a show. One evening he arranged a pair for

Gertie and Banya in the front stalls. The stage door keeper, Molly, was a complete contrast to Jimmy at the Palace: a twinkly-eyed old lady with her hair in a bun, her hunched shoulders covered by an ancient but still presentable cardigan.

'She may look like an old dear, but she's sharp as tacks,' Ralph told him, after he'd introduced Molly during Tommy's first-day tour of the building. 'I think of her as theatre's answer to Miss Marple. She doesn't miss a trick. Keep her on side and she'll be your most valuable ally. Apart from me, of course!'

The other main character was Teddy, the commissionaire. He stood, resplendent in his military-style uniform on the steps of the theatre entrance as the first audience of the evening (or matinée) arrived, then moved into the foyer when things got busy, serving as a cross between an information desk and a bouncer-bodyguard. A veteran of the First War, he was small, stocky and the proud possessor of a handlebar moustache. Teddy had a life-long faith in authority that even the First World War generals couldn't shake, and he treated Tommy with all the respect he'd have given a young subaltern on the Western Front.

With these as the core people in the team, Tommy knew he'd landed on his feet. He had survived a potential scandal over Ivor's death, thanks to Bobbie Andrews' mastery of keeping unwanted details out of the press, and had been given his dream job. The Civil Service was just a memory. As he walked down the stairs to the foyer, ready to take his position before the doors were opened to the public, he caught sight of himself in one of the gilt-edged mirrors that lined the staircase. He was happy with the elegant figure he cut. This was his world. He belonged.

Chapter Twenty Seven

Guy kept in touch with Tommy via letters sent to the stage door. Transatlantic telephone calls were simply too difficult, especially with the time difference and Tommy inevitably working in the evenings. The American stamps on the envelopes caught Molly's attention, though after her first comment on this foreign correspondence - 'A friend of the Trumans, are we?' - she did no more than raise an eyebrow when handing over Guy's envelopes. Tommy quite enjoyed receiving them as Guy was an entertaining correspondent, but so intense was his immersion in his new role that Guy and the time he'd spent with him seemed almost unreal.

Guy's other correspondence was with Auden, to whom he boasted that his meeting with Tommy at the Royal Opera House, and subsequent inveigling into writing an occasional answer to his letters, was as much a tribute to his sex appeal as Shakespeare's portrayal of Richard III wooing and winning Lady Anne, the widow of his slain enemy.

Guy's last note to Tommy suggested they meet at Rules for dinner to celebrate his final return home. His hidden agenda was to lay Ivor's ghost to rest by dining in a restaurant Tommy would previously have associated only with him. He was confident it would work, especially given the little twist to the evening that he had in mind.

He booked a table for Tommy's only night off during the week. Arriving exactly on time, Tommy half-expected to see Guy leaning nonchalantly, in his favourite pose, outside the restaurant entrance. There was no sign of him, however, so he went in, to be greeted, asked for his name, and have his overcoat and hat taken. He was then led, by an elderly waiter, away from the main dining room, up a narrow wooden staircase to an upper floor.

'Mr Burgess has booked a private room for the three of you, sir.'

'Three of us?'

'So I'm told, sir.'

'Good heavens. The third isn't a young lady, by any chance? Dark hair? Very pretty?'

'No, sir.'

'It wouldn't by any chance be Mr Auden? The poet?'

'No, sir. Here we are.'

The waiter knocked on the door to the private dining room - a relic of late Victorian London, when the Prince of Wales and numerous aristocrats entertained buxom actresses to dinner and sex, safe from prying eyes. Knowing this, Tommy wondered what Guy had in mind. A threesome, on his first night back? Not what you'd expect from an ex-lover desperate to be reunited. From inside the room the knock was answered with an exuberant: 'Enter! Enter!' It was, unmistakably, Guy. The door was opened and Tommy was ushered in by the waiter, who then left, closing the door behind him. Seated on a divan in the corner of the room - a divan which would have a fascinating story to tell, Tommy thought, if it was really as much of an antique as it looked - were Guy and another man. The stranger was very slim, with a long, lean head. He wore a beautifully-cut suit but the immediate impression he gave was of intellect rather than wealth. Tommy, who had an instinct for these things, immediately spotted the loneliness underneath the *hauteur*.

'Tommy! How lovely to see you!' Guy strode up to Tommy and kissed him, but gently and only on the cheek. Aware that he had to play his cards carefully - and far more skilfully than before - he deliberately toned down his usual behaviour. There was none of the lip-smacking lewdness he'd displayed to Barry and Tom at the Stag's Head. Seeing this, Tommy began to relax.

'Welcome back!' he replied. 'Good to see you.'

'Thank you! Now, let me not forget my manners... May I introduce you to an old friend from my Cambridge days? Anthony Blunt - the Surveyor of the King's Pictures.'

Tommy blushed becomingly as Blunt shook his hand. Guy knew that an introduction to someone so close to the heart of the Establishment would impress Tommy. It was a good start to the evening. Another card well-played. Private conversation could wait until later, when he would, if things went according to plan, take him the short distance over the road to the Savoy.

'I've heard so much about you', said Blunt, giving Tommy his toothy smile. 'I hope you don't mind my being a gooseberry! I rather bullied Guy into inviting me. I have to go to Windsor for a few days from tomorrow and I couldn't manage any other time to meet you at last.'

'At last?'

'Your name is rarely off Guy's lips.'

'Not just his name, Anthony.' Burgess couldn't resist the quip. Damn. Two steps forward, now one back. Fortunately, Tommy didn't seem to mind.

'Guy!' Blunt laughed. 'You'll embarrass Tommy! May I call you Tommy?'

'Please do!'

'Splendid. Call me Anthony.... Now, come and sit down. You there, next to Guy. I'll sit opposite. I'm being bossy because I insisted to Guy that I pay for the evening.'

Burgess was delighted. Things had got off to a good start. He poured another drink and settled back in his chair. Looking around the room he felt a rush of pleasure at being back in London in such agreeable surroundings. This truly was the greatest city in the world. Once he'd helped Moscow over Maclean, he vowed that, apart from the occasional short holiday or long weekend, he would never leave London again.

Chapter Twenty Eight

Though nothing was specifically mentioned, it became clear, through body language and an unspoken understanding, that Tommy would spend the night with Guy. This wasn't what Tommy had planned, though the possibility was present when he accepted the invitation. It was always easier to fall into bed with an old flame, even when the flame had been extinguished in a welter of recriminations, than to agree to sleep with someone you'd never met before. Sleeping with an ex was less charged and could be written off more easily than heading off into the night with a stranger. Drink always helped and Burgess had made sure the wine flowed.

At the end of a convivial evening, outside the restaurant, as Burgess and Tommy walked away, the older man's arm thrown over the younger man's shoulder in a proprietary way, Blunt stood quietly watching them. As he did so, he pulled out a cigarette case with an exquisite jade decorative device and removed a Balkan Sobranie - his favourite brand. With the cigarette between his lips he replaced the case, then produced an equally elegant lighter, lit the cigarette and took a long, deep, draught of it. The sight of the two men on the way to spend the night together in bed, while he went home, alone, to his icily minimalist apartment, made his mind up for him.

Ignoring the people walking past, he continued to stand, alone with his thoughts, as he so often found himself, whether at Buckingham Palace or Windsor Castle. A loud rattling of keys was the only thing to distract him. It was the verger of the Roman Catholic church on the other side of Maiden Lane. He must have been working very late, thought Blunt. Busy at his devotions, or making sure the place was fit for other people's, first thing in the morning. Then he remembered. One of the waiters had mentioned the church was staying open all night. Some sort of saint's day. All-night confession. The verger had been making sure the church door was properly wedged open, the little candle on a nearby shelf still alight; a gentle advertisement of the unusually late access to God.

As if awake after a dream, Blunt turned towards Charing Cross and walked away from the church, the restaurant, and the hotel where Guy would have his way with Tommy. He was surprised at how visceral his reaction was to the idea. It wasn't as if he didn't have sex occasionally himself. It was a need, though one he felt far less urgently than most. Hence Guy's periodic teasing, which Blunt shrugged off when it happened. For he prided himself on living a life of the mind. It was why, he liked to think, he had become involved in spying for the Russians in the first place. A brilliant mind applying the logic and analytical skills that made him so distinguished an art historian, to the principles of politics and economics. He genuinely believed this, blocking out the youthful idealism of his school and university days and the true nature of his early commitment to communism. For though he had indeed found it intellectually stimulating as a concept, his interest in the cause of world revolution had been fired by a romantic desire to be part of a 20th century version of the French Revolution. An expert on 18th century art, he had thought, like Wordsworth, that to have been young at the time of those tumultuous events must have been very heaven. He'd been too young for the Russian Revolution, but he could at least commit himself to its continuation. He might more or less live in a library but, through passing on the secrets that came his way during the war, he felt he'd made a real contribution to the struggles of the rough, violent world that he otherwise shrank from. The idea of himself as a marcher, a demonstrator, let alone a street fighter was laughable. But an elegantly-uniformed spy, helping the revolution by outwitting its enemies? That was simply delicious. Now he had done his bit. The war had ended at last. Fascism had been defeated. He continued to help where he could, but he knew the royal tittle-tattle he passed on was essentially gossip. No more agents would end their lives in pools of blood in basement punishment rooms because of his betrayals. No more families would find themselves listed as Enemies of the People and enslaved in labour camps. Those days were over. He could concentrate on the most important thing in his life. Art. Besides, he enjoyed the social position he now held. He saw no contradiction in this, because he regarded (and he was nothing if not self-regarding) his position, his money and his prestige as the honours due to his intellect and to the art that it served. It was only a matter of time before he was given a knighthood. At last, he would be a social cut above Guy. Marlborough, his school, was a good one, but not in the same class as Eton. He would enjoy teasing his old friend about it.

His friend… He had always liked Guy, since they first met at Cambridge. Guy was better-looking, better-built. An extrovert. A leader of men. And seducer of them. Their own sexual encounter had been pivotal in Blunt finally releasing himself from a misguided chastity and, in doing so, finding a maturity that had previously been lacking. It gave him the experience of human nature that was crucial to understanding the representation of it on canvas and in stone. He owed Guy a lot. And he had repaid him, on many occasions. Guarding his back, giving him (rarely taken) good advice, smoothing ruffled feathers in Moscow as well as in Whitehall. He did this out of gratitude and friendship - but also from a desire for self-preservation. It was a good idea to keep an eye on Guy, to know what he was thinking, what he was likely to get up to next. As the years passed, his friend had become an increasingly loose cannon, now verging on a liability. His infatuation with Tommy could only increase the risk.

Which was why he decided to make the phone call. That, at least, was the justification in his own mind, as he walked down the Strand, but, as with his passion for the Russian Revolution, there was a personal element as well. Though he would never admit it, this was the real motive, or at least the one that tipped the balance. For, like many men before, he had been captivated by Tommy. His fresh good looks, his easy chatter, his delightful habit of touching one's arm as he talked, to emphasise a point... A young man who was so evidently in love with life - with the theatre, with London, with his body and the pleasure it gave him. Blunt realised, in the course of the dinner, that he was completely hooked. At one point, when Tommy's attention was more closely on Guy, Blunt, gazing at the boy's profile, had even allowed himself a brief fantasy of how he might shape his future. He imagined taking him to galleries. Introducing him to the right people. Being the Eddie Marsh to Tommy's Novello. Or the Henry Higgins to his Eliza Doolittle. Madness... Or was it? Why shouldn't he? After all, Guy was a dead end for a boy like Tommy. Fine for now, perhaps, but before long he'd be a busted flush - and a ruined liver. Or possibly in jail, as a traitor. No, that last could never be allowed. He would drag others down with him. If only to have some like-minded company in prison. The very thought made Blunt shiver. And confirmed a decision that had been forming throughout the evening. Burgess would have to go.

He reached the telephone kiosk, near the top of Craven Street, which ran south from the Strand towards the Embankment. It was close enough to the main road not to look furtive, but far away enough to be quiet. Blunt had never seen a queue there. He would not be overheard. The Soviet Embassy agreed to it as safe to use. He picked up the receiver, inserted a coin then dialled a number. The phone rang for some time before a click on the line suggested it had been picked up. There was a brief pause, then it was answered by a man with an East European accent.

'Yes?'

'This is Palace. For Dacha.'

'Carry on.'

'I thought you should know... Our mutual friend seems to be getting very reckless since his return. He is, in my opinion, a liability.'

'Will he still be able to help his friend go on holiday?'

'Barely, but yes. Though I think, for the sake of his health, he should join him there.'

'That is quite a big step. Long holidays can be expensive.'

'He needs it. As do we, if our health is not to be risked, too.'

'You are sure?'

'Sure enough to be concerned that The Man's health might well be compromised. And you know what that would mean.'

'The Man's health must be protected at all costs.'

'Quite so. Hence my call.... Can you arrange this?'

'He may not wish to go.'

'It could be a surprise. Once he's already begun taking his friend abroad.'

'Perhaps. It may be better he knows before the planning begins.'

'I think not.'

'Is there a complication?'

'He has a friend he will be reluctant to leave.'

'The one he has seen much of recently?'

'Precisely.'

'That can be arranged...'

'No! I mean, no, that would not work. The young friend is known to many people.'

'Then he should be left out of this?'

'Absolutely. Very wise…'

'Anything else?'

'No. Goodnight, Dacha.'

'Goodnight, Palace.'

Blunt's forehead had a sheen of cold sweat when he put the phone down. He hadn't been sure how the Russians would react. The coded mention of Kim Philby seemed to do the trick. They would not have wanted Blunt himself revealed as a spy, but Philby was vital to their entire, ongoing penetration of British intelligence. Less cold than Blunt but far more controlled than Burgess, he was their best, highest-placed agent. The trump card in Blunt's betrayal. The thought of Tommy, alone once more after Guy's disappearance, in need of another older man, brought some warmth back to Blunt's face. As he left the telephone box, the petrol fumes and open air banishing the tart, intrusive tang of stale urine splashed about the floor and the lower glass panels, he felt a sudden relief. An anticipation. And yet, ashamed. Suddenly unsure of himself, he thought of the all-night vigil at the Catholic church back in Maiden Lane.

Ten minutes later, Blunt was sitting in a confessional. Though technically an Anglican, he had been to many Roman Catholic services in his university days and had once spent the night with a seminarian. He could easily pass himself off as a Catholic, from dipping his fingers in holy water at the entrance and crossing himself, to genuflecting as he passed the altar on the way to the confessional, where he sat in a comforting half-light, waiting for a priest to slip into the neighbouring compartment. A slight shuffling noise, a click, and then a dim light coming through the speaking holes in the dividing wall indicated a priest had now arrived. They both said some prayers and then came the moment of truth.

'What have you to confess, my son?'

'I have sinned, Father.'

'In what way?'

'A dozen minor infractions of courtesy or kindness, moments of self-regard, temptations of the flesh - mainly my own… all the usual.'

'But that is not why you are here at this hour?'

'No, Father. It's because I have betrayed a friend's trust. Because, by sending this friend away, which is not something he would want, I hope to befriend another person, one very close to him, of whose relationship with him I'm jealous.'

'You say you will send him away? How so?'

Blunt knew of the sacredness of the confessional. The priest would repeat nothing. But Roman Catholics were notoriously anti-communist. He would have to obscure the exact truth. Something he was used to, after all.

'My friend works for the government. He would like to stay in London, with the young friend I have mentioned…'

Add detail to every lie, he thought. As he had been trained to do.

'But I have had a word with his superiors and he will be transferred overseas. Unlike the friend, whose career is very much here in London. This will break up their friendship.'

'Leaving the way clear for you?'

'Yes.'

'So you did this for purely selfish motives?'

'I could pretend otherwise, but yes.'

'Then you should own up to your friend. Apologise. Warn him, so he can take action to plead his case, against going abroad. Besides, this is a free country. He isn't being exiled!'

'Indeed, Father.'

'There you are, then. Say four Hail Marys and contemplate the power of friendship among Our Lord's disciples. Try to imitate the selflessness they showed, as recorded in the gospels. And confess to your friend. Ask his forgiveness. Rebuild the trust that your jealousy has damaged. You will feel so much the better for it.'

'I will, Father.'

The priest gave absolution.

Blunt left the confessional. As far as he was concerned the whole thing was mumbo-jumbo, but he felt better for having got it off his chest. Mission accomplished, he thought, as he headed down to the Strand, looking for an available taxi. He hoped his Soviet handler would soon be saying the same thing about getting Burgess across Europe to Moscow, leaving Tommy alone - and needing a new friend and mentor.

Chapter Twenty Nine

At the Savoy, Guy was about to bare his soul, too. Though his confession was even more of a riff on the truth than the one Blunt, unknown to him, had just delivered a few hundred yards away. He was lying in bed with Tommy. The curtains and one of the windows were open, letting in the moonlight, the fresh air (despite the cold) and the distant sound of barges on the Thames below. It was a river view room and so several times the price of the one he normally hired for sex, but tonight was a special occasion. Tommy lay beside him, his head on Guy's chest, while Guy gently stroked Tommy's shoulder.

'Tommy, there's something very important I want to tell you.'

'It's OK. I know you're mad about me!'

'Not that, my dear, though it's certainly true. No, it's about the real reason for my coming back.'

Tommy, who had been feeling pleasantly sleepy, simply snuggled further into him. Guy took this as encouragement to continue. If Tommy was listening but drowsy, so much the better.

'You know I work for the government?'

'Yes, though you're always so vague.. 'Diplomat' covers a wide range of activities.'

'It does. And it my case, that means intelligence work.'

Tommy had wondered about this, but kept silent. Guy's next words were delivered in as casual a way as he could manage.

'And the thing is, I may have mentioned a friend and sometime colleague of mine. Called Donald Maclean. Nice man, but a martyr to his nerves - and the bottle.'

Tommy had no recollection of this, but given he was half-asleep, he might have been mistaken. Besides, most of Guy's friends seemed to drink like fishes.

'You may have… I can't remember right now.'

'Oh, I'm sure I will have done. The thing is, and you must swear to keep this to yourself…'

Tommy squeezed Guy's arm in assent.

'It seems poor damaged Donald is a spy. For Russia.'

'God!' Tommy sat up in bed, looking directly at Guy.

'The last thing on his mind, I imagine, when he began his career.'

'How does this affect you?'

'I've wormed my way into his confidence. My widely-trumpeted communist sympathies helped there. So he thinks I'm a friend.'

'Does he think you're a spy, too?'

'Good Lord, no! But he does think I'm sympathetic to him. He's been very ill recently. Something of a nervous breakdown. He's cracking under the strain, you see. And I've offered to help him get out of the country. On government orders of course, though naturally he doesn't know that. He's too ill - mentally as much as physically - to travel, but I've told him I'll go with him to the continent. Hand him over to the Russians.'

'But how would that help our side?'

'Because we'll be handing him safely and secretly over to the Russkies in return for their releasing some brave Hungarian friends who took against the Communist take-over of their country at the end of the war. One of them is a friend of Tomas.'

'The man in the pub?'

'Yes.'

'So your helping Maclean is a sort of bluff?'

'Very much so. There are other aspects to it, but I'm afraid I can't go into them. The point is, it's crucial, absolutely crucial, he never suspects. He must believe I'm just an old friend doing an incredibly good turn. If he were still entirely in his right mind he'd see through that, but he isn't - which is why he needs to go in the first place. And to keep up the front, it's got to appear as if we're leaving the country secretly. That we're going to France. All rather exciting.'

'You bet!'

'Which is where you come in.'

'Me?'

'I'd like you to come with me. It'll look less odd having a few friends travelling together rather than just the two of us. More of a sightseeing trip, with a young man in tow. I'll leave you in Brussels, which *entre nous* is our first stop, take him further east, then a day or so later come back and you and I can have a short holiday in Amsterdam, before heading home.'

'Why Brussels?'

'Because, traditionally, Englishmen who flee abroad have always headed for France in general and Paris in particular. Nobody will expect Brussels, which is safely dull and uneventful. Plus, I'll get to show you the Musée des Beaux Arts.'

'The one in Auden's poem?'

'The very same. I can't wait to see it again, with you at my side.'

'You're forgetting that I have a job now. A career.'

'Far from it. But I think you said earlier that the theatre is 'dark' for a few days between shows?'

'Yes, but…'

'Ralph sounds a very reasonable man, and from what you've told me he likes you. I can't see him objecting to you having a spot of foreign travel. You'll only mention me, of course, not Maclean.'

'I suppose it might just work.'

'And the first evening you'd be free?'

'Not long now. Friday the 25th.'

'There you are. When better than May, to see the sights?'

'What if things go wrong? What if it's thought you're actually a spy, too? And what about me?'

'It won't go wrong. As I've said, I'm doing all this on behalf of His Majesty's Government. Who will be pleased you helped. Not officially, of course, but it'll be a good mark. And I'm sure if there were some weird mix up, Anthony would put in a good word.'

'He did seem very friendly…'

'Doesn't everyone, where you're concerned?'

'Only if they're queer.'

'Indeed. As a friend once remarked: 'All the world's a stage - and most of the actors are poofs!''

Tommy laughed. Burgess had got what he wanted.

'Then it's a deal? You'll come to Brussels?'

'If Ralph's O.K with it. And one other thing.'

'What's that?'

'Auden's poem about Banya. It's high time you handed it over. Why haven't you?'

'I've been away. And we were barely on speaking terms until the day before I left. Commissioning it - and giving it to her in due course - are both favours on my part. Favours I was happy to fulfil when the time was right. Now you're coming to Brussels with me….'

'I am?'

'Aren't you?'

'I said, it's up to Ralph.'

'Then ask him tomorrow. Now, be a good boy and move your hand a little further down…'

Chapter Thirty

Tommy cleared the trip with Ralph, who reacted with typical goodwill. Tommy claimed he was going to Paris. Brussels was never mentioned.

'I have to say, I'm rather jealous! A family man can't just up sticks and cross the Channel for a few days. And I haven't been abroad since before the war. Used to go cycling in France. Fortunately.'

'Why fortunately?'

'Because plenty of people between the wars enjoyed visiting Germany. Before the First War, it was the French who were our enemies, after all. Until we got worried about the Kaiser building up the German fleet. But after the Armistice many people tried to let bygones be bygones. Reconnected with German culture. All those music festivals. Walks in the Black Forest. Beer and Rhine cruises. Very embarrassing when the last war started. A couple who lived near my wife's parents used to spend their summer holidays teaching English at Hitler Youth camps. Had a whale of a time apparently. They saw it as a more glamorous version of the boy scouts. Egg all over their faces once the Krauts were the enemy. Again.'

'Politics aren't my thing Ralph… I'm very grateful you're letting me go.'

The other crucial person he had to tell was Banya. Because he shared everything with her, he told her where they were really going.

'And you'll see Auden's painting?'

'Of course! But Guy's got something else up his sleeve. I'm not supposed to tell you, but Auden's written a poem about you.'

'Really?'

'Really! Guy says he asked him to - and, having met you, Auden was happy to oblige.'

'Well, darling, in that case, I'll come as well!'

'What?'

'You're not the only one who'd like to see that painting in the flesh. And if he's got an Auden poem about me, then it's high time he gave it to me. Where better than the Musée des Beaux Arts? You mustn't let him use it as some sort of permanent bribe. Not if you have any self-respect. Which I rather wonder, given you're sleeping with him again. Didn't you learn anything from what happened to Ivor?'

'You know I did.'

'You're not exactly showing it.'

'It was a great evening, he behaved himself, I'm not seeing anyone else, I had a lot to drink…'

'In other words you let alcohol and hormones lead you down what has already been proved a very dark path. And it wasn't just your feeling horny. Guy knows you. He used, as a very obvious bait, an introduction to someone working directly for the King. Plus the chance for a trip abroad.'

'My first ever trip abroad. Of course I jumped at it! And I was acting in your interests too. I'll make it clear we're having a little fun again, but that's as far as it goes. And, believe it or not, I'm going to dump him when I get back.'

'Before or after you cement your friendship with the Surveyor of the King's Pictures?'

Tommy's laugh, which Banya joined in with, was a mixture, on his part, of embarrassment and bravado.

'Now then,' she said. 'Back to that trip. Safety in numbers. What better way to avoid suspicion than having a woman along? Besides, if this friend of his is in a bad way, having a girl in the group might help. You say he's not, you know?'

'No. He's married and all that.'

'There you are, then. Besides, if you're having an adventure I don't see why I can't. I'll leave you men in Brussels and carry on to Paris to see Peter.'

She lit a cigarette and enjoyed a long drag on it, during which she looked upwards, as if in deep thought. When she lowered her gaze to look straight at Tommy, there was a mischievous glint in her dark green eyes.

'Now I think about it, getting the poem in the museum's rather cheesy. I'd rather have it presented to me on the high seas.'

'It's a cross-Channel ferry, Banya. Not the Queen Mary!'

'It's a ship and we'll be at sea. The very waters where the Spanish Armada was scattered by the Protestant Wind. Where pirates have sailed and Dreadnoughts steamed to keep the Kaiser's fleet at bay…'

'Is there something more than tobacco in that cigarette?'

'I'm just high on the adventure of it all. You don't begrudge me a little excitement, do you?'

'Of course not.'

'Then you're glad to have me on board? I won't be in the way?'

'I'm amazed at the idea, but I can't think of anything nicer.'

'Good! That's the right answer. When do we sail?'

'The 25th of May. First night I can get away.'

'Excellent. Now let's order a bottle and pretend we're already at sea…'

Chapter Thirty One

The time between Guy raising the idea of travel and the day itself passed very quickly. Tommy threw himself even harder into his work, keen to let Ralph feel he had earned the short holiday.

Guy was astonished at Banya's suggestion she join them, but as it would be perfect cover he agreed with as good a grace as he could manage. Tommy then confessed he'd told her about Maclean, Brussels, the lot.

'She knows everything?' asked Guy, when Tommy told him.

'Yes.'

'Well, at least you've told me.'

'You're not angry?'

'Not enough to make a fuss, but certainly enough to give you a good spanking later this evening.'

'Then I'll have to find something else to confess!'

'Naughty boy!'

On the afternoon of Thursday 24th of May Guy had lunch with Tommy and Banya.

'The Three Musketeers!' Guy raised his glass in a toast.

'One for all, and all for one!' they chorused.

'I'm so looking forward to our little adventure. But there is one important change of plan. We are to meet, tomorrow evening, at

Dover, to get the night ferry to Ostend.'

'I thought we were going from Southampton?'

'I've changed the plan. Two men have been hired for the occasion to drive to Southampton and get on the night boat to St Malo, flashing passports purporting to belong to Burgess and Maclean. Just to throw people off the scent.'

'What people?' asked Banya.

'Our friends in Moscow, of course! We may be giving them the traitor Maclean, but we don't want them to know our processes as well. Might interfere with any later operations if they do.'

'How very cloak and dagger!'

'That's the nature of the game…'

The next evening Banya and Tommy, each carrying a small suitcase, their passports and some cash, waited at the Dover ferry terminal for Burgess and Maclean to arrive, which they did, ten stressful minutes after the appointed time. Guy made brief introductions. Tommy thought Maclean had a pleasant face, overlaid by a mask of nervous tension. Both men had been drinking, which, given Guy had to drive all the way, wasn't the best preparation for a long voyage where time-keeping was essential. All four flourished their passports. Guy and Maclean were carrying false documentation - 'the Secret Service thinks of everything!' confided Guy to Tommy and Banya as he showed them the brand new, wholly fictitious documents before they got to the control post.

'It can't be that easy, surely?' asked Banya.

'Don't you believe it! If British prisoners of war in Colditz could, with almost no resources, make false German identity papers, then for our government to come up with a couple of British passports can't be too much of a challenge.'

The ferry was basic but somehow elegant. The cabins were similarly functional rather than luxurious, but had something jaunty about them. Everything suggested a sense of adventure. From the portholes to the style of furniture, the whole ship spoke of the sea, of travel, of new horizons. Guy and Maclean were sharing a cabin, while Tommy and Banya had cabins to themselves. Maclean was helped to a seat in the restaurant for a modest dinner. During the meal Banya cut through Guy's dissimulation and asked him directly about the poem. He whipped it from his jacket pocket, knelt at the side of the table - to the delight of a group of elderly women, who assumed he was proposing to Banya - and presented her with the manuscript. He had hoped to hang on to it for longer, but had kept it within easy reach for just such an eventuality, so he could pretend that he had planned to give it to her then, all along. After a toast to Banya, they tried to do justice to the dinner that was provided, but were too tired to have much of an appetite. In fact all four were exhausted and, with an early start ahead of them in the morning, they kept the meal brief and went to their cabins by nine o'clock.

Tommy had thought Guy in a strangely depressed mood, far quieter than usual and with a preoccupied look about him, but when he realised he was being observed, Guy dredged up some *bonhomie* to match Banya's resolutely cheerful manner. He maintained this on the way to bed, propelling Maclean down the corridor to their cabin, while looking back over his shoulder and saying, with a roguish grin:

'Good night, my dears! Tomorrow, the Continent!'

Chapter Thirty Two

The ship was making easy going of the Channel crossing. The waves were minimal. Guy, who had suffered many rough journeys on ocean liners during Atlantic storms, thought it more like being on a lake than at sea. He had telephoned his embassy contact at Dover, as arranged, and been given the appalling news that he had to go into exile with Maclean. He had started to protest but was told, curtly, that his name was now known to British intelligence and that he was in imminent danger of arrest. The Soviet Union would welcome him with gratitude and make life as comfortable as it could for such a distinguished servant. Guy, whose class consciousness stood in direct opposition to his politics, winced when he heard the word. However metaphorical the usage, it was not a term he would ever associate with himself.

He tried to keep up a brave face over dinner, but, having put Maclean to bed and watched him fall almost immediately asleep, his worries kept him awake. The prospect of not just the next few days, as he had planned, but the rest of his life away from England, was unbearable. On the other hand, long years in a high security prison would be worse. Unless he could cut a deal with the authorities. Too late now. And what of Tommy? That was all over, too. Unless… Might he be persuaded to share Guy's exile? No. A mad idea. Or was it? Realising it would be a sleepless night, he dressed as if getting up in the morning and made his way along the corridors and up various steel staircases to the deck.

He had always found something incredibly soothing about looking at waves while leaning over the white-railed balcony at the back of a liner. When travelling, he affected not to understand nautical terms like port or starboard, winding up ships' officers by pointedly referring to right and left instead, and insisting on calling a ship a boat. Deliberately upsetting people who couldn't answer back was an unattractive habit, he knew, but the boredom of frequent trans-atlantic crossings brought out the worst in him. As he stared over the railings at the churning wake the ship left behind, he wondered what officialdom in Russia would be like, and if his status as a spy for the Motherland would give him any of the leeway over there that being an Old Etonian had done in his own country. Lost in his thoughts, he was startled at hearing someone give a gentle cough behind him.

'Good God! You scared me!'

It was Banya. Like him, she was dressed, though less completely. She had put trousers and a jumper over her pyjamas (she couldn't bear nightdresses) and thrown a raincoat on over them. A silk scarf completed the outfit, while she wore slippers rather than shoes.

'Couldn't sleep either?' she asked.

'No. Unless I'm sleepwalking.'

Guy pinched himself, as if to check.

Banya laughed. Doing so broke the tangible discomfort caused by each other's presence on what each had hoped would be an empty deck where they could clear their heads. Her laugh transformed them from awkward intruders into conspirators.

'There's a lot to think about', she said. 'What with this little outing, then Paris, Peter - and the poems.'

'I can imagine.'

'And what about you? You look as though you have a lot on your mind.'

'You're a perceptive girl.'

Burgess's sarcasm was unmissable. Was he bitter, she wondered, because she had spoiled his solitude? Or her having joined the little group on this voyage? Perhaps he envied her Tommy's attention. Or was he just tired and worried? Faced with such imponderables she decided to rely on female intuition - the instinct that had given her a flash of insight back on the dock at Dover, and which had brought her on deck to have time, space and the fresh salt air to think. Guy's presence made the latter impossible, so she decided to jump in and hope she was right.

'Guy, as we're here, in this sort of in-between place between the sky and the sea, in the dark before dawn, can we talk frankly? Beginning with a question?'

'If it's as eloquent as the preamble to it, then why not?'

'You're not just giving that poor broken man to the Russians, are you?'

Burgess looked at her, coolly, without answering.

'You're going with him. And the only reason you'd do that is because you're one of their agents, too.'

The silence between them seemed to affect their surroundings as well. The splash of the waves against the sides of the ship, the background hum of the ship's engine, all seemed to fall quiet, as if the sea and the swift vessel were both waiting, like her, for Guy's reaction.

He reached into his overcoat pocket and for a sudden, freezing moment she thought he was going to pull out a revolver. Instead, with a flourish, he brought out his cigarette case, followed by a lighter. He silently offered her a cigarette, which she gratefully accepted. Slowly, Burgess took another from the case, tapped it against it, then, with it in his mouth, at the sort of angle she associated with handsome American movie stars, he leant forward, lit hers and then his own. He drew a deep pull on the cigarette then tilted his head back and blew a plume of smoke into the air, where they both watched it seized by the breeze and taken away. Only then did he speak.

'The answer to both your questions is, yes. I am.'

'But Tommy doesn't know?'

'Of course not. He wouldn't have come if he did. It took all my skill to wrench him away from that bloody theatre of his, as it was.'

'If I'd known, I wouldn't have let him come.'

'But you didn't - until too late - so he did. As did you, rather complicating the picture. As for looking out for him, are you telling me you're more concerned for him than dear old England and its various shadowy secrets?'

'Yes. King and country can look after themselves.'

'You see yourself as a mother figure? Or an elder sister, perhaps?'

'There's a hint of the sister about it, I suppose, but no, I see him as a friend. And, though he's twenty he's not quite the man of the world he likes to think he is. I don't want to see him hurt. Which is exactly what you've lined up for him.'

'Not me. The men in Moscow. I only found out I had to go when I phoned them from Dover.'

'You certainly looked as though you'd had bad news.'

'Did I? I tried to appear calm.'

'You looked poleaxed.'

'The others didn't notice?'

'I doubt if Mr Maclean would notice anything much at the moment, and Tommy was too busy looking forward to the journey. And helping you.'

'Do you think he loves me?'

'No. As you're bright enough to realise, unless your feelings have completely blinded you. Which, given the way you play the rest of the world, is unlikely. You went a bit mad in the run up to Novello's death. As people do when they're in love. But I imagine you've calmed down since then. Or are you still pretending?'

'A little calmer. Though being in bed with him sets it all off again.'

'He has that effect on people.'

'Including you?'

'No. It would ruin eveything. And my sense of self-preservation is very well-developed.'

'As is Tommy!'

'That's not the sort of thing a gentleman should discuss, is it?'

'One likes to share one's good fortune.'

'Mr Burgess, are you trying to shock me?'

'I don't think I could, even if I tried.'

'Then please don't. As for Tommy's mind rather than his manhood, you know he doesn't actually love you or you wouldn't have asked. To be fair, he's amused and excited by you. Partly because you make it very clear to him you can open the sort of doors he'd like to walk through. Though even that's a bit of a charade, isn't it?'

'In what way?'

'Because he's not the right class or temperament to be accepted in your world. Once his looks go, they won't let him onto the steps, let alone into the building.'

'You resent the class system?'

'That's the sort of question asked by people who think they're on the inside sneering at those who aren't.'

'Sorry. I never sneer on purpose. It screws the face up so.'

'It would be wasted on me. The English side of my family are what most people would call grand and the Burmese are minor royalty, so social insecurity isn't my weak spot.'

'I wonder what is?'

'Let's stick to Tommy. I'd like you to keep him from getting any further into this mess.'

'How?'

'We're going to Brussels. Fine. You can show us the painting. Fascinating. But give him a break. When you and Maclean run away, leave a letter or something he can show the authorities when they question him. To prove his innocence in all this. It'll be bad enough being labelled as a homosexual. You can spare him being tarred as a traitor.'

'There is another way.'

'How?'

'He can come with me.'

'You're mad!'

'I need him!'

'That's your tragedy.'

'Haven't you a heart?'

'Haven't you a brain? Everything he really cares for is in London.'

Burgess stubbed out his cigarette on a railing then threw it into the sea.

'You're forgetting me.'

'I'm excluding you.'

'Kipling had it right. The female of the species is more deadly than the male.'

'We have to be, as the odds in life are so stacked against us.'

'You've got the vote, haven't you?'

'Finally. But there are plenty of other areas where...'

'OK, OK. Spare me the political lecture.'

'That's rich, coming from a Communist.'

'*Touché.*'

'So, do you agree?'

'To a letter stating his innocence?'

'That, and to not asking him to go with you. To putting him first. The way one does with people one loves.'

He looked away from her, in the direction of a now vanished England.

'Greater love than this…?'

'That sort of thing.'

He turned round again, to face her.

'I seem to have little choice.'

'You have a simple one. To do the decent thing or the selfish, desperate one. Surely you'll choose the first?'

'I fear you know very few Etonians.'

'Just the one. Uncle Herbert. Who wouldn't hesitate to do the right thing for someone he loved.'

'Then I concede defeat with as much grace as I can muster. Shall I kiss your hand to clinch the deal?'

'No. Save that stuff for the continentals… Tell me. Do they kiss hands in Russia?'

'Not since the Revolution.'

'A shame… May I ask you another question?'

'You've kicked in the door. You may as well enter.'

'How will a man like you manage in a country like the Soviet Union?'

'I'm not sure. To be honest, it's what's kept me awake tonight. It's not what I would have chosen, but then greater men than me have been forced into exile.'

'You see yourself as Napoleon?'

'A nice image, but no. He actually tried to apply for exile in England. I was thinking of someone less grand but equally romantic. More like me.'

'Yes?'

'Byron rather springs to mind. A sexual misfit. A penchant for abroad. A dedication to the cause of another country. Of course, there was one fundamental difference between us.'

'His club foot or his title?'

'Neither. He went to Harrow.'

'Shocking bad taste.'

'Nobody's perfect. But you have to admit his poetry's sublime.'

'It is.'

'I was thinking of one of his lesser-known works before you appeared. A little self-indulgent, but very apt. Would you care to hear it?'

'So we'll go no more a'roving?'

'No, not that one.' He paused. 'Though you've given me an idea.'

'Which, then?'

Guy turned slightly, giving Banya a view of his profile. He looked out to sea while reciting Byron's brief farewell to England:

'Adieu, adieu, my native shore
Fades o'er the water blue;
The night winds sigh, the breakers roar,
And shrieks the wild sea-mew.
Yon sun that sets upon the sea
We follow in his flight;
Farewell a while to him and thee,
My native Land, Good Night!
A few short hours, and he will rise
To give the morrow birth;
And I shall hail the main and skies,
But not my mother earth…'

As he finished and turned to face her again, she saw tears in his eyes. About to ask another question, she stopped herself.

'That was lovely. I'll leave you to the sunrise. And your thoughts.'

Guy nodded his agreement and, as Banya walked away, he looked up at the sky as the first faint streaks of light made themselves seen. Safely alone, he let the tears fall freely, weeping partly for the thought of Byron heading off to Greece and an early death, but mainly for himself.

'Adieu,' he repeated, pushing aside fears of what was to come by conjuring up images from his past: his study at Eton, punting on the Cam at Cambridge, visiting his tailor, walking through the leaves in St James's Park on an autumn afternoon. The happy highways where he went, and could not come again.

Chapter Thirty Three

At lunchtime on the day the group sailed from England, Sir Edward Marsh was joined at his table at the Savoy Grill by an exhausted-looking Bobbie Andrews. For all his competence, he had found dealing with the professional fallout from Ivor's death a huge strain. To which was added his personal grief, which he kept under control in public but was almost overwhelming in private. He had found, as Gertie had predicted, some comfort from not standing in the way of Tommy's career and in allowing him to attend the funeral. Magnanimity had been empowering. But his hatred for Burgess not only continued, it grew. It was a focus for his resentment, an added layer of frustration when he dealt with business problems, and of bitterness when he went home to an empty flat and a bed where Ivor's absence was as noticeable as his presence used to be.

Sir Edward was also in mourning. Even more so than when Rupert Brooke had died. He had known Ivor longer and Brooke was at least a casualty (albeit from blood poisoning rather than a bullet) of war. Ivor's death, years after the end of the Second World War, having survived the bombs that narrowly missed his flat and damaged so many theatres, was a doubly upsetting event. It stirred him from a comfortable retirement and gave him the strength and determination for a last exercise of the behind-the-scenes power that he had been a minor but effective practitioner of for over fifty years.

The table Bobbie arrived at had been largely cleared of the evidence of the lunch that had just ended. Sir Edward's guest had left ten minutes earlier. Bobbie was joining his old friend for coffee. Sir Edward waved a hand at the empty chair. Bobbie sat down, and as he did so a waiter arrived with fresh coffee and a plate of assorted cheeses, with bread and crackers.

'Hello Eddie!'

'Bobbie!'

'I thought I was coming for coffee?'

'You are, but I felt you might need feeding up. Looking at you, I was right.'

'Thank you.'

'My pleasure. Now, you'll want to know what's happened.'

'Yes.'

'I spoke to Sir Herbert about our concerns.'

'And was he receptive?'

'Very. His department have been on to several suspects over the last few months. One of Burgess's friends is among them. Burgess himself has always been treated as more of a joke than a risk, as you know. Over the last few weeks I've done some lobbying and that attitude has begun to change. Though, like turning a battleship round, it takes some time. Can't spin on a sixpence.'

'No. So what action is anyone suggesting?'

'Observation. Surveillance.'

'Is that all?'

'All? It's a huge amount. Don't you see? We want the bastard hammered. Whatever his politics, whatever he may or may not be up to, he's highly sexed and he's going to be picking up men. At which point the police will move in and arrest him. Bingo! Career ruined, public disgrace and a year or two in jail. Unwelcome for ever more at school reunions, which sounds superficial but would be a real blow to him.'

'That's more like it.'

'And, springing from that, there's something else.'

'Yes?'

'The surveillance has paid off. It seems he's booked tickets to the Continent. From Southampton to Calais. Tonight. In his name, and that of his friend. The one they're sure is an enemy agent.'

'Ah! Will they be arrested as they try to board?'

'No. Two reasons. One is that the government is happy to bang Burgess up for sex but they don't want a public trial where our dirty laundry is washed in public.'

'But the other man? Is he…?'

'No. Married and all that.'

'Then what about him?'

'He's under suspicion, is aware of it and is fleeing the country.'

'What then?'

'We follow them and hope Burgess is helping the man run away. Which gets rid of his chum. Then we get him when he comes back. Unless he's planning to go, too, which would be perfect.'

'But he'd have escaped justice!'

'The rest of his life in the Soviet Union? Don't you see the poetic justice in that? He'd hate every minute of it. It would be a glorified prison camp. And with any luck Stalin might find him an irritation in the end and put him in a real one. Especially if we feed the Russians a bit of disinformation about him being a double agent. Which would neutralise the value of a lot of what he'll no doubt tell them.'

'Then everything's better than we could have dared hope.'

'There's just one fly in the ointment.' Sir Edward toyed with a salt cellar, meditatively.

'What's that?'

'That boy has started seeing him again.'

'After everything that happened?'

'I know, I know. What I don't know is why, or how serious it is. But who cares? Except that the boy and his woman friend have tickets in their names for the same crossing.'

'What a bloody little fool. Tommy, that is. The girl, I thought more highly of.'

'I dare say she's only going to keep an eye on him.'

'How does it - do they - affect what you were saying about getting Burgess?'

Sir Edward stopped playing with the salt.

'I want Burgess out of it. But I don't want the boy getting involved, publicly, in any fallout.'

'Serve him right, surely?'

'Bobbie, think for a moment. We're doing this to avenge Ivor. As things stand, his name won't be associated with any trial that Burgess may face. The boy, however, is another matter. His defence lawyer would have a field day. Young man led astray by Burgess - and Novello. Gang of perverts preying on the impressionable new arrivals in London.'

'Yes, I see.'

'We can't allow it.'

'So, what have you and Sir Herbert come up with?'

'We carry on as before. The girl has a boyfriend. Some sort of minor film star. Currently in Paris. It may be she and the boy will head there and leave Burgess and Maclean - that's the name of the other man - to do whatever they're planning. It may be Burgess takes the boy with him. If the former, it'll be easy. If the latter, the team on the ground will need to separate him from the other two, show him the error of his ways and bring him back to London. Sir Herbert says he's got one of his best men working on it.'

'So, the girl won't be involved in any fallout?'

'No. He was very clear on that.'

'What a gentleman.'

'More to the point, what an uncle.'

'Lucky girl! And Tommy? What'll happen to him?'

'He'll go back to his job at the New. It's what Ivor wanted, after all. He's been a fool. But given Burgess charmed the best minds in the Foreign Office for years, when his treachery was more or less staring them in the face, perhaps we shouldn't be too hard on a twenty-year old with little experience of the world. He may learn his lesson and move on. Or he may fall in with other undesirables. But we'll have done our best, Ivor won't be part of any future disaster and we will have clear consciences if he ruins himself.'

'Eddie, this is brilliant!'

'I wouldn't go that far, but it's pretty good. And better than we might have expected. So, without wanting to jinx things, I think a glass of port might be in order, don't you?'

Bobbie did.

'Splendid!' said Sir Edward. 'Waiter!'

Chapter Thirty Four

They reached Ostend a few hours after sunrise and were in Brussels by lunchtime. Customs officers had shown no interest as they disembarked. The train journey - 'Isn't Thomas Cook's wonderful!' - went smoothly. There was a long line of taxis waiting at the station when they arrived and one took them straight to their hotel, the Metropole. A vast late-Victorian building and one of the grandest in Brussels, it was a favourite with well-heeled international travellers.

'Isn't it a bit risky?' asked Maclean, when Burgess mentioned the hotel's name and address to the driver.

Surprised his fellow spy had taken anything in, given his near-comatose state during the rest of the journey, Burgess patted him reassuringly on the leg.

'As I've said to my friend Tommy here many times, the safest place to hide anything is under the light. It doesn't get much brighter than at the Metropole.'

He checked the party in, though Banya had no room as she was going on to Paris. Burgess and Maclean shared a room, while Tommy had his own, inter-connecting with the other men's.

Banya and Tommy followed them into their room. Maclean declared himself exhausted and needing to go straight back to bed.

Banya wondered whether Burgess had put anything in his colleague's coffee at breakfast, but she remembered having once met the sister of a friend, a few weeks after she had had a nervous breakdown. She had been even more withdrawn than Maclean was now.

Having tucked him in, Burgess told him where they were going.

'Just to let you know, Donald, we're off to Aux Armes de Bruxelles for lunch. But first, we're going to look at Wystan's painting at the Musée des Beaux Arts. I've always wanted Tommy to see it, and Banya really must, so she can tell her boyfriend Peter all about it when she joins him in Paris.'

Maclean grunted, then turned over and fell asleep.

The museum was a vast, imposing structure with a classical facade, a few minutes' walk from the royal palace. The tickets having been bought, Guy led the way up a large marble staircase to the gallery where Breughel's Fall of Icarus, the inspiration for Auden's poem, was hanging. All three stood looking at it intently. Guy, thinking fondly of Anthony Blunt, began an art historian's brief guide to the painting. In the foreground a farmer was ploughing a field with a carthorse. A field that looked perilously close to a clifftop, with a view across the sea to a fortified island and, beyond it, the harbour of a wealthy-looking coastal city. Near the farmer a shepherd looked resolutely away from the sea. In the bottom right-hand foreground, unnoticed by either, or by a nearby fisherman casting his line (rather unrealistically, given the picture's perspective), was a pair of legs, belonging to the Greek youth Icarus, whose attempt to fly had been wrecked by his climbing too high in the sky, where the heat of the sun melted the wax holding the feathers of his makeshift wings together, sending him plunging to his death in the ocean. The only person in the painting looking in the right direction, as Guy pointed out, was a lone sailor, climbing the rigging of a passing ship. He was frozen, as if astonished at the sight. Was he clinging to the rigging, taking reassurance from the thick, strong ropes that he wouldn't also plunge into the sea? If so, though he, unlike anyone else, had seen Icarus fall, his thoughts were nonetheless entirely centred on himself. Tragedies and personal disasters often took place almost within touching distance of passers-by who were entirely focussed on their own joys and worries.

'So, there it is. And now, for lunch!'

Another taxi was taken, to the restaurant, which had been one of the smartest in Brussels since it opened in the 1920s. A table for three had been booked by the concierge, though given the restaurant manager welcomed Guy like an old friend, it seemed an unnecessary precaution.

During lunch they talked about everything: art, poetry, Banya's trip to Paris, Peter's burgeoning film career, his potential as a writer, Tommy's experiences with some eccentric old ladies in a matinée performance the previous week. Anything rather than Donald Maclean or the Russians. Banya took the envelope containing the poems from her handbag, then placed the individual poems like trophies on the white linen tablecloth. Her delighted anticipation of Peter's pleasure at seeing his own work again - and discovering Auden's - lit up her face, and as she read them out loud Tommy thought she had never looked so beautiful. Guy listened politely until she finished, then, as she returned them to the envelope and took a sip of water, he started talking to the prettiest young waiter, pretending to need advice over which dessert to order. Taking the hint, both Tommy and Banya announced they needed to wash their hands, leaving Guy a clear field.

'Don't you mind?' she asked Tommy as they negotiated their way between tables.

'Not at all. Takes the heat off me.'

'Still bloody rude.'

'Don't be like that. He's been very nice to you.'

'It's how he is to you that worries me.'

They reconvened some minutes later at the table, where the waiter was still standing, teeth flashing in a wide grin at Guy's innuendo. Seeing their return, the manager discreetly signalled that enough was enough. The boy made his excuses and left to look after another table.

'I've paid the bill and now I'd better head back to the hotel to check on our friend. I'll sit with him awhile. Banya, my dear, you should get a cab to the station if you're to meet your train…'

Banya checked her watch. 'Good Lord! You're right! I'd no idea….'

She stood up, grabbing her handbag, flustered that she hadn't been more aware of the time and irritated that Guy, whose line of sight included a large wall-mounted clock, and who knew the importance of her catching the train, hadn't said anything earlier.

'Hang on! You don't want to forget these!'

Burgess handed her the envelope she had left on the table in her rush to leave. She thanked him profusely and pushed it into her handbag. Her little suitcase was in a small cloakroom near the entrance to the restaurant and a waiter was already bringing it over to her, sensing her need to leave.

'Now, I really must go!'

Guy and Tommy escorted her out into the street and towards the nearest taxi rank, which was a couple of minutes' walk away. Having got there and secured a cab, they said their goodbyes in a flurry of hugs, kisses and laughter. A final word: 'Remember, Guy! Look after Tommy!' and Banya was off to the station, waving cheerfully at them from the back of the cab.

'What was that about?' asked Tommy.

'She's just playing the big sister. Women can't seem to help it. And, to be fair to her, it *is* your first trip abroad. And you don't speak French…'

'That's very sweet of her.'

'She's a nice girl, I admit, but after today I'm not sure sweet's quite the right word.'

'What do you mean?'

'Never mind. Look, let me walk you to Grand Place. You can have a quiet coffee in the prettiest square in Europe - after St Mark's, in Venice, of course - while I look after Sir, back at the hotel.'

Reaching Grand Place, they grabbed a spare table when a tourist couple got up to leave. Guy sat down briefly.

'Give me an hour or two at least. I have some… arrangements to make.'

'Phoning Whitehall? Letting them know things are going according to plan?'

'That sort of thing.'

'Great. Though that's a long time to sit over a coffee. I don't think the management will be pleased.'

'They won't. May I make a suggestion? Central Brussels is very charming. So many little squares, antique shops, galleries, churches. Just set off by yourself and have a look at whatever takes your fancy. Here…' He produced a small map of Brussels like a conjuror producing a rabbit. 'It's an essential item if you're not to get lost…'

From another pocket he brought out a wad of notes.

'And you'll need some Belgian francs.'

'Thanks! Are there any theatres shown on here that I should have a look at?'

'Theatre Royal de la Monnaie. An opera house. From where a crowd of middle-class Belgians, inspired by an opera, emerged to start the revolution that gave birth to the country. The power of art…'

'Like I've said before, if all else fails you could get a job as a tour guide.'

'You have. And it's a reassuring thought. Now, I must love you and leave you. We'll embrace the Belgian way.' So saying, he hugged Tommy then gave him three kisses, two on one cheek, one on the other, before walking purposefully towards the hotel.

Chapter Thirty Five

Tommy ordered his coffee and sat back to enjoy some people-watching. Grand Place was indeed a beautiful square, with a grandeur usually only seen in churches and cathedrals. Most of the late medieval guild buildings and the town hall had been destroyed by bombardment - not by the Germans but centuries earlier, by the army of the French king, Louis XIV. The Bruxellois, used to foreign invasions, doughtily rebuilt the mansions afterwards. Tommy was just relaxing into the experience when a large man with a lived-in face sat down in the empty chair opposite him.

'May I join you, please? I am a friend of Mr Guy Burgess.'

'Oh! He didn't mention…'

'No. He doesn't know I'm here.'

'Then how did you know who I was?'

'I followed you, from the restaurant.'

'Ah! You work with him!' Tommy looked around, to see if they were being listened to. 'So you're with British intelligence, too!'

The man laughed.

'No!' he chuckled at the very thought. 'I'm not with British intelligence.'

'Now you mention it, your accent…?'

'I am with Soviet intelligence.'

'Oh! The chaps Guy's handing Mr Maclean over to? It's all right, he told me about it. Mum's the word.'

'I hope so. You see, Comrade Burgess is with Soviet intelligence, too.'

Tommy suddenly felt sick. A burning heat, beginning with a bright red flush on his whole face, then a feeling of icy cold and a clenching in his stomach, for he realised in an instant that the man wasn't bluffing. And if Guy had been a Soviet agent all along, then he, Tommy, was in deep, deep trouble. Prison, at the very least. A ruined career. He suddenly saw Ralph's face, peering over a copy of the Daily Express, with headlines about Tommy's arrest for helping a spy flee the country. What on earth had he been thinking of, going out with a man who was an avowed Communist?

As if reading his mind - which wasn't difficult, given how shocked he looked - the Russian carried on.

'You realise your reputation in England will be ruined? As will you. Life imprisonment, or twenty-five years at least. And though English prisons are less harsh than our labour camps, most people would not care to endure one for a month, let alone a quarter of a century.'

'The bastard! The bastard!'

'Do not be too hard on him. His life has been…complicated. In the service of a noble cause. And now he will begin a new phase of that life, and a different form of service. Moscow rather than Mayfair.'

'He's welcome to it.'

'He would be lonely without you.'

'Tough.'

'Yes, it would be tough for him.'

'That's not what I meant…Garçon! Some water. Water, s'il vous plaît.' Water was brought and Tommy drank. He immediately felt the need to throw up, but somehow stopped himself, gagging and spluttering instead.

'You have had a bad surprise.'

'Yes.'

'Like Comrade Burgess. He would rather have stayed in England. But he must come to our Soviet Union. A recent decision, taken at the highest level. An end to his hopes of enjoying a foreign holiday with you. Earning your approval and gratitude. All a dream, dissolved in the daylight. He must leave for Moscow in a few hours' time. With poor Comrade Maclean in tow, of course. And, we hope, you too.'

This time Tommy was actually sick, a stream of water and vomit, which he managed to direct into a trough of flowers and earth that marked the border of this café and the start of the seats belonging to its neighbour.

Was this why Guy brought him on this mission? Did he *want* him to face disaster? Was this a punishment for sleeping with but not loving him? Or was it some horrific form of blackmail? Forcing him to flee with him? To live with him, with no hope of ever leaving?

'Here.' The Russian offered him a clean napkin, which Tommy wiped his mouth with, while the Russian waved away a concerned-looking waiter. 'My friend is fine, now. Thank you.'

Tommy was anything but fine. The vomiting had been an essential release from the tension but made no difference to the hideous situation he found himself in. He thought of Ivor's warning. Tommy's insistence on continuing to see Burgess had in effect ended Ivor's life and now, in a sort of poetic justice, it looked as if it was going to end his, too. What made it worse was that the current situation only happened because he had stupidly gone back to Burgess. What had he been thinking? Why hadn't he learned the most painful lesson life had ever taught him? He hated himself almost as much as he hated Burgess. Not least because he could see see no way out. The Russian tried to sweeten the pill.

'Consider, please. In Russia you will be the friend of an honoured man. A Hero of the Soviet Union. You will be given a job. A senior job. In one of our state theatres. After all, you have experience, do you not? We have much theatre. And ballet. And opera. You will have a freedom of movement not many in my country are permitted. Such an opportunity! Warsaw, Krakow, Prague, Budapest, East Berlin… So many places to see! And there is another consideration.'

'Which is?' Tommy asked, in a bitter voice.

'There is a great deal of tension in Europe. Another war may well be possible. One where good will, at last, triumph and capitalism be thrown in the dustbin of history. The Red Army will be unstoppable. And you, comrade, will be on the winning side.'

'I… I can't… I can't even think right now. I need some time on my own. Fresh air. You out of my hair. Please.'

'But of course. I saw Comrade Burgess give you a map. You will be able to find your way back to your hotel?'

'Yes.'

'Then I will leave you to it.'

'I wish you would. But one question?'

'Please.'

'Did Burgess ask you to ask me to go with him, or is it your idea?'

'Mine. He thought the choice would be too hard for you. You see what a good man he is? You could have a good life with him. And he is amusing, no? Good company?'

'You'll excuse me if I don't find anything remotely amusing right now. Not him, this trip or your forthcoming war. Nothing fucking amusing at all.'

The Russian stood up. He placed a large note on the table and summoned the waiter with a nod of his head.

'Keep the change.'

'Thank you, sir!' said the waiter who then spoke to Tommy. 'I hope you enjoy your visit to Belgium?'

'No', replied Tommy. 'So far the whole thing's a disaster.'

The waiter's English was limited to a very few phrases so he gave a polite smile over blank eyes, pocketed the note and walked back to the kitchens with the empty coffee cups.

As Tommy stood up, the Russian passed him a piece of paper. On it was written a telephone number.

'What's this?'

'The number you will dial to contact me. At the hotel. Direct to the room, where I will be waiting. I see this is not easy for you. I too would need a little walk in such a case. We are not bad people, whatever your capitalist propaganda tells you. Go. Walk. Think. Then call me in an hour. At the most, please. Then I will arrange a car to collect you.'

'And if I don't want to come back to the hotel? Or ever see Guy Burgess again?'

'Then we will know, and will not wait any longer before getting our comrades to safety.'

Tommy didn't believe a word of it, but it might be useful to at least have a way of reaching the Russians. Who was he kidding? He was a little pawn in a bigger game. There was nothing to negotiate. He had no bargaining chips. His only options seemed to be to go with Burgess to Moscow, which was inconceivable, or be thrown to the wolves as an accomplice, left to the mercy of a furious British government. The only thing he could do was take the Russian's advice - and Burgess's earlier - and walk the streets while this waking nightmare unwound around him. The contrast between his horrific position and the cheerful faces of sightseers soaking up the architectural glories of Grand Place made everything worse. It was as if a thin but impenetrable pane of glass separated his world from theirs.

The Russian offered him his hand, which Tommy ignored, walking away in the direction of the taxi rank by the Stock Exchange building that he and Burgess had strolled past on their way to Grand

Place. He pushed his way through the crowds, grateful for the anonymity they offered within their ranks. His hopes were almost immediately dashed as, only a few yards further on, another Russian, who had been pretending to look at the endless lace souvenirs that decorated nearby shop windows, began to follow him. Tommy decided to lose him by getting into the first cab he could find.

Realising this, when Tommy reached the taxi rank the Russian moved closer, so he could hear where he was asking to be taken. Suddenly a large man, with the solid build of a rugby player, slammed into the Russian, knocking him to the ground. As he fell, the huge man bent over him, ostensibly to apologise - saying very loudly 'Are you OK? So sorry! Are you OK?' so the fallen man was both disorientated and unable to hear anything Tommy might say to one of the drivers. As he pretended to check the Russian for injuries, he forcibly held him down on the cobbled street. At the same time a much slighter, older man, dapper in a double-breasted suit, tapped Tommy on the arm and quietly but firmly, in an unmistakably English accent said:

'You're having a bad day, old chap. But take a taxi to the Abbey and things may start to look up.' He pressed a business card into Tommy's hand. It had the name and contact details of an official at the British Embassy. The man let Tommy glance at it, then turned the card over, to reveal a hand-written address. He opened the taxi door and almost pushed Tommy in, telling the driver the passenger would tell him where to go in a moment. For now, just drive!

The car pulled away, with a bemused but obedient driver who had decided to follow the Englishman's instructions, on the basis everyone knew the English were eccentric but that they had money, so it should be a good fare.

After a moment looking at both sides of the business card, Tommy read out the address.

'Monsieur, you speak English?'

'Mais oui!'

'Good. Then please take me to the Abbey de la Cambre. In Ixelles.'

'The Abbey de la Cambre, Monsieur? Then you know our city?'

'No. But a friend suggested it.'

'A good choice! *Bien sur*! A very good choice.'

Tommy hoped so. As far as he could see, he had very few choices left, about anything.

Chapter Thirty Six

The driver dropped Tommy in a road which was lined by imposing houses divided into grand flats on one side, and what seemed like a small park or garden on the other. He had noticed a forest, the Bois de la Cambre, on the map Burgess had given him, but that was a little further south than the Abbey.

'Are you sure this is the right spot?'

'Monsieur, but of course! The most attractive way in. Down the little path. Look! Just there! The entrance!'

Tommy saw. He made his way down the path's steep incline, passing through a screen of trees towards what was in effect a little valley, in which the Abbey de la Cambre was situated: an oasis of cool lemon-yellow walls and green gardens. The ancient monastery had been closed down by French Revolutionary troops when they invaded in the 1790s but some monks had returned when the Allied armies retook Brussels from Napoleon. These days the buildings were used for a variety of purposes. Tommy had always thought of monasteries as medieval, and as romantic ruins. This place, though founded in the Middle Ages, had been rebuilt centuries later: it was now a collection of what looked to him like an eighteenth century barracks, or the various wings of a rambling mansion. The Abbey's religious origins were not forgotten, thanks to the presence of a large church - plain but imposing. Tommy found the main door opened quietly and easily when he tried the large iron ring that served as a handle. It was as if the place was inviting him. 'Unlikely to have any Russians lurking inside,' he muttered to himself as he opened the door wider before going in. Once inside he looked around the simple, elegant building, where a handful of mainly elderly women were at their devotions, scattered about various points on the long wooden pews. An organist was practising gently, the music creating a calming atmosphere. Just what Tommy needed. He wasn't remotely religious, despite childhood years at Sunday school and hymns every morning at school assembly, but there was something reassuringly familiar about the architecture and the sense of peace that it offered.

He sat down, a few rows behind the nearest huddle of women - far enough not to arouse their interest or an approach, but near enough to feel comforted by their presence and the sense of security their faith generated. He didn't hear the footsteps getting nearer, until he felt the pew move slightly and realised someone had sat down near him. Very near. He turned, prepared to say something sharp to the Russian who, he feared, had somehow followed him and was about to have him dragged into a car and off to Moscow. As he turned round, he saw that his companion wasn't the Russian at all. It was a man he hadn't seen before. He looked as if he was in his mid to late fifties, with a military bearing and immaculate in an expensive-looking suit. He had already placed his hat beside him on the pew.

'Delightful church!' said the newcomer. His voice was educated and authoritative but lacked the cut-glass edge of Burgess's accent. 'And such nice music. Wonderful when it all comes together, isn't it? Makes one think of higher things.'

Tommy examined the man's face. It bore the lines of a life full of experience, and a certain amount of danger. It had a firm, well-shaped nose but the most immediately striking feature was the intensely blue eyes. The hair must have once been blond, given the yellow tinge that was still discernible in the grey that it had become some years back. He had the aura of a man who could be trusted. Who would look after you.

'You mean God?' replied Tommy.

'I mean England.'

'I'm not a traitor.'

'And I'm not counsel for the prosecution.'

'Who are you, then? A friend of the man who gave me this card?'

He showed it to the stranger.

'Yes. Though he and I have rather different… specialities. But well spotted.'

'Look, I've done nothing wrong. Not deliberately, anyway. And if you'll let me explain…'

'No need, old boy. Though as you'll have gathered, we know all about your chum Burgess. Rather a scrape you've got yourself into. Luckily for you, I'm here to offer a solution. Allow me to introduce myself. Windermere. Edward Windermere.'

'I'm…'

'I know who you are. Can't say I understand your private life, but live and let live… I quite like the theatre myself. Specially Terence Rattigan. My wife and I loved The Browning Version. And she's very keen on the ballet. Can't say I'm quite as enamoured of it, but I enjoyed The Red Shoes. Mainly for Moira Shearer. Always had a bit of a thing for redheads!'

Shearer had starred in the film, as a young ballerina who falls under the spell of an impresario - based on Diaghilev and played by Anton Walbrook. Tommy had always had a bit of a crush on Walbrook, a handsome older man, but thought this wasn't the moment to mention it.

'Now,' said Windermere, 'I'd like a few words, if I may, and out of respect I suggest we have them not in church but outside in the grounds. We can perch on one of the benches.'

'OK.' said Tommy, who for the moment had lost any sense of control over his life. He wished, suddenly and intensely, that Banya was still in Brussels. She would have known what to advise. What to say.

Windermere led the way and as he did so Tommy noticed, automatically, that he had a good, athletic physique underneath the Savile Row tailoring. He was slightly shorter than Tommy but carried himself with the confidence of a much taller man. He imagined he had had an active war. In other circumstances he would have been attracted to him. They soon came to a bench, shaded by some of the many trees that ringed the Abbey and its grounds.

'Let me get straight to the point. You must be under a lot of strain, which as I've already said I understand. But there is a way out. Which I can offer you. After all, even if you were a traitor…'

Tommy opened his mouth to protest his innocence, but a gesture from Windermere stopped him. 'Even if you were, I can't see what you'd have to offer the Reds. I doubt if they're very interested in green room gossip.'

Tommy felt a sudden rush of relief. This man seemed to know everything, yet to be on his side. What was the catch? What would he have to do? Whatever it was, thought Tommy, there must be a way out or Windermere would have simply had him arrested. Did he know about the Russian's approach to him earlier? Should he tell him? Unsure of himself, he played for time.

'You want to help me?'

Windermere glanced at Tommy as if he found himself dealing with someone less intelligent than he had been led to believe. Then, perhaps allowing for the stress of Tommy's situation, his look softened.

'Actually, my primary concern is for you to help us. But if you'll play the game, then we'll play fair by you. After all, we're not ogres. That's the other side, whatever tosh your lover may have told you.'

'He's not…' Tommy began an automatic denial, born of the need for any homosexual man to deny having broken the law by sleeping with the same sex, but Windermere's ice-blue eyes warned him to shut up, which he did.

'We're trying to avoid a third world war. Yet, having bankrupted ourselves and lost the Empire - or India, which is much the same thing - to beat the Nazis, we're not going to throw away the peace by letting the Soviets run their tanks all over what's left of us.'

Windermere looked at Tommy, expecting some verbal or visual expression of understanding or agreement. Instead, Tommy stared resolutely at his feet. Windermere coughed. Reluctantly, Tommy looked up.

'I'm not really into politics, Mr Windermere.'

'Maybe, but at the moment you are, like it or not, very much in the thick of it. Burgess planned to help Maclean escape before we arrested him. By doing so he has confirmed our rather belated - but that's another story - suspicions about him. And now, politics or not, I take it you are a patriot?'

'Yes, of course. But the theatre is my world. Politics don't come into it.'

'Aren't you leaving something out?'

'What?'

'Men. You're very interested in men.'

Tommy turned a deep red. Windermere carried on.

'Sorry to bring it up, but it is rather to the point here, isn't it? And one of the men you were very interested in was dear Ivor, as my sisters used to call him.'

'Yes. He was a great man of the theatre and I'm proud he was my friend.'

'Very good. One should stick up for one's friends. He was a patriot and I'm sure he'd expect you to be too.'

'He's not been long dead. Do you have to use him as some sort of lever?'

'He would have hated what Burgess represents. Wouldn't he?'

Tommy thought back to the fatal row in Ivor's flat. 'Yes.'

'And given a choice, you wouldn't want to do anything that could help the King's enemies?'

'Of course not!'

'Good. I thought so, but I needed to hear it direct from the horse's mouth. So I can put it in my report.'

Windermere heard something and turned his head towards the sound. He tapped Tommy on the knee to get him to look up again, then having got his attention nodded towards a small group, chatting animatedly and taking photos of the gardens.

'Those tourists will be in earshot in a minute or two, so I suggest we carry on nearby. While walking. I always find a gentle stroll clears the head, don't you?'

'Where to?'

'I had thought the park here, but on reflection let's stroll round the Etangs d'Ixelles. Those little lakes? Green grass leading down to water. Easy on the eye. Reminds me of England.'

Chapter Thirty Seven

Tommy looked, as unobtrusively as possible, at Windermere as they walked through the small park towards the southernmost of the two Etangs. This man held his life, or certainly his freedom, in his hands. At this thought, and with the sun breaking through the clouds, in a way whose symbolism wasn't lost on him, Tommy couldn't help but feel a huge surge of relief. The nightmare, that half an hour or so earlier had loomed over him, was now dissolving in the sun. The only nagging worry was whether he was going to have to see Burgess again. He assumed not, but what if he did? What if he had to testify against him at his trial? Would he be granted anonymity, or would he appear in public court as himself? In which case, surely, his life as a homosexual would be blazed all over the popular press and his career ruined. Theatre owners didn't care about their manager's private lives - their own were often far from blameless, whatever their sexuality. But to have an illegal way of life confirmed in public was socially and professionally unacceptable. Even the rumour of homosexuality was a cause for dismissal in many jobs.

While this was shooting across his mind, he and Windermere crossed the road that divided the edge of the Abbey park from the head of the southernmost lake, and carried on walking with the lake and the smooth green bank that led down to it on their left. There was a sign, in both French and Flemish, prohibiting the feeding of birds, but an elderly man had ignored this and was contentedly sharing several sandwiches, wrapped in tin foil, with a group of ducks and a pair of young swans.

'Having been stationed in the British zone in Germany, it's rather refreshing to see someone disobey an official sign. One of the many charms of Belgium…'

'Charms? I thought it was famous for being dull?'

'Unfairly so! It's cosy, welcoming, pro-British, has marvellous beer and the best chocolate in the world. What more could one ask for?'

'You've been here long?'

'Just a couple of weeks. I was here for purely routine reasons when your pal decided to come over *en route* to Moscow. The powers that be gave me the job of talking to you.'

'Your organisation… whoever they are, how did they find us? Guy switched ports to avoid detection.'

'Oldest trick in the book. Hardly likely to throw us off the scent.'

'But…'

'We watch all the main ports, on both sides of the Channel. And he's pretty easy to spot.'

'His colouring?'

'Yes. And that, traitor though he is, there's something about him. A sort of battered charisma, that stands out in a crowd.'

'Not ideal for a spy then?'

'Not normally, no. But then as you'll have gathered, he was rather clever in that he never tried to do anything other *than* stand out. A sort of bluff.'

'Hiding under the light.'

'Sorry?'

'A phrase he liked. That the safest place to hide is in plain sight, as that's the last place anyone searching for someone shadowy would look.'

'It didn't work this time... Isn't this charming?'

They were now approaching the second lake, the one that led to Place Flagey, one of the largest squares in Ixelles, around which were a large variety of cafés and restaurants, as well as a radio station and a large, dark Roman Catholic church.

'Very pretty', Tommy agreed. 'A bit like St James's Park... but without the sex.'

To Tommy's surprise, Windermere laughed. He clearly knew of the park's night-time reputation. Now feeling slightly more connected, the men paused, both looking at the lake, with the Avenue des Eperons d'Or and its row of Art Nouveau townhouses at their back.

'So, what next?'

'A bit more information on the Soviet agent who approached you would be a help. Yes, we saw him in Grand Place. What did he say?'

'That Burgess is going to Moscow with Maclean. That hadn't been the original plan - or not according to Guy. But everything he's told me has been a lie.'

'But the Russian...' Windermere prompted.

'Wanted me to go with them. He more or less ordered me to go back to the hotel to meet up with Burgess before he and Maclean start their journey east.' As if remembering something, he suddenly looked at his watch. 'I told Burgess I'd phone him if I had any trouble. And the Russian demanded I call him at a number he gave me. I have to find a phone.'

'There are several in Flagey or you can use one in a bar. Did he threaten you?'

'Not specifically. Just a heavy hint about a coming war. Should you tell someone? I mean...'

'No. That's part of the propaganda they're fed by their own side - except they present it as a pre-emptive strike against the West before we repeat what the Germans did ten years ago. All a lot of tosh.'

'But if they tried something?'

'Let's let the generals and admirals worry about that. So, you have to phone him and let him know whether you'll go with Burgess?'

'Yes.'

'Any details? Time? Train? Station? I imagine it'll be by rail. Less conspicuous than by plane…'

'No details at all - other than that they'll be moving soon. They'll need to, as Maclean's cracking up.'

'I'm not surprised. Wouldn't you?'

'I wouldn't put myself in such a situation in the first place.'

'Ironic, then, you're currently at the heart of the biggest spy scandal of the century.'

'I don't belong here. I want to go home.'

'You will. Now, about this phone call. When you get him on the line, what do you plan to say?'

'What should I say? You tell me.'

'All you need is to repeat that you're not going to Moscow. That's it. Tell him Burgess will have to fend for himself. Don't get drawn into any conversation. Short, sharp and to the point.'

Tommy started to shake. Windermere tried to calm him.

'I know it's an ordeal, but at least this way you're spared having to tell the man in person. Once you've done your bit, we'll have a well-deserved drink. During which we can have a chat about arrangements to get you home.'

'Thanks. Can I shake your hand?'

'We're not saying goodbye.'

'I know. But it'll settle me. Before the call.'

'Then of course you can.'

They shook hands, briefly but firmly. Tommy let go of Windermere's then walked beside him into Place Flagey. Outside the radio station was a public phone. Windermere rummaged in his pocket and pulled out several coins, which he passed to Tommy, who then called the number the Russian had given him, having placed the scrap of paper on the little ledge beside the phone.

'Hello?'

The voice at the end of the line wasn't the Russian's. It was Guy's. The last thing Tommy had expected. He was horrified.

'Is that you, Tommy?'

'Yes. I wasn't…'

'If it was the Comrade you're after, he's in the lavatory. I wasn't supposed to answer the phone, but then I never did pay much attention to authority figures. Apart from Mummy, of course…'

'Guy, this isn't the time for jokes.'

'*Au contraire*. Humour is a crucial part of tragedy. As a theatre buff you should know that.'

'I can't come to Russia with you.'

'I rather thought you'd say that. Look, if we can just meet up I can explain so many things to you…'

'I don't want a fucking history lesson. I want to go home.'

'Home is where the heart is, surely?'

'And mine is in a tiny office in a West End theatre.'

'Look, it's all a bit of a shock. I entirely understand. It was to me, when they told me I had to defect. A permanent move rather than a temporary assignment. But go I must. And I can't, without seeing you one last time.'

'I really don't…'

'Surely I deserve at least a goodbye?'

'No! You're a traitor! You've lied to me. Put me in danger. You don't deserve a goodbye. Anyway, the Russian won't let you.'

'He will, when I explain how important it is to me.'

'And you think someone like him will be moved by something like that?'

Windermere appeared at Tommy's shoulder. He passed him a note, which read: 'See him. Find out what he wants.' Tommy gave

Windermere an anguished look but knew he had to keep him happy at all costs. He was his only way out.

'Alright. Where?'

'That's better! Where are you now?'

'Place Flagey. Do you know it?'

'Very well. A good place for a drink, looking at the lakes. There's a cab rank on one side of the square. Get in one and ask for the Place du Petit Sablon.'

'The …?'

'Sablon. It's a little garden. Pretty, central but quiet and private. I'll be there in twenty minutes. Join me. And be prompt. Please. Now, I must go. I think Boris has finished his ablutions.'

The line went dead. Tommy replaced the receiver then turned to Windermere.

'He wants to meet. To say goodbye.'

He told him where and when.

'Can you cope with that?' asked Windermere.

'Do I have any choice?'

'Let's just say I'd appreciate it. Even if it's only a case of my seeing who he has with him as back-up.'

'And then you'll arrest him?'

'That's not the plan at all. The last thing we want is a public trial. What he and his pal Maclean have been up to is mortifying. Ideally we'll keep it under wraps, so the Americans don't find out. They'd give us hell, and these days we need them. But even if it does come out eventually, we'll have bought some time, rooted out any others and be able to show the Yanks we've been cleaning up our mess.'

Tommy reached for Windermere's arm.

'You're not going to shoot him, are you?'

'Sadly, no. Not our line. In peacetime. Now, if you'll excuse me, I have to make a call of my own. If you could just give me a minute?'

Tommy took the hint and walked away, towards the church at the end of the square. He felt like going inside, but Windermere was focussed on his call and Tommy couldn't catch his eye to point to the door. Besides, he couldn't waste any time. He had to find a cab and go to the Petit Sablon as soon as possible.

Not long after, Windermere finished the call and hailed a cab. As they sat on the back seat, Windermere patted Tommy's hand, in an avuncular way. He managed to be physically reassuring without being in any way sexual.

'It'll be all right, you know.'

'I can't see how. But thank you.'

'When we get there, jump out and go into the park. I'll get the driver to drop me off a short way further on. Don't look for me, but rest assured, I'll be very close.'

Chapter Thirty Eight

The taxi pulled up near the southern entrance to the garden, which was on a little hill surrounded by old buildings and cobbled streets. It was some twenty minutes after the phone call with Burgess.

'Charming little spot,' said Windermere. 'And rather appropriate. Dedicated to two aristocrats who were executed as traitors to the imperial power of their day. Burgess obviously has a sense of history… Good luck!'

There were a handful of people in the garden, including a young family. An engaging scene. A little apart from the others, sitting on a bench, striking a nonchalant pose with a newly-lit cigarette, was Guy. Tommy saw Guy's chest discreetly heaving. He must have run some of the way to make sure of being there on time. The idea of him running would have been funny in other circumstances. A little breathlessly, Guy spoke first.

'You came!'

'Yes.'

'Good of you.'

When he offered a cigarette, Tommy shook his head.

Guy shrugged. 'Ah, well… Look, I don't have long. I know things are bloody at the moment, but please, won't you reconsider?'

'Guy, you know my life is in London. Having been given this job, which is what I've always wanted, I can't just walk away from it into a life of exile. And as an enemy to my country.'

Guy tightened the knot of his tie.

'Whatever happened to *amor omnia vincit*?'

'Sorry?'

'Love conquers all.'

'Latin won't be any use in Russia.'

'Actually, they're very receptive to a bit of culture.'

'But will they be to you?'

'Of course! I'll be a Hero of the Soviet Union!'

'You don't belong there. You belong in St James's.'

Guy looked away.

'Ah, yes. All those things I'll miss about London. The cold, the rain, the sexual repression.'

'And Russia? Not exactly sex at the seaside, is it?'

'Actually, I plan to spend my summers chasing boys on the Black Sea coast. Which has plenty of Greek and Roman remains. Latin tags practically *de rigeur*...'

'Shouldn't we just say good-bye?'

Guy reached out to touch him but Tommy took a step back to avoid contact. Guy winced.

'I had no choice, Tommy. I was trying to protect you. Had I been arrested, you'd have been in the clear. Able to tell the authorities you'd been hoodwinked. Can't you see that?'

He stepped forward again. This time Tommy stood his ground but brushed away Guy's hand.

'I'm sorry, but I can't believe anything you've ever said, or will say to me again.'

'Then you really won't come with me? Share the adventure? A new world, another way of life?'

Tommy said nothing.

Burgess threw his last reserves into the battle, though knowing that doing so would damn rather than save him.

'What a shame. And I had hoped to give Banya her poems.'

'You did. You reminded her when she nearly forgot them. She's taken them to Paris.'

'No, she took the envelope to Paris. I have the poems.'

'But how?'

'At lunch. When you both went to the lavatory. Took them from her bag. Popped a menu into the envelope so she didn't notice the different weight.' Burgess looked positively malevolent.

'But why? For God's sake…'

'Punishment, I suppose. Revenge. An underrated emotion.'

'Revenge for what?'

'For having you. For having her actor. Who's also a good writer. For being young. For standing up to me on the boat across the Channel… Oh, ask her about it another time… For being part Burmese yet backing King and Country. So that I can take Wystan's latest poem into exile with me, as a reminder of our long friendship… A whole host of reasons, really.'

'If you think I'm going to throw away my life to save a few pieces of paper, then you're mad as well as bad.'

'Then I'm in good company.'

'You're not Byron. You've created nothing. You'll leave nothing.'

'I've influenced the world. Kept parts of it safe for Communism. The politics of the future. Shelley called poets the legislators of the world. Typically over-the-top of the boy. Now it's spies. We change things. Or help to. Ah! I'm afraid it's time to go.'

Walking towards them were two very large men, neither of whom Tommy had seen before.

'Where's your minder?' asked Tommy

'Probably nursing a black eye for having let me slip the leash for a while. The comrades will have been rather vexed. Even though

I phoned them once I got near here. Just in case. Best to keep on their good side, especially as I'll be living with them.'

Tommy pointed at the men, who were getting closer and seemed larger and more intimidating with every step.

'And that's the sort of people you're going to live with?'

'Silver linings come in black clouds, I'm afraid. Always did. You're sure you're not coming?'

'More than ever.'

'Then give me a hug goodbye.'

Tommy let Guy put his arms around him and, as he did, Guy's physical presence, his smell (a unique combination of himself, tobacco, alcohol, garlic and an expensive cologne that couldn't quite mask the other aromas) and the imminence of his departure, caused Tommy, suddenly overwhelmed, to burst into tears. They were triggered by the appalling stress of the situation, his rage with Burgess, his rage with himself, his still fresh misery about Ivor's death, his fear of what the Soviet agents might be about to do to him. Love for Guy was nowhere in the mix, but Burgess, desperate to salvage some shreds of self-respect before he was dragged into exile, chose to see this as proof that Tommy had really been in love with him all along. The basis of a romantic construct that would both sustain and torment him in the years ahead. Guy held him tight, then pulled back slightly, with tears in his own eyes, which had lost the startling hardness they'd shown while he spoke of Banya.

'Tommy, you *do* still care.'

Unable to summon the energy for a denial and in any case frightened by the approaching Russians, Tommy said nothing.

'Come here,' said Burgess. 'Come here.' He pulled him to him again, then kissed him gently on his lips. As he did so, Tommy felt a pressure against his chest.

'Your tears have won the lady back her poems. To those who

have,' Guy quoted the Bible, 'more shall be given. To those who have not, even that which they have shall be taken away.'

He stepped back slightly and patted Tommy's jacket, as if in affection but actually to check he had transferred the poems safely.

'Couldn't let the comrades see', Guy murmured, 'Or they'd think I'm hedging my bets by handing over something useful to London.'

Just then the two Soviet agents reached them.

'This is the boy?' asked the older of the two.

'It is. Isn't he lovely? But I'm afraid he won't be joining us, after all.'

'Yes he will. Orders.'

A firm, authoritative voice broke in on them.

'Then you'll just have to report he ran away.'

It was Edward Windermere, who had, unnoticed, acting like just another person strolling in the gardens, approached the group.

'Quite a little party we seem to be having!' said Burgess, trying to cover his alarm at this latest development.

'There are plain-clothes gendarmes at both entrances to the park,' said Windermere, ignoring Burgess and focussing entirely on the older of the two Russians. 'You can take this piece of rubbish with you, but the boy stays here. Unless you want to be arrested? I assume you're both armed, but so am I, so are the gendarmes and we have other agents ready to assist them. You'll die in this park.'

The Russian looked at his colleague as if for agreement, then at Burgess. 'Come, then.'

'Then this really is goodbye?' Guy moved forward as if to give Tommy, who had dried his tears, a hug for a second time.

Windermere stood between the two men. 'You've already done that. Just go! Think yourself lucky you haven't been arrested, tried and hanged.'

Guy turned to leave but looked, theatrically, over his shoulder, to make eye contact with Tommy.

'Do write, darling. It'll be a sort of lifeline. Like when I was at school. Letters from home were always such a tonic.'

The young family Tommy had noticed earlier, of twenty-something parents and a toddler, enjoying the summer afternoon's sunshine, were crossing the park, the child running about happily while her mother and father beamed at her. The contrast between their domestic happiness and the international incident that had manifested itself in the same place, suddenly struck everyone in the group, including the Russians, who both had families they were looking forward to seeing when they got home at the end of this mission.

Guy looked at Tommy again but offered his comment to the wider group, almost as if he was thinking out loud.

'You see? Just like Breughel's painting - I've fallen to earth. Yet this happy little group don't know and wouldn't care…'

With a wry smile and flanked by the Russians, he walked to the north entrance of the gardens, past the watchful gendarmes with large shoulders and crew-cut hair who stood at the gates, in civilian clothes but massively conspicuous.

Tommy felt Windermere's hand on his shoulder.

'You all right?'

'I've been better.'

'Not quite what you expected when you first bumped into him back in London, I imagine.'

'No.'

'I also imagine you could do with that drink.'

Tommy turned to face him.

'Thank you. And can I then go home?'

'Not tonight. But you will, first thing in the morning. I've booked your ticket.'

'And you?'

'I'm going to Cologne tomorrow. Other fish to fry. You'd be surprised how many people the Soviets have got on their payroll.'

'And the Metropole? My suitcase?'

'All looked after. You're in another hotel. Ask for the keys at the reception desk when we drop you there. There'll be an embassy minder staying with you, so I hope you don't mind sharing a room. Separate beds of course.'

'Is he attractive?'

'That's for the ladies to say, surely?'

'Oh, come on, Mr Windermere.'

'Yes. He's a good-looking young man.'

'Specially chosen for the task?'

'Not by me. And I'd have thought you'd had quite enough adventures for one day.'

'For a lifetime, actually. And you? In your line of work…'

'I've had plenty.'

'I'd be fascinated to hear about them.'

'That would take longer than a quick drink.'

'Then how about dinner? I don't know about you, but I'm starving. Must be the excitement. The King can run to dinner for two, surely?'

Windermere smiled.

'As it happens, I've booked a table at the same place you had lunch today. You're welcome to join me. If you don't mind starting with a little more debriefing about Burgess. *Quid pro quo* for a good meal. And my anecdotes.'

'Thanks. There's just one other thing…'

'Yes?'

'I need to send a telegram. To a friend in Paris. Reassuring her that I'm safe and, almost as important, so are some personal possessions of hers.'

'The young woman on the ferry?'

'Yes.'

'She left her purse?'

'She left some poems.'

'Then she'll be very pleased to hear from you.'

'She will.'

'The hotel concierge will arrange it.' The men had now reached the gate on the south side of the garden, where a large car, with a driver and another British agent, were waiting for them.

'Then let's get that drink!'

The bar he chose was a heavily Art Nouveau-inspired café at the side of the Brussels Stock Exchange, just a few minutes from the hotel. As he walked through the café, the old-world decor reminded Tommy of Rules and therefore of Ivor. The world he had wanted to join. Windermere excused himself to make a phone call from a booth near the bar. Tommy assumed he was calling his superiors back in Whitehall. Which he did, but in a brief conversation in which a code word was spoken, confirming a successful mission. He then phoned his wife.

Left on his own, Tommy opened the envelope Burgess had given him. He checked the contents, in case there was some further final twist to the deceptions Guy had lived by for so long. Inside were Peter's poems about Banya, and Auden's, too. Tommy was delighted by it. He recognised its quality and the truth of what the poet had identified about Banya's personality. He felt far better for having read it - almost as if had been with her while he was doing so. Then he found, crumpled because of the way it had been pushed into the envelope, a single page, on Metropole notepaper, with a message from Guy:

Dearest. If you're reading this then you've left me behind. Or rather, I've had to leave you, for after all it's I who am embarking on a long and permanent journey. So this is goodbye. And how better to say goodbye than with a poem? By the Master. Not Noël Coward, who I know will have sprung to your theatrically-inclined mind, but Lord Byron. As ever, he says what needs to be said, the best way possible. Guy x

So, we'll go no more a roving,
So late into the night,
Though the heart be still as loving,
And the moon be still as bright.

For the sword outwears its sheath,
And the soul wears out the breast,
And the heart must pause to breathe,
And love itself have rest.

Though the night was made for loving
And the day returns too soon,
Yet we'll go no more a roving,
By the light of the moon.

Tommy re-read the note. When he got to the signature for the second time, Guy's name written in a larger, more exuberant hand than usual, he felt an almost overwhelming sense of relief. It was over. Once Burgess was in Russia, he might as well be dead. He would have no further contact with him. He thought, by association, of Anthony Blunt. That had been an enjoyable evening at Rules. The Surveyor of the King's Pictures! A man who could open doors. And would, Tommy had realised at once - seeing through the coolly ascetic exterior and the declarations of devotion to art - expect Tommy to open himself in return. Before the events of the last twenty-four hours, Tommy would have jumped at the opportunity. Blunt would not have been his natural choice of bedmate, but the things the man would want to do to him would, nevertheless, still give him pleasure. So the price for the galleries, the meals, the introductions to other well-placed people, would have been worth it. But now, that was impossible.

He had met Blunt through Guy. He was one of that circle. Obviously not dangerous in the way Guy had been. No connection with the intelligence services. Safely isolated from all that, behind the palace walls and within the long cool galleries of museums and art collections. Still, he was taking no chances. He had to leave behind everything to do with Guy Burgess. He would follow Ivor's advice and stick to the theatre. Not so much lowering his sights, as focussing them where they served him best. The only good thing about mistakes, as Ralph had told him over a glass of port after the show one evening, was what they taught you. Time to learn from this huge mistake, which he made, almost suicidally, not once but twice - *twice!* - as he drew the firmest possible line under it. He would ignore any notes or calls from Blunt when he got back to England. And if the newspapers got hold of the scandal of Burgess and Maclean's defection, he was sure that Blunt, as one of Guy's oldest and closest friends, would want to keep a very low profile. Far from anyone who might compromise his position. There would be no hearing the chimes at midnight with the King's art historian.

He saw Windermere thank the manager for the use of the phone and make his way through the café's little round tables, a friendly smile and more relaxed expression suggesting a successful call. So, thought Tommy, things had gone well for both of them, these last few minutes. Ivor's death and the saga of Guy's defection had been exhausting, but he was young, he had energy, he had ambition. He would spend the night in a grand hotel then go back to London, the slate clean, to a job he loved, with a new government in the offing and the Festival of Britain promising a bright new future. Windermere sat down beside him.

'Everything OK?'

'Yes!' said Tommy, tucking the envelope safely back into his jacket pocket and picking up the drinks menu. 'It looks as if it is.'